S0-BYV-672

BLOOMFIELD TOWNSHIP PUBLIC LIBRARY

3 1160 00530 6837

7-DAY BOOK

Bloomfield Twp. Public Library
1099 Lone Pine Road
Bloomfield Hills, MI 48302-2410

ALSO BY LESLIE EPSTEIN

Ice Fire Water: *A Leib Goldkorn Cocktail*

Pandaemonium

Pinto and Sons

Goldkorn Tales

Regina

King of the Jews

The Steinway Quintet Plus Four

P. D. Kimerakov

SAN REMO DRIVE

SAN REMO DRIVE

A NOVEL *from memory*

LESLIE EPSTEIN

BLOOMFIELD TOWNSHIP PUBLIC LIBRARY
1099 Lone Pine Road
Bloomfield Hills, Michigan 48302-2410

HANDSEL BOOKS
an imprint of
Other Press • New York

Copyright © 2003 Leslie Epstein

Design by Miko McGinty

This book was set in Caslon

10 9 8 7 6 5 4 3 2 1

All rights reserved. No part of this publication may be reproduced or transmitted in any form or by any means, electronic or mechanical, including photocopying, recording, or by any information storage and retrieval system without written permission from Other Press LLC, except in the case of brief quotations in reviews for inclusion in a magazine, newspaper, or broadcast. Printed in the United States of America on acid-free paper. For information write to Other Press LLC, 307 Seventh Avenue, Suite 1807, New York, NY 10001. Or visit our website: www.otherpress.com.

Library of Congress Cataloging-in-Publication Data

Epstein, Leslie.
    San Remo Drive : a novel from memory / Leslie Epstein.
        p. cm.
    ISBN 1-59051-066-6
    1. Hollywood (Los Angeles, Calif.)—Fiction. I. Title.

PS3555.P655 S26 2003
813'.54—dc21

                                            2002035547

Parts of this book have appeared in *Princeton University Library Chronicle, Partisan Review,* and *Five Points.*

The events and characters of this novel have passed through the magnetic field of the imagination—or perhaps it is the other way around, and all that is fanciful has been caught in the seine net of memory; in any case, the reader would be making a mistake if he or she assumed that any resemblance between an incident or character in this book and an event or person from real life, now dead or still living, was anything other than coincidental.

For my brother

JUL 2 2 2008

E. T. A. Hoffman used to explain the wealth of imaginative figures that offered themselves to him for his stories by the quickly changing pictures and impressions he had received during a journey of some weeks in a post-chaise, while still a babe at his mother's breast.

—Sigmund Freud, *Moses and Monotheism*

Contents

PART ONE

MALIBU

(1953)

I

The sun was where it always was, high overhead, though on the particular Sunday I have in mind it had to force its way through a thin layer of cloud that stretched above us like a sheet of wax paper. I assume it was Sunday: we weren't in school, Barton and I, and it wasn't warm enough yet for summer. In spite of the cool weather, I'd put down the top on the Buick we owned back in the Fifties. As we made our way in traffic along the Pacific Coast Highway, Sam, our spaniel, leaned out from the back seat, nose up, ears blown inside out. My brother hung onto his leash, lest at the sight of a skunk or a cat or—rising out of the haze-hung ocean— a silvery dolphin, he leap into the opposing stream of cars. Lotte, our mother, sat beside me, clutching a scarf over the permanent wave she'd set in her hair.

"It's going to be a nice day," she declared; as if in obeisance one corner of the milky overcast peeled away. At once the windows of the houses atop the right-hand hilltops began to shine, winking down on the sudden checkerboard of the sea.

"No, it is not," said Bartie.

I glanced back in the mirror: his face was buried in dog fur, the wind socks of the animal's ears twirling just above his own. He wasn't, I knew, referring to the climate.

"Why are you being so negative?" Lotte replied, though I doubted Bartie could hear her in the rush of air. "René is looking forward to the afternoon and so am I and you should be too. He is a wonderful cook. He is going to a lot of trouble to make a special treat. And his house is a little dream."

"A little dream on stilts," I muttered.

"Well, of course it's on stilts, Richard. It's a beach house. I hope you're not going to be in a negative mood too. Let's relax. Everybody just relax. We're going to have a good time."

I pulled around a Bekins van and was able to speed up after Carson Canyon. Lotte twisted her pale green scarf under her chin, and in that clamp fell speechless.

Bartie, in back, said, "It's too soon." Which might, from him, have meant anything: *Slow down, we're getting there too soon*; *Too soon for the three of us to start fighting*; or, and here's where I put my money, *Too soon to have a good time.*

I took a quick look over my shoulder. Barton stared back at me, grinning, a little gap-toothed, a little bucktoothed, which is what he got for sucking his thumb. "They don't have a King of England anymore. Everyone there wears black clothes. I saw it on the Zenith. They are sad because there isn't a king."

Lotte: "Yes, they have been very sad. But now they are going to have a queen, Bartie. The Princess Elizabeth. You can watch her coronation next month on television. No one will be wearing black, I promise you that. Isn't that how things should be? The king is dead. Long live the queen."

"But they waited a year. More than a year. That was February. Next month is June."

Our mother didn't answer. In Barton's mind, she knew, our father was the king—king of Hollywood, king of comedy—and it was a scandal not to mourn him for at least as long as the English had George VI. Instead, she pointed through the windshield. "There it is. Slow down, Richard. We'll go by."

The row of beachfront properties fell away on the left, caught between the highway and the public beaches. I coasted past the Sweetwater turnoff, trying to distinguish one of the sagging shacks from the other. None looked as if it had been painted since before the war: faded pastels, cheek by jowl, like a tray of melting sherbert.

"It's that one!" said Lotte. "See? That's his car."

She meant, I saw, a blue Plymouth coupe parked in front of what looked to be little more than a cabin of crème de menthe. I swung in behind it and turned off the ignition. A dog was barking nearby. A piece of tar paper on the place next door was slapping against the rooftop. And of course there was the thump of the waves on the hidden beach below. I opened my door at the same time René stepped out of the little house and made for us.

"Ah, Lotte, I have been waiting. You are late, just like today the sun. Welcome! Hello, boys! *Comment allez-vous?* All is well?"

He had, as always, his thin Frenchman's moustache and his thin Frenchman's hair, slicked down with the brilliantine we all could smell when he leaned over the passenger door and gave our mother a Frenchman's double kiss.

"We got a late start, darling," Lotte began, though René had already moved to the rear, where with what I knew was called *bonhomie* he was kneading Bartie's neck.

"And how is this one, eh? My sailor! My marine!"

Barton's lashes dropped over his eyes, which when open were a startling blue. He smiled. "We brought Sammy," he said.

"I see! *Bonjour, monsieur,*" he said to the dog, patting him once on the head, so that his eyes closed reflexively too. "What a fierce beast. That is why I have put Achille on the rope. You hear him? Barton, what is he saying?"

"*I want that spaniel for lunch—*" That was my contribution, which I covered with a chuckle.

René laughed aloud, with his head back, so that his short-sleeved shirt, circles of yellow, circles of blue, split over his belly. "Ha! Ha! But no! Ha! Ha! Lotte? You heard? *Pour le déjeuner!*"

"He didn't ask *you,*" said Barton. A button of flesh, a red-colored welt, rose on his brow. "Why did you answer?"

Lotte slid off the bench cushion to the gravel of the drive. "And you wouldn't believe the traffic. At least, I can't believe it. Norman and I moved out here in 1935. Practically with the covered wagons! There was hardly a car on the road back then. Honestly, you blink once and the population doubles. We were the pioneers."

I got out the driver's door and turned toward where our mother's lover—I hadn't much evidence for that, aside from his diplomatist's kisses and a single embrace that I had spied through the windblown curtains of our living room window—now approached me, his pink hand out. The lids of my own eyes dropped at his touch, so that I found myself staring at the wrinkle-free material of what people were beginning to call Bermuda shorts; his bowed, tanned legs; and the oddly pale and oddly small feet, crisscrossed by the leather straps of his sandals. "Richard," he said, "I feel embarrassment because I am going to show you my latest paintings. I mean, I cannot hide them, eh? They are not in your style. They are more—what do you call it, chèrie? More of *l'expressionisme.*"

My mother had leaned back over her side of the Buick, to fish out her beach bag, which was woven from the same washed-out colors, in straw, as the dwellings along the shore. "Darling, why do you apologize? There's certainly no reason for *that.* Your work *is* expressive. Did I tell you that Betty is considering the new oils for her gallery? She has the best taste of all my friends."

"What do you mean, *pioneers?* You and Daddy came out on the Super Chief! With an observation deck, for Christ's sake, Mom. Do you know what the real pioneers, the ones who *did* have covered wagons, went through?"

"Well, I wasn't suggesting that we were cannibals."

"Why do you have to put yourself—I don't know, at the head of the line."

"Richard—" This was René. "You must not speak with this disrespect toward your mother. I implore you."

"*Disrespect?* I am just trying to make a point. Have you read *Grapes of Wrath?* It's a great book. A John Steinbeck novel. The Okies, the people from Oklahoma—do you even know what that is?"

"It is a province of the country. I know that of course."

"A province! Ha! Ha! Ha! Did you hear that, Bartie? I bet he couldn't be a citizen, even if he wanted to. No French guy is going to know who signed the Declaration of Independence."

"Richard, you are always so smart. Do you know that we wouldn't even have our independence if it weren't for the help of France? Lafayette, we are here!"

Lotte beamed at René across the cooling hood of the automobile. Then her smile disappeared. "Oh, no, Barton," she cried. "Not now! Please don't!"

Bartie had donned a pair of dark glasses, wire-rimmed, and now he put a cold corncob pipe in his mouth. "I shall return," he intoned, in a voice deeper than his own.

"Ha, ha! This boy: he makes for us a masquerade?"

"I'm so upset. Oh, René. I don't know what to do. He's had that pipe for a year. And he has a cap too! *Barton! Please!* He keeps pretending he's that terrible MacArthur."

As if on cue my brother took out a visored cap and placed it over the mop of blond curls that, with his blue eyes, reinforced the romance that he was not from our dark-haired, dark-skinned family, nor from any other line of Jews. He got to his feet and through some kind of trickery—jutting the jaw, sucking in his plump, pink cheeks until they sank in like the septuagenarian's—transformed himself into the great man, the darling of the Republicans, as he drove down Fifth Avenue.

"Old soldiers," he declared, around the pipe-stem, "never die—" Then he threw out his arms, as if to catch the streams of ticker tape, the snowstorm of the confetti, the roaring crowds that were simulated by the cymbal crash of the oncoming sea. But in that instant the dog's leash slipped though his boy's-sized hand; Sam flashed over the side of the Buick and disappeared yipping and yapping down the side of the bluff that separated René's green house from the plum-colored bungalow next door. A howl went up: the beast on the rope!

"Sammy!" cried Bartie.

Lotte: "Stop him! René!"

"I'll get him," I shouted; but I knew, from the torrent of animal growls, the two different pitches of the barks and bays, that I was too late.

René's cabin was indeed supported on stilts, four long iron poles sunk into the sand. Achille, a big German shepherd, black and brown, was tied to one of them. He lunged, gasping from the pressure of his collar, at our little spaniel. Each time he did so, the rope caught him, standing him upright, so that the saliva flew from his mouth. Again and again Sammy, his fur standing on his back, dashed forward, teasing and taunting. The din, in that cavern, was tremendous.

"It's a Nazi dog! A Nazi dog!" Barton was screaming the words. He scooped handfuls of sand and threw them at the crazed Alsatian. The breeze blew them back in his face.

"Richard! Richard!" cried Lotte, from atop the bluff. "Can't you do something? Catch him!"

I tried, hurling myself full-length at the darting dog. But Sammy dodged easily and came at his antagonist from a different angle. Achille turned, rearing, only to have the spaniel run beneath him, nipping at his hocks. After a series of feints I saw, or thought I saw, a method in this madness. Sam kept moving to his left, which meant that each new stand that Achille took tended to wind him clockwise around his iron pillar. It took less than a minute for his tether to be cut by half. His breath was shorter too, coming out in human-like groans. The fierce barking had stopped.

"Don't cry, Bartie," I shouted, glancing back at my brother, whose face was covered by a mask of sand crystals and zigzagging tears. "He's going to win!"

It seemed, for an instant, to be true. The big brute was strangling himself. He breathed now with the hacking, wheezing cough of a smoker.

Barton saw this. He thumped his chest with his balled-up hands. "It's David," he cried. "David and Goliath!"

But this time the giant was the clever one. Sammy came in at five o'clock, like a Spitfire attacking a lumbering German Junker. Achille didn't leap; instead he remained in a crouch close to the ground, and Sammy in amazement tumbled to a halt before the snot-smeared snout. In an instant the Alsatian shot forward and took the spaniel in his open jaws.

Lotte screamed. Bartie cried, "No-o-o-o!" For a heartbeat I thought that Achille, like a python, would swallow him whole.

Then René strode forward. "*Assez! La ferme!*" Without breaking stride he kicked his dog in the belly, not with the leather toe of his sandal but with the much harder bone of his shin. The shepherd buckled, spitting out his prey, who dragged himself off, whimpering, whining. "*Cochon!*" cried the Frenchman. He kicked the animal again, this time against the heaving rib cage.

Bartie ran toward his own dog, who stood slick and shaking, like a miniature of a newborn foal. He took him in his arms.

"Don't kick him anymore," I said, fighting tears myself. "Please."

"What? You ask me to spare him? This pig of an animal? It will be as you wish. We will show mercy."

Lotte came down the bluff, stumbling a little. "Is everyone all right? Is anyone bitten?"

"Wasn't Sammy great, Mom?" said Barton. "He's a brave boy!"

"What is this?" asked René, pointing to his nose.

"A nose," I answered.

"*Le nez. Oui.* And it smells something. Wait. A moment. Ah, it is the crust of the saucisson. Come. Up the stairs, my friends. Our luncheon is burning."

The Frenchman led the way up the wooden planks that served as the back staircase. Bartie followed, holding Sam against his chest. I moved to the first of the unpainted steps. Lotte touched my arm.

"I didn't mean anything," she said. "You and Bartie, you're the real Angelenos. The natives of the land." Then she leaned closer, though her lover, I realized, was still close enough to hear. "You mustn't worry. You know I'd never do anything you didn't approve."

2

The smoke filled the whole of the little house. René opened all the windows and pushed up the skylight. A column of soot corkscrewed from the open door of the oven and out into the pale patch of sky. He stooped to remove an aluminum pan, at the center of which lay the charred log of our feast, a log with juices spurting from it in little golden arcs. The truth was it smelled delicious. "Ah, we have arrived just in time," declared the chef, an oversized oven mitt on either hand. We three guests applauded. He grinned. "It is only necessary to peel from the top a bit of the dough." He leaned over the dish, expertly flaking away the burnt layer, like a scab from a healed wound. "Ah, it is as I thought. Only the butter was burning. We shall eat! Lotte, you will toss the salad?"

Our mother went to the sink, where the greens were waiting in a colander. She poured oil from one bottle, rose-colored vinegar from another. René, meanwhile, had laid out the sausage-filled crust on a platter and was slicing it into sections. "You notice here the pattern of the ingredients: the veal; the pork; here the pistachio, the strips of the ham; the darkness, it is the mushroom and the chicken livers. What you see with the eye, this helps us with the sensation on the tongue."

"That's why you are an artist, darling," said Lotte. "Everything you do is a composition."

"The funeral-baked meats," I said, giving my brother a nudge. But he looked up, entirely blank.

"I tell you what, Barton," said René, holding up a chunk of the paté. "You may give a taste to *le chien*."

Bartie took up the *saucisson* and shifted the hot meat—gray and green, pink and red, swirling with steaming black bands—from hand to hand. He brought it over to where Sam lay trembling in the corner.

For a moment everything was calm. The last of the smoke whisked out the windows. The haze over the ocean was lifting too. A sailboat went south to north on the horizon; another sideslipped the breeze a little closer in. I could make out the fishermen throwing their lines for mackerel at the end of the Malibu Pier. A few hardy swimmers were testing the waters. The breakers crashed to pieces before them and rolled sizzling about their feet and ankles, like animal fat. Lotte, heaping salad onto each plate, hummed, a little pointedly I thought, *I love Paris in the springtime*; and René, standing directly behind her, arranging a line of mustard at the rims, came in on *I love Paris in the fall*. You couldn't turn on the radio without hearing the lyrics. I moved from the kitchen area and walked the walls, white and stucco, to examine the paintings of our host.

"Mommy! What's wrong? He won't eat!" Bartie was kneeling on the floorboards. He was pushing the meat at Sammy, right up against his nose.

"Perhaps he is a true Jacobi, eh?" said René, with a belly laugh. "Ha! Ha! Ha! He must not eat what is forbidden."

Bartie wheeled to face him. "That's not my name. *Jacobi*! My name is Barton Wilson."

"Don't say anything," said Lotte. "It's a phase."

"But why? Is it because he has shame?"

"That is one thing I am thankful for. That Norman didn't see this behavior in his son. He wasn't a religious man; he just laughed at the rabbis. But he was proud of his family, and of his people too."

"To change your name, this cannot be allowed." René pounded a fist into his turned-up palm. "It is I think terrible."

Lotte replied lightly, so that her laugh mingled with the tinkling knives and forks she set at the table. "Oh, it's not so terrible, sweetie. Didn't I change my name to Jacobi? And what *about* the Jacobies? That wasn't their name when they came to Ellis Island. Richard, you know: didn't Grandpa Leo take the name of the man who was ahead of him in line?"

"Hee, hee hee! Ha! Ha! Ha!" I couldn't control my laughter. It had nothing to do with the old family joke—how Leo had exchanged the family name, *Ochsenschwantz*, "oxtail," itself bestowed upon *his* father's father by a jesting German; and why couldn't the stranger in line be a Belmont, an Adler, a Vanderbilt even. *Ha! Ha! Ha!* I burst out again at the sight of René's paintings—a half-dozen canvases on which the paint had been laid on by the blade of a knife, a thick, multicolored impasto out of which emerged something like daisies or magnolias or meadowlands, a tree, a horse.

"Why are you laughing, Richard? It's impolite."

I only half knew myself. I turned toward the last painting in the row. I glanced from it back to the painter: *this cannot be allowed.* I saw how his little moustache was suddenly drenched by the sweat on his lip. His hand, as he screwed the cap on the bottle of mustard, was shaking. He could not bear the thought of changing a name. This last work was of a sad-eyed clown: chalked face, reddened cheeks, lipsticked smile. The great thing was the nose, not the red bulb of a Bozo but a long, pointed schnoz, *le nez,* which literally grew out of the canvas, layer upon layer of dried, stiffened paint that thrust precariously a good six inches into the air.

"Ha! Ha! Ha!" I couldn't control myself. I knew, and I saw that René knew too, that this was a self-portrait: a picture of a name-changer, a fraud. Impasto? Impostor! But I only said, or rather bellowed, a single word: "Pinnochio!"

"Ah, it is a pity. Richard does not like my effort."

"Of course he does. He wasn't laughing *at* them. Were you, Richard?"

"Not exactly."

"No, no, no—I see that I have in your eyes made a failure. This makes me sad."

"René, darling. Don't be silly. Betty loves your paintings. Richard likes to be a know-it-all. Mr. Know-It-All. Mr. Snob. But he's only a boy."

"A boy! Yes, a boy who has sold his paintings in that same gallery whose patron, this *Betty,* only talks with repetition of hanging mine."

"Oh, those were just drawings of our neighbor—"

"Mademoiselle Madeline. *La petite jeune fille.* I have seen all the series. I have no choice but to bow to the critique of such a master."

I didn't like the French word *Mademoiselle.* It didn't fit Madeline. I remembered the patch of dark down at the nape of her neck and the thin line of hair—not like Sammy's, more like a shadow—that ran down her spine almost to the flesh of her buttocks. I didn't like *petite jeune fille.*

My mother laughed. "A *master*? Richard? Those were nothing but charcoal sketches. Betty only—"

"Lotte, *tais-toi!* Eh? I warn you."

"What does that mean, *tais-toi*? Shut up? Don't tell her to shut up!"

"Richard, it's all right. He's upset."

"Don't you see he's a fake? *René*? Is that your name? *René Belloux*? Joe Blow I bet!"

"But what are you accusing me of—?"

"I bet he didn't make this—what is it? *Saucisson en croute.* Where did you get it? At the Farmer's Market? At Chasen's?"

Now it was René's turn to laugh. "I assure you this recipe has been in my family, the family Belloux, for generations: yes, and we did not change this name for the Germans or for the immigration. We are not ones to wander the earth. But believe what you wish, my young friend. I am happy to see that the repast is being enjoyed by Monsieur Wilson."

He waved toward where Bartie had taken his seat at the table. He was stuffing the food into his mouth with both hands. "*Oui! Oui!* Mr. Barton Wilson. *Oink! Oink!* A Jew wouldn't eat all this pork."

"Now look," said Lotte. "I want everyone to sit down. There is no reason to continue this bad temper. We have a lovely meal. And I happen to know there is going to be a special dessert. Isn't that so, René?"

"Yes, the éclairs. About this I confess they are from the store. We can have them after our swim. Do we agree to this plan?"

Lotte took her place at the table. "That would be wonderful. And the sun is burning brighter and brighter. It's almost like a summer day. Richard, aren't you going to eat? Come sit next to me."

I did as she asked. I cut into the warm meat with a fork. We passed around a pitcher filled with the halves of lemons. The ice cubes bounced musically off the glass.

"I can't wait to get out on the beach," said Lotte. "There hasn't been any sun since I don't know when—since last fall. I've no color. You'd think I was a character in Tennessee Williams. A pale Southern belle."

"Richard and I will go out in the boat," René declared. "Would you like that?"

"Oh, I know he would."

"It is just a modest rowboat."

"What about Barton?" Lotte asked, smiling; there was a trace of lipstick on the white of her teeth. "Bartie, would you like to go too? Or would you rather stay here with your paper and pencils and write?"

My brother had put down his knife and fork. I saw the rouge-colored welt rising between his eyebrows. Tears formed a bell of light over the blue of his eyes. "Why did I do it? It's wrong for me to eat. Poor Sammy! He's sick. He won't eat. He's going to die. The big dog killed him!"

We all turned our heads to the corner where Sam lay flat on his side. For an instant it seemed he was no longer breathing. Then he sighed, with a great heave of the ribs, and slapped the floor with his tail. I would have thought he was dreaming, but his eyes were wide. Again, the pause; again, the slap, the sigh. *Brrr* was the sound that he made through his vibrating lips, like a man who is warming himself in the midst of a snowstorm.

Our mother was the first one onto the beach. She didn't put on a swimsuit. "This is a sunsuit," she announced. "The rays come right through and the wind stays away." Then, as she sometimes did, she said something odd and striking. "I can't think the last time I went into the ocean. It's so unconscious." With her scarf tight over her head and her straw bag over her shoulder, she clutched the handrail on her way down the weather-worn steps.

From that same bag she'd pulled trunks and T-shirts for my brother and me. René, at the sink, had his back turned; Bartie dropped his pants and his shorts, and hopped into his trunks—blue with a white stripe down one side. When he struggled with his shirt, arms upraised, I saw the remains of the baby fat that puckered his chest and hips; then his head, with his bucktoothed grin, popped through the V neck.

"What's so funny?" I asked.

"You," he answered.

At the exchange, René turned around.

"I have to use the bathroom," I told him. "To urinate."

He gestured with his head and his shoulder, over which he wore a checkered dishtowel. "It is there. Past the bedroom."

I took up my things and headed down the short corridor. The bedroom door was open and the bed itself, more expressionism in confused blankets and sheets, was on the floor. The bathroom had a stall shower surrounded by opaque glass. A pedestal sink stood beneath a flat mirror. Toothbrushes, hair brushes, a shaving brush too, along with a soapy razor and a bottle of that sweet-smelling pomade, were scattered across a single shelf. Over the toilet hung a smaller version, a study, of the clown painting I had seen before: sad eyes, crimson mouth, eggshell skin. I stripped off my clothes and stood before the bowl. Nothing came out. I ran the water in the sink. Nothing still. I closed my eyes, to shut out the gaze of the clown, with his pointed, protruding nose. But of course I knew the painting was there, like a man in an adjacent stall. I turned my back altogether and pulled on my swimsuit and elbowed my way into the shirt. When I stepped back to the living room, René and Bartie were gone.

3

The belated sun had brought a small crowd to the public beach. People lay on their blankets, in couples, or families, or quite alone, but always each equidistant from the other. Here and there a radio played snatches of popular songs: *Baubles, Bangles, and Beads*; *Wheel of Fortune*; *Ebb Tide*, though I saw that in reality the tide was coming in. Small children ran from each other, screaming. The breeze came hard off the ocean, stringing out the fringes of the beach umbrellas and kicking up little whirlwinds of sand. A lifeguard stared out to sea, though no swimmer had dared venture past his knees. I trudged steadily ahead in my unlaced sneakers until I saw Bartie digging not far from where the last wave had coughed up a bellyful of kelp.

He squinted up from what was already a hole the size of a sailor's trunk. "Want to dig too?" he asked.

"Sure."

He stooped and with a little green shovel—had he found it? swiped it?—tossed a new helping of sand onto the barrier he was erecting against the oncoming sea.

"That won't work," I said.

"Yes, it will."

"Don't you see? You started too far down."

"You don't know anything."

"But the water will come around the sides."

Even as I spoke there was a thud, I felt it through the rubber soles of my Keds, and in no time a wave came snarling and snapping to within a foot of the redoubt.

"No, it won't!" shouted Barton, standing upright and pointing skyward with the blade of his plastic shovel. As if he were Neptune, the sea retreated.

I shouldn't have been surprised. Bartie had always been an imperious god. Ten years earlier we'd driven out to the pier for a Sunday brunch, only to find all the restaurants closed and barbed wire strung clear across the dock. At the end, hundreds of feet away, barrage balloons bobbed on thick wire cables. More of the antiaircraft devices were tethered well out to sea. A trick of the light, the perspective of a three-year-old child, the taut lines gathered on buoys or barges, made it seem that these fat blimps, a mile off shore, were street-corner balloons. "Want one! Want one!" Bartie cried, stamping first one foot then the other. Down he went, rolling on the planks of the pier. Norman plucked him up and ran for our Packard sedan. A terrible wail trailed the fleeing figures, so loud, so piercing, and adamant too, that I half-expected the whole of the fleet to nose about and follow him dutifully home, like a herd of cows that were lighter than air.

There was another thump, hard enough to send sandslides down the walls of Bartie's excavation, and the next moment the wave came rushing up, biting at the bottom of the barricade with its slick white fangs. Bartie jumped from the pit and began inexplicably to scoop at the mud that the wave had left behind and pile it up on the untouched sand.

"What are you doing?" I asked. "What are you making now?"

"It's Jolie's pyramid," he answered. "You know, at the cemetery."

"You mean his shrine? It's not a pyramid."

"It is too! The same as in Egypt."

"Well, how do you know that?"

"How do you know it isn't?"

He had a point. Neither of us had gone to our father's funeral, yet like almost everyone in Los Angeles we had a vague impression of the Jolson Monument, which could be seen on the hillside, white and blazing, by those driving to the airport on Sepulveda. "What is this?" I asked, with foreboding. "This hole in the ground?"

"A grave."

"A grave. For who?"

"For Sammy. He died."

I stood for an instant, shivering in the sea spray. "What do you mean? What are you saying?" But I had understood clearly enough. I suddenly realized that he had not been at the house when I left it. Poor Sammy! Where was he? In the garbage can? Waiting for the garbage truck?

Bartie was patting down the sides of the singer's memorial. "He did it. The Nazi dog."

I turned toward the highway, where I could just make out the brown and black Alsatian, prowling at the end of his leash. Then I turned seaward again and dropped quickly to the floor of the grave. On all fours, dog-like myself, I pawed at the hardened sand. "Dig! Dig deeper!" I cried. "We've got to bury him! Before the sea comes in!"

Bartie squeezed in beside me. Like a slave on a chain gang, he threw shovelful after shovelful onto the top of the embankment. We kept at it for a minute, a minute more, though the thunder of the surf seemed to be clapping directly over our heads. Then we glanced at each other and broke simultaneously into laughter.

"Not a pyramid!" Bartie guffawed.

"No, a tower!" I answered.

Then we both yelled together: "The Awful Tower!" You would have thought that the strength of our shouts alone would have brought down the walls of Sammy's tomb. "The Eye-Full Tower!"

We were both thinking of the great monument in Paris, down the stairs of which we'd seen the actor Alec Guinness come running. That is where we were during Norman's funeral, at a movie, a comedy, where we laughed our fool heads off. Everyone in Hollywood was at the cemetery; a thousand people saw how Lotte had jumped into her husband's grave.

The oncoming sea covered us with its spume. We hadn't much time. Frantically we dug until with a boom like artillery a final wave seemed to break at point-blank range, eradicating the retaining wall and, with a torrent of water, collapsing all four sides of the grave. "Oh, Sammy!" I cried, as if the poor spaniel had actually been disinterred. I pushed the meat of my palms into my eyes to dam the welling tears. Then, with a sucking sound, the wave retreated and the water drained from what was now no more than a shallow depression.

"Look," said Barton. "Listen." About our covered feet and across the sodden landscape there now opened ten thousand tiny holes, inside of which we thought we could hear the faint clicking membranes of the buried animals, the crabs, the clams, the periwinkles, unhappy insects and spiders, each of them gasping for light and air.

4

It was already mid-afternoon. The haze, which had only half-lifted, holding itself in a thin suspension, now began to drop like a curtain on our matinee. The bathers retreated from the edge of the ocean. Outward, toward Malibu Point, a surfer rode a large wave, green and milky, like water in a glass of absinthe. A second surfer paddled seaward, windmilling his arms. I walked the beach, zigzagging about in a fruitless search for our mother. People had begun to pack up, calling in their children, shaking the sand from their own beach towels onto those of the groups farther inland. A biplane flew by, dragging a banner for Zesto.

On a nearby blanket two men, both shirtless, with barrel chests and hair-covered bellies, had the ballgame from Gilmore Field on their portable radio. The Stars were playing the Beavers. I stopped to listen. Portland was up 4–2, but we had Gene Handley on first and Ted Beard at the plate; only a few weeks before he'd hit four home runs in a single game against the Padres and right after that tied a league record with twelve straight hits. On this Sunday, however, he went down on three pitches. Frank Kelleher, my favorite, hit a long foul and then grounded to short. How Lee Walls got on base I didn't know, because the biplane had banked round and buzzed so low I could see the streaming hair of the pilot; but when the noise of the propeller had faded the bespectacled outfielder was on first, Handley on third, and Dale Long had the count against him, one ball and two strikes. He sent the next pitch over the left field wall. The roar that went up from the radio was much like the sound of the surf. I gave a little jump, instinctively mimicking the leap I used to take from my seat to hug my brother, my father, the perfect strangers in the rows before and behind.

There would be no embrace of these two fans. Neither of the men had reacted at all. They didn't even seem to hear the crowd as the hero circled the bases. Each remained propped on an elbow, looking northward to where a woman in sunglasses lay flat on the sand. Her dress was hiked over her open knees, and her head was pillowed on the woven straw of her basket. It was Lotte. I walked over and knelt next to her sleeping form. She lay parallel to the coastline, one arm by her side, the other flung outward. In sleep, all the lines had disappeared from her face. A sheen of perspiration clung to her cheeks, her brow. I saw that she had slipped both straps of her bodice from her shoulders. When the wind puffed in off the sea it lifted a flap of her sundress, so that the pink nipple was plainly visible on her breast. The breeze lost its grip, the cotton dropped down, only to rise upon the next breath of air. Behind my back, I knew, the two men still lay on their haunches, unabashedly staring.

I ran. First uphill, toward the house, the highway, the car; then to the left, along the rows of pilings; then back, at an angle toward the ocean. All too soon my chest, my throat were burning; I could barely lift my high-topped sneakers from the sand; I staggered to a halt.

"Richard! Hello! Have you come to assist me? That is admirable."

It was René, dressed now in an old-fashioned black swimsuit, clinging tights and sleeveless top. He was dragging a rowboat from the inland lagoon toward the sea. Its brown wood was slathered with lacquer. The oars were stowed inside. "You are strong? *Fort*, eh? Let us carry her together. It is not good, you know, the friction of the sand." He threw the rope into the boat and strode from front to rear. For some reason the nautical terms came to me: the prow, the stern, the painter. I gave a little laugh: *more of a painter than you are.* He squatted and without straining lifted the heavy back. "Now you. Not with the torso. With the muscles of the thigh." I wanted, now, to laugh out loud, to walk away, as a spectator might from the strongman in a circus. Instead, like a zombie, I did exactly as commanded: moved to the front of the rowboat, took hold of the—*gunwale*, was it?—and raised my half of the craft. The two of us walked crabwise to the foaming shore.

Timing the breakers, we made our way out to where the boat floated freely. The Frenchman, up to his waistline, steadied her while I climbed aboard and took the seat at the rear. Then he hauled himself over the side. Without a word he grasped the oars, turned our prow to the open sea, and began to row. Immediately I felt seasick, though I did not know whether the wave of nausea was caused by the motion of our little boat across the troughs and swells, or by the fact that each time the rower raised his oars from the ocean, I smelled the brilliantine on the head of hair that thrust nearly to my lap. I bit my lip. It may be that I had turned a shade of green. For beneath his furrowed brow René glanced upward. "Ha! Ha! Ha!" he laughed. "The *mal de mer.*"

He did not break his rhythm. If anything he rowed with more determination. Sweat dripped from his hairline; droplets of it formed on his shoulders. His black shirt was soaked through. I heard how, at the start of each stroke, he grunted. It was as if he were in a race, rowing against others, and not on an outing for pleasure. Suddenly, as if we'd crossed a finish line, he slipped the oars, so that the shafts lay at the waterline and the blades rose on either side of me, neck-high. For a moment he panted. His fingers, I saw, were curled, as though he were still gripping the wooden poles. Then he turned and reached into the prow, where an oilskin pouch was hanging. He took out a pack of Chesterfields and a book of matches. What was left of the breeze blew out the flame in his hooked hands, repeatedly. But just as I was about to bark with derision, he drew the flame into the end of his cigarette.

"Lotte," he said, with the Gallic shrug. "She does not permit me cigarettes, though she smokes herself. Her opinion is that it was this habit that killed your father." I did not reply. The boat remained motionless amid the whitecaps, like a decoration on a frosted cake. René exhaled a blue, diesel-like cloud from his nostrils. "Richard, I did not know your father—except, naturally, through his work. During the war it was not possible to see American cinema. *Les Boches,* you know. And then we had our hands full, as you say. But I remember, in Nineteen Thirty-Nine, and also in Nineteen Forty, how the laughter rang out in the theaters of Paris. Not to mention these last years, when according to my taste he created his finest films. Well, I have not had the opportunity to tell you I am very sorry at your loss, which is also I understand very well a loss for all the world."

I had, at these words, to fight back a surge of tears. I turned my head. I brought my fist down on my knee. "Selfish!" I said out loud. But I kept to myself the source of this sorrow: *Poor Stanley,* those were the words I was thinking, furious that the pale, pudgy attorney, Norman's pal, had been forced to drag Bartie and me all around the city, to the museum, to the movies, when of course he wanted to be at the funeral of his friend. "Selfish!" I said once again, this time without tears, and perhaps even with some gratification that the Frenchman was bound to misunderstand.

With a quick motion he flicked his cigarette over the side. "*Oui.* Selfish. It is true. Your loss, it was also my opportunity. I have been enabled to meet Lotte. Yes. Ironic." A pause. The waves slapped and sucked at the watertight boards. René took a deep breath, as if upon his abandoned cigarette. "Richard, it is important that you know something. Allow me to tell you I love your mother very much. She is the delight of my life. My intention is to marry her. I offer you the promise that I will do all in my power to make her happy. As she makes me happy now." Another pause. Another inhalation. "In this case I will be for you and Barton a kind of father. I do not speak of Norman. I know what he meant to you. But you should know this, Richard: I will work to make up this loss, and I will make the attempt to be for you a good parent. I hope that in the course of time we shall perhaps respect each other and experience love among the members of our family."

"What you mean, *respect? Love?* Don't make me laugh!" All I could think of was his arms on my mother's back, she leaning into him, the blowing curtains that had exposed them. *The Kiss,* by Rodin. "I know you're living in sin!"

At these words René plucked up the oars, leaned forward once more, and dipped both blades into the ocean. I felt the same thrill of triumph that

I supposed Dale Long must have sensed when the sweet spot of his bat struck the fastball. I had won! Humbled, defeated, the Frenchman was taking me back. But then I noted that he had swung the prow westward and that, more leisurely now, effortlessly even, we were drawing still further from the coastline. I peered ahead, to the horizon, only to discover that there was no longer any demarcation between sea and sky. I wheeled to look over my shoulder. The very continent had disappeared! The hills were gone and so was the highway, with its stream of cars. There was no bluff, no row of houses. The beach itself was dissolving, as if inundated by a great, gray wave. Here and there I could make out a figure, half dismembered, or an article of clothing: a bathing suit in red; a parasol, orange; a scarf, green or greenish, held aloft. Was that Lotte? Waving a greeting? Signaling danger? In a few more strokes even those shreds had vanished. It was dead calm. There was nothing but fog on every side. Soon even the tips of the oars, the dripping blades, grew blurred. René rowed on.

"This is far enough." The words, my own, in that bell jar, sounded like a shout.

René, not halting, glanced up. "Far enough for what?" he answered.

I had no idea why I said what came out next. "For whatever you want to do."

He did not respond. He pulled the oars six more times. Then he sat upright, letting the shafts dangle in the water. "Yes. It is far enough."

I did not dare speak, because I feared my voice would tremble, not so much from fear as from the force of an inexplicable sadness. René spoke instead.

"It is a pity. I have offered you friendship. But you make a mockery. I row, you know, to release the anger in my arms." I stared at those arms, which hung at his sides, and at his fingers, which once more remained tense and curled. "You are a boy, a child, nothing, Richard: there is in you no experience of life. But in your work, that is where you are already a man. Poor René, eh? He looks in the mirror. He paints a clown. Much life. Little talent."

Now, as he spoke, he began to pull on one of the oars. The boat turned on its axis, and kept spinning about in its own little whirlpool. Then, singlehandedly, he removed the Chesterfields from his tightly stretched shirt top, popped like magic a single cigarette from the pack, and placed it in his mouth. Another trick: he struck with one hand a match on his matchbook and in the calm allowed it to burn. "So, Richard, if you will attend my words. This Mademoiselle Madeline. The *petite jeune fille*, eh? The little neighbor girl. You will tell me how you persuaded her to take off her clothes."

That was the instant I realized René was going to kill me. I had read with absolute certainty the contents of his mind. The movement of the boat in a dizzying circle; the match that burned in the gray and gloom; his voice, *you will tell me, attend my words*—it was all a form of hypnotism. And I was the one sleeping, nodding, willing to obey his command: *squeal like a pig! rear like a horse! throw yourself into the water!*

René drew up the oars. He got to his feet, towering above me. One by one, I understood, he was going to kill us all. Starting with poor little Sammy. Then me, the hurdle, the obstacle: *I'd never do anything you didn't approve*. Next crazy Bartie. Poor crazy Bartie. And Lotte too, though only after he'd married her. For her money. Norman's money. His Oscar that looked as if it were made from gold.

He raised the oar, streaming with the wet of the sea. "*Ecoutez!*" he commanded, continuing the fiction that he was a Frenchman. "On your feet." I obeyed. "Turn around." I followed those instructions too, turning my back on him. I had no idea whether I was facing Malibu Beach or the islands of the Pacific, MacArthur's Philippines, the far-off lands of the East. He moved directly behind me in the tipping boat and grasped my shoulders. I took a breath, to prepare for the moment I hit the water. Now I wanted to live. Not for myself. To warn the others. Could I swim for it? But in what direction? And would he not beat the life from me, as one might club to death a swimming rat?

"Don't budge yourself," he said, his grip like iron. Then I smelled something familiar. The sweet wisps of tobacco. He had lit his cigarette.

Suddenly he was by me, sitting in my place at the stern. "Hold these," he said, extending the grips of the oars. He gestured for me to take his empty seat. "You will teach me from your knowledge, all the secrets of art. Perhaps one day, in a future we cannot know, this Betty will also hang a work by René upon her walls. And I? I will teach you. My friend, you have much to learn. So. Straighten your arms, if you please. Lean from the waist. Up. Lift the oars up. Now dip them. Pull! Pull! Pull for *la Californie!*

5

I rowed us in. The breeze, ever capricious, started up again, easing my task. The sun, well down in the sky, began to burn through the thinning haze, like the bulb of a projector scorching a strip of film. We caught a wave into the shallow water, then carried the boat over the gravel and across the beach to its mooring in the lagoon. René headed off to the pastel cabins along the highway. The hills were again in plain view, brown even in springtime, with patches of white yucca. There were still a few people lingering on the beach. I trudged back along the shore. Before I reached the spot where I'd left Bartie, he came running toward me, trailing a dancing and darting maroon-colored kite.

"Where'd you get that?" I asked.

He looked up to where the kite tugged at its taut, white tether. "It was under the house. He's got a box of stuff down there."

Just then a dog came rushing out of the surf and made for us. "It's Sammy!" I exclaimed. The spaniel, half normal size in his wet coat, leaped at me, happily barking. Then he shook the salt water from his body. "You said he killed him!" I screamed at Bartie. "That Achille killed him! It was a lie!"

My brother was still looking up, to where the kite was diving toward the ground. He pulled on the cord, which sent it swooping skyward again. Then he turned the wet and glittering marble of his eyes on me. "I didn't lie. You don't know the truth. It's possible to come back from the dead."

"Oh-hoo! Yoo-hoo!" I knew that cry. Lotte was making her way toward us from the foot of the tumbledown house. Behind her, René followed, carrying a small four-legged tray, like a Japanese table for tea. He'd changed back into his shirt of concentric circles, blue and yellow, and had on a pair of white tennis player's pants.

"Éclairs!" he shouted. "Éclairs!"

Lotte waved her grass-green scarf. "Well," she exclaimed, as she drew closer. "If Mahomet won't come to the mountain—"

I saw that she'd washed out her hair, which now hung loose and dark to her shoulders. Sam dashed by her, making for René. He leaped three feet in the air, hoping to snatch one of the cream-filled pastries.

Bartie grabbed my arm. He put the spindle of string into my hand. "It's you who made the mistake," he said, starting up the beach to get his dessert. "It was all inside your head."

I remained alone for a moment, while the three of them, the four counting Sammy, arranged themselves around the lacquered tray. Motionless, I stared across the ocean. There was no way I could know that just two months later René and Lotte would be married. Or that, after another two months, she would discover that he had looted all her accounts. In the British comedy Alec Guinness is led off in handcuffs. In real life René and my mother only divorced. But by then much had irrevocably changed. Bartie and I were sent off for a few months to a private academy; when we came back we discovered that Sammy, irascible, not to be reconciled with Achille, had been put to sleep. He had seen clearly what, on that far-off Sunday, I could only imagine.

At Malibu, on the empty beach, the kite continued to jerk back and forth above my head. At my feet a wave broke into pieces, like a hundred thousand silvery minnows, or beads of mercury that soon reassembled themselves beneath the shining mirror of the sea.

DESERT

(1952)

I

Wild Red Berry rebounded from the ropes and, though only half the size of his opponent, seized him by the leg and by the neck. With the strength of Hercules he lifted him over his head.

"Uh-oh," said Arthur, our butler. "That Gorgeous George in big trouble now."

Indeed, Wild Red threw down the heavy wrestler, like a stevedore hurling a bale or a barrel into the hold. The tremendous thud rattled the speaker of our brand new Zenith, and dust rose from the canvas square on the screen.

"Get up, Gorgeous! Get up!" My brother, Bartie, as blond as the fallen gladiator, was bouncing on the springs of the couch.

How could he get up? The wiry Berry had thrown himself across his antagonist's chest. All you could see was the curl-covered head of the giant, along with his helplessly flailing legs.

"Sure looks like the end this time," said Arthur.

"No, no, no!" wailed Bartie. "Don't say that! I'll kill you if you say that!"

But fate in the form of the referee was already kneeling, preparing to slap the surface of the ring.

"Why you let these boys watch your trash?" That was Mary, Arthur's wife, who had just opened the door. Her gold-rimmed glasses flashed as she walked in front of the set.

"Move, Mary. I can't see."

"You the one to move, Mister Barton. And your big brother too. Don't you have the sense you were born with?" That last was addressed to her husband, who, save for the white of his collar and the whites of his eyes, was nearly invisible in the darkened room. "These children got school tomorrow. I's the one to get them out of their beds. Do you know what time it is to be watching this show?"

Barton: "Get out of the way! You fatty! He's escaped! I know!"

Mary clicked off the TV. "You boys, you bet—"

She did not have a chance to finish. Bartie was bounding across the den. "You big black Aunt Jemima!" He pushed the heavy woman aside and pulled the knob of the set. "Didn't I tell you? Bartie knows. Bartie sees."

What we all saw was that the fallen gladiator had not only, Houdini-like, escaped, but had turned the tables. Now the head of Wild Red Berry protruded backward from the thighs of Gorgeous George, almost as if the big wrestler were in some fashion giving birth to the little one.

"Watch out," warned Arthur. "Gorgeous George going to give him the pile driver."

Which he did, dropping onto his buttocks with such force that the face of Wild Red Berry was smashed against the mat.

"Oh," said Mary. "That poor man."

"Kill him," cried Bartie. "Kill him, Gorgeous!"

"Don't worry," I said, to no one in particular. "It's fixed. It's all an act."

But I was worried myself, since only a few weeks before I had hauled Wild Red's clubs around the back nine of the Riviera Country Club. If anything was an act, it was my imitation of a caddy. Berry, however, never said a word as I rattled the sticks in his bag or suggested an eight iron when, on the famed 18th hole, he had two hundred yards to the elevated green. I didn't need the twenty-dollar bill he pushed into my hand. I was trudging the course to build character. The minute the wrestler dropped his final putt I went to the clubhouse and put a chocolate malted, with whipped cream, onto my father's tab.

"You aiming to stay up to the hour of midnight? Miss Lotte know, she'd whip me with that tongue of hers worse than those two men beating each other." Mary wrapped her nightdress around her thick figure and once again bent to turn off the Zenith.

My brother grabbed for the knob. "You don't know the rules. You're the servant. You obey Bartie."

The two of them struggled for a moment. Mary fell back against the set, which unaccountably came on—not to the wrestling match, at least not the one in Santa Monica.

Would you state your name for the record? a voice intoned.

Even before our father could reply, Bartie said, "Look, it's Daddy."

"Sure enough," said Arthur. "It's Mister Norman. On the television from Washington, DC."

Between them, I realized, Mary and Barton had changed the channel. This was the kinescope of that day's testimony before the House Committee on Un-American Activities. Norman, in a dark suit, with his trademark handkerchief pouring from his suit pocket, sat behind a microphone. Our friend Stanley was beside him, whispering something into his ear. I saw that Norman's hat was on the table. What was left of his hair looked damp, and was pressed against the tanned surface of his skull.

"Would you spell that for us, sir? Is it Jacobi with an *i* or a *y*?"

"Yes," said our father. "It's with an *i*. J-a-c-o-b-i."

I looked for Lotte, but everyone in the crowd behind the table was blurred.

The same man, Mr. Walter according to the plaque on his high desktop, leaned into the microphone. "Mister Jacobi, we hope to take only a few minutes of your time. It won't be necessary to do anything more than repeat here the questions you agreed to answer in executive session. I assume that arrangement sits well with you?"

My father nodded.

Mr. Walter: "You understand that your employer, Mister Jack Warner, indicated that you were suspect in his eyes because, and I quote, 'He is always on the side of the underdog.' Do you wish to respond to that? Or do you wish to make a statement?"

"No, I have no statement. I am ready to answer the questions."

"Mister Wood."

A second camera surveyed the congressmen in their leather chairs, including the one who was just now putting on a pair of reading glasses.

"I have just one question for the witness," he said, "though it comes in two parts. *Have you ever been a member of a subversive organization?* That's part one. And part two is, *If so, name that organization.* May we proceed with your answers?"

It was like a movie. The four of us, the two sons, the two servants, watched entranced as the camera caught Norman in a medium close-up. He nodded again. "In response to the first part of your question, the answer is, *Yes.*"

There was a gasp from the crowd, which was suddenly no longer out of focus. The camera panned through the committee room: there were the crouching reporters with their notepads, the photographers with their flashbulb reflectors, the tangle of dark cords on the floor; and there too were the rows of men and women, among whom, in a pillbox hat and with slightly smeared lipstick, sat our mother. She was arm in arm with Betty, her childhood friend.

"That's Lotte," said Bartie, putting his finger on the glass of the screen. Then he put his lips there. "Here, Lotte. Here is a kiss for good luck."

Arthur said, "Best turn the machine off, Mary. No good coming from it."

Norman was already leaning forward again. His handkerchief, I thought, looked as white as a flower. "The answer to the second part of your question is, *Warner Brothers.*"

There was a pause, whether of puzzlement or shock I could not say. Then someone cried, "Oh, my *God!*" The next thing I heard was laughter, ripples of it, then a roar of it. Mr. Walter was calling for silence, to no effect. Stanley had his hand cupped to Norman's ear and was shouting something. Someone's microphone was making a ringing sound. A policeman moved in front of the photographers, as if to block with the bulk of his body the rays from their flashing bulbs. I saw Betty with her head back, laughing. A veil, pocked with dark dots, had fallen over Lotte's face, so that it was impossible to know if she were laughing too.

"What's *subversive?*" asked Barton. "Is it something funny?"

A Mr. Frank Tavenner had the word *Counsel* on his nameplate. He was the one banging the gavel. "Come to order! Come to order!" he shouted. "Come to order or we'll clear the room!"

The noise, if it did not stop, subsided.

"Did you wish to say something, Mister Jackson?" Mr. Walter asked.

"I just wanted to say that everyone knows Mister Norman Jacobi is a great humorist. I've had my share of fun at his films, too. But this is not the time for cutups, sir. The country is in danger. Do you wish to answer our questions or do you want to play the wiseacre? Because if he's going to be a wiseacre, Mister Chairman, I'd just as soon dismiss the witness without further testimony."

That sobered the crowd. In the ensuing silence Norman said, "I am sorry, Congressman. It's a flaw I have. You correctly bring attention to it—that even at the most inappropriate times I can't resist. I'm afraid that what Chairman Walter said about Jack, about Mister Warner: well, I think he named everyone on the lot he couldn't get under contract. I apologize. I let my feelings run away with me."

I felt, at those words, a hollow sensation in the pit of my stomach, as if Gorgeous George had butted it with his head. *Apologize?* To *them?* I could not believe it. I watched my father wipe his hands on the side of his pants and then, under the hot lights of the television cameras, use his handkerchief to wipe his brow. It was like a flag of surrender.

Mr. Jackson: "I think I speak for the membership when I say we understand how in times like these feelings run high. We appreciate your patriotism and your spirit of cooperation. Now Mister Tavenner has told us that in executive session you expressed your conviction that the United States of America is under attack and that its enemies are undermining our institutions and our Constitution."

Another congressman, Mr. Doyle, said, "Would counsel read the pertinent passage from the executive transcript? We are being broadcast by the medium of television. I think all Americans should hear it."

Tavenner had been prepared. His thumb, I saw, was at the proper page. He did not need glasses. "I have it here, Congressman. Mister Jacobi states, 'I have come to believe the country is being undermined by a small but determined group of fanatics who have no respect for our liberties or our way of life. They have no respect for our laws. They mock our free institutions. They have done great damage and threaten to do more. They are more powerful now than they have ever been before.'"

Mr. Doyle said, "That's the part. About being more powerful than ever before. It's the very point we've been trying to establish."

Mr. Jackson: "And did the witness declare that he was willing to give us the names of those he rightly calls fanatics?"

"Don't you think we should change the channel?" I asked in a voice plainly cracking. "Arthur, we won't know who won. I'll bet on Wild Red Berry. What about you, Bartie? Want to bet a quarter on Gorgeous George?"

But the chauffeur sat unmoving. My brother rocked from foot to foot, a bulge of concentration forming on his brow. Even Mary stood with her fists on her hips, as if to express her indignation. Meanwhile Mr. Tavenner was confirming for the committee that our father had indeed promised to disclose a list of names.

It was the turn of Mr. Wood: "Very well, sir. Are you prepared now to give us these people by name?"

"I am."

There was, in that paneled room, as in our own stucco den, a perfect silence. Norman, from an inside breast pocket, took out a piece of paper folded in squares. As he spread it open, Stanley, his pale, plump attorney, shaded his eyes. "Clyde Doyle," my father began. Then, a little louder: "Donald Jackson. John S. Wood. Francis E. Walter. Frank Tavenner—"

The room was already in an uproar. Mr. Walter, red-faced, was smashing the gavel down all over the surface of the desk in front of him. Flashbulbs were going off like lightning. The audience was laughing even more loudly than before. Mr. Wood was on his feet now. "Why, he's giving the names of this committee!"

Norman said, "Oh, I can do better than that. Martin Dies. J. Parnell Thomas. John Rankin. Jack Tenny. Joseph McCarthy. Richard Nixon—"

"He's under oath! Under oath! Cite him for contempt!" Mr. Jackson, in lieu of a gavel, was pounding the desktop with his fists.

"Remove the witness." That was Tavenner. "Sergeant at arms! Remove the witness from the room!"

Arthur said, "My, oh my. Going to be the devil to pay now."

"You got no call saying anything about Mr. Norman, the man be so kindly toward us these years."

"Those men are big men, that's all I'm saying."

"Do you get it, Bartie?" I asked my brother. "Ha, ha, ha! Do you see how he turned them into fools?"

Barton ignored me. He bent to the Zenith and switched back to the live broadcast from the Santa Monica Auditorium. Wild Red Berry was gone. So was Gorgeous George. This was a tag team match. Two men wearing masks were bouncing off the ropes and hurling themselves against two other men wearing capes. They were throwing fists. They were throwing chairs. It was mayhem. It was pandemonium. The referee ran about like a puppy jumping at the humans' knees. The open-mouthed crowd was hooting. Bartie stood up; he turned around. Even in the near-absolute darkness of our little room I could see that his uneven eyes were sparkling with delight.

As Mary had feared, it wasn't easy getting us out of bed the next morning. The telephone, ringing incessantly, woke us, not my old Donald Duck clock. There wasn't time for breakfast. Mary packed a bag with peanut butter and jelly sandwiches, the crust cut off the way Bartie liked them. Arthur had his chauffeur's cap on the dark dome of his head.

"I am thinking I best drive you boys down to school in the Buick."

That wouldn't please Bartie, I knew, since he sat in the seat behind the bus driver, Mrs. Rakotomalala, who was from the island of Madagascar, and who always kept up a conversation with him, in English and French, which he gave every indication of understanding.

"No, no. I want the bus," cried Barton. "I won't ride with old Uncle Ben."

We compromised: Arthur pulled the Buick from the garage and drove us through the morning mist to the stop, which was at the corner of Sunset and Capri. The bus was already there, its stop sign extended, the warning lights flashing. We ran to the steps.

The Coveney brothers stood in the open door. "You aren't getting in," said Pat.

Peter, his sibling, said, "Un-Americans not allowed."

Barton stared up at Mrs. Rakotomalala, but she peered straight ahead, as if mesmerized by the metronomic sweep of the windshield blade.

"Keep them out!" shouted someone from the rear. To our amazement the dark-skinned woman pulled on the lever and the door closed in our faces. The school bus pulled away.

Arthur remained next to the buttermilk Buick, which was spilling its exhaust over the ground. I got into the back. Barton climbed in next to the chauffeur, where he could pretend to steer and pretend to step on the gas. We started down Sunset but turned surprisingly onto Sepulveda, well before Westwood Boulevard.

"Arthur, where are we going?" I asked. "Aren't we going to school?"

"No, sir, Mister Richard. Got no time now to take you to the Junior High. Miss Lotte and Mister Norman took the midnight airplane. Got to hurry or we going to miss them."

Which explained why he wove through the morning traffic and uncharacteristically sped through the yellow lights. We pulled off at Century Boulevard and after only a few blocks the canvas top of the convertible began to ripple and a huge Constellation passed overhead, its propellers whirring and its flaps fully down.

"There they are! It's them!"

I watched the landing gear descend. I watched the three rudders fishtail and sink from view. "Maybe it is, Bartie. Maybe that's the plane. They always fly TWA."

"Don't be stupid. Lotte was in the window. She had a hat on. With a feather. Not like the one on TV."

All any of us knew for certain was that by the time we'd parked the car and made our way to the gate, Flight 1212, Washington to Los Angeles, had landed. There were, as yet, no passengers in sight. Or, if they'd started down the red carpet, we couldn't see them because of the press of photographers and reporters. There were more of them here than in the hearing room. For a moment I wondered which statesman or movie star they'd come to greet; but at the sight of Hedda Hopper, licking the point of her pencil between her painted lips, I understood they were all here for my father. There were rope lines, just as there were at one of Norman's premieres. At the rear on the opposite side I saw Arthur holding his cap up, the way other people held signs.

There was a stir. I ran to the end of the carpet, where the crowd had thinned out. Two men in uniform, with a stewardess between them, were coming down the aisle, pulling their luggage behind in wire carts. Pilots, perhaps. Then the first-class passengers began to come through the gangway and onto the carpet. They were laughing, most of them, as if relieved to be on the ground. Even the solitary travelers seemed to be smiling at some private joke.

Stanley came out of the tunnel. His mouth was set and his skin looked green, as if he had been sick on the plane. I always called him Pear Shape, after the Dick Tracy character that I followed in the comics. Betty and Lotte came next, arms linked, just as they had been in the hearing room. The next thing I knew Bartie was running the length of the carpet. "I saw you up in the air!" he shouted. "I saw your hat!" Indeed our mother wore a light brown hat with a dark brown feather. She knelt, holding her arms out. The light from the flashlamps washed over her like water. Everyone was shouting, wanting to know what she thought of the hearing and whether she had heard that her husband had been suspended by the studio, and if the family was going to issue an apology. By way of reply she said, "Do you know my son Barton? He's the younger one. Just look at these curls! Did you ever see anything like them? And the blue in his beautiful blue eyes! Oh, this is my fine big boy!" She put both arms around him and kissed him on the cheeks and on the forehead. She wasn't done speaking:

"And so talented! I used to think he'd be a painter. He did such pretty drawings. But nowadays he goes up to his room and stays there for *hours!* Do you know what he's doing? Writing! Such wonderful stories. They make me cry. I'll be happy to give the press a statement. Jack Warner may think he has silenced my husband, but the real writer is going to be my son!"

The trouble was, no one was listening. That was because Norman had emerged from the gangway. The crowd surged toward him. The stanchions went over, pulling the ropes along with them. Betty gave a shriek. I saw Stanley turn and try to make his way back to his friend. A policeman began to wade through the throng. I followed him until I could break through to where Norman was standing. He crouched upon seeing me and held up his hands. This was a regular greeting: I threw punches and he, once a champion bantamweight at Penn State, expertly blocked every one. The crowd stepped back as I swung away. My fists splatted against his open palms. We both were grinning.

"You were amazing!" I told him, puffing already. "You almost fooled me. Except I knew you were no fink. You showed them up. Now the whole country knows."

"You want to fight, eh? Eh?" He seized my fists and, as if performing some new form of jujitsu, bent my punches back toward my face.

"I know why you did it," I said, ducking as best I could from the impact of my own blows. "You had to, right, Norman? It's what you always say. Hey! Ouch! Don't!"

The harder I struck, the greater the force he directed against my cheek, my chin. I tried to finish what I wanted to say. "You know, about the mirror? About shaving? Ow! That hurt! You always have to look at yourself in the morning."

For another half minute he redirected my punches, so that I struck myself hard on my nose and on my eye. Then he dropped his hands and pulled me forward in what I thought was a boxer's clinch, but which I soon realized was an embrace.

"Sorry, Rich," he was saying. "Sorry, Richie, sorry, sorry, sorry."

I hugged him back. I remembered what he smelled like. I felt the day's growth of his whiskers against my scalp and against my skin.

Then the battle was rejoined. But it wasn't I who was striking at Norman and it wasn't Norman fighting back. I realized that it was Bartie who had set upon him. He was leaping forward, windmilling his arms. His face was red, both from emotion and from the lipstick kisses with which Lotte had covered him. All during the attack he was screaming like a banshee:

"You're a traitor! A Communist! A Benedict Arnold!"

2

At the parking garage we said goodbye to Stanley, who was going to drive Betty home in his new Mercury coupe. "Is Norman going to be blacklisted?" I asked him, sotto voce, while formally shaking hands.

"Not to worry," he answered, though his skin was still ashen. "We're going to sue Jack's ass off."

Betty came over, bearing her usual gifts. Mine was a pair of cuff links, clearly gold. "Don't thank me," she protested. "I am going to make oodles out of your drawings. Don't tell your mother, but I'm planning on opening the show early next year."

That's when Arthur came round in the Buick. We locked our suitcases in the trunk; Norman got into the front, and Barton and Lotte and I slid into the rear.

"Where's Sammy?" my father asked, as if he had just realized that our little spaniel was not there to greet him. Then the greater realization struck him: "Hey, why are you guys not in Emerson? I hope you're not skipping classes."

"Didn't have no time to fetch that dog, Mister Norman. I thought to myself these boys going to find unhappiness in that school."

"I see," said Lotte. "It's Subpoena Day. Citation Day. A national celebration."

"Do you know what Mister Murphy said?" Bartie asked. "He said that I am the fastest boy in P.E. He timed me with a stopwatch."

No one responded. Norman looked out his window, squinting against the sun's attempts to make its way through the last of that morning's clouds; and Lotte looked out of hers.

There were more reporters in front of our house. Their cars were parked on both sides of San Remo Drive. They besieged us when Arthur rolled down his window to unlatch the gate. There were another twenty or thirty people stretched along the length of the metal fence. They were shouting and waving their homemade signs.

"I didn't imagine this in Riviera," Lotte said.

"Don't kid yourself," Norman answered. "They never wanted us here in the first place."

We drove by the front of the house to the open space between the two wings. Sammy, in greeting, ran in Sambo-like circles around the pecan tree. Mary stood at the back doorway, her hands pressed against her white uniform. We could hear the phone ringing in every part of the house. Then, as if seized by the same breeze that was tossing the feather-shaped leaves, the family Jacobi blew off each in his own direction. Lotte said, "I don't care about the weather. Let it rain! Let it shine! I am going for my swim." Off she went to the bedroom to change into her suit.

"Take the phone off the hook, please, Arthur," Norman said. "I'm taking a ten minute nap. Don't let me sleep any longer. I've got a mountain of scripts." He climbed the stairs to the library, to lie down on the leather couch. Bartie took Sam through the arch to the yard in back, where they could play catch with figs from the hedge. Mary thought she'd better prepare for lunch; and Arthur took off his cap and his jacket, then rolled up his sleeves and started to polish the silverware with a stained yellow cloth.

I snuck out the side gate and crossed Romany Drive to Madeline's house. I hadn't seen her through the window of the bus that morning, which meant that she was probably still in bed with the flu. The Italian maid grudgingly allowed me upstairs. I once heard Norman say she had had to leave Rome because her family was connected to Mussolini. "You should see the grin on Patrizia," I said to Madeline, by way of greeting. She was in bed, with my copy of *The Grapes of Wrath* propped on her knees. "Our downfall is her triumph. I thought she was going to laugh in my face."

"Did you ever hear of knocking? It's the gentlemanly thing to do."

I saw that she wasn't reading—or that, while reading, she was also painting her nails.

"Who's a gentleman?" I replied.

"That's right. You're the bohemian. Exempt from society's rules. Maybe the *artiste* will do my right hand. I'm no good with my left."

I took the little bottle and began to paint the index finger she extended toward me. Her wrist, where I held it, was warm with fever. "I've got news," I told her.

"Yes, I read in the paper. What's the matter with you? Why don't you sit down?"

I eased myself, a little primly, onto the edge of the mattress. "I don't mean that. I mean I saw Betty this morning. She said we have enough drawings already. She's going to hang them in her gallery. It's going to be a one-man show."

Madeline pulled her hand away to clap it against the other. "Oh, that's wonderful! You'll just be starting at Uni. You might be a genius like Picasso."

"Yeah, well, Picasso didn't have Betty as his mother's best friend. Everything comes down to luck."

"It's a good thing you have enough of the sketches. Daddy, he— well, he doesn't want me to pose anymore. He never liked it. I told him it was only my back, mostly, but that's not what's bothering him. I heard him this morning hollering down at breakfast. *What a bunch of Communists! I always knew it! A bunch of Commies!* Ha, ha, ha! It makes you sound like bananas."

"It's not true. Even if it was, I'd have no apologies. I know some Communists, ex-Communists actually—at least I think they were. They are idealistic people. They wanted to change the world for the better. Are you reading this book? Or is it a prop—?"

"Of *course* I'm reading it. I'm already up to how they are treated when they get to California."

"It wasn't just California. It was *everywhere*. On the East Coast, in Massachusetts, half the workers in the cranberry bogs were children. It was terrible. They were up to their chests in the water."

Madeline put both hands—the seven painted nails, the three I hadn't got to—to her face and tee-hee'd like a little girl.

"*What* is so funny? There weren't any child labor laws until the Forties. Roosevelt tried but the Supreme Court wouldn't let him. *Will* you stop giggling?"

"I'm sorry, Richard-boy. I really am. Bananas and cranberries. I didn't think we were going to talk about fruit."

"We're not. We're talking about children's lives!"

"No need to shout, Richard-boy. I'll pose for you, no matter what Daddy says, even if you are a Communist."

"I told you, that's a canard. Lotte and Norman, they didn't even vote for Henry Wallace. Don't you remember? How I rang all the doorbells in the last election? Your father, he said he was voting for Dewey. Dewey! That's practically treason."

"I don't know why I'm not angry with you when you say something like that. I love my father just like you love yours. He is an outstanding businessman and provides jobs for almost a hundred people, even if he's not famous for his wit and hasn't won an Academy Award. I guess if I'm not angry it must mean that a little bit anyhow I also love you."

She took my hand, the one with the little wet brush in it, and drew it toward her mouth. First she blew on her nails, which now were the color of eggplants, and then she kissed each one of my fingers. The voice of the people was speechless; but she said, "How many times do I have to say it, Richard-boy? I love your artist's hands."

"You've got a fever," I lamely replied.

"No, I'm almost better. I could have gone to school today. I'll go tomorrow. But here's the thing. What I want to say. Besides your hands, it's your mouth I love. Not the shape of it even though the shape is very nice. It's the words that come out of it. All your angry words. About the workers and the Rosenbergs and Senator McCarthy and even the Republican Party. They're like songs. To me they're like love songs. Do you know what I mean? You're the speaker, the orator, and I'm your crowd."

Her breath, as she spoke, washed over my knuckles. That, or her words, made me feel an excitement that I feared was all too visibly sexual. I pulled away, twisting in my embarrassment toward the foot of the bed.

"Oh," said Madeline brightly. "You can do my toes, too!"

I watched as her foot slid out from beneath the little cotton-tufts that decorated her covers. I had painted it often enough. In fact, I was sure Betty wanted one of those studies to go along with the countless charcoals of Madeline's buttocks and Madeline's back. The toes, the arch, the shadows of the hidden bones: none of that had meant any more to me than a peasant's shoe had meant to Van Gogh. This time, however, I wasn't painting a portrait of a foot but, with my tiny brush at the end of the tiny wand, the foot itself.

"Hold still," I said, to stop her from playfully wiggling her toes. She did. I leaned forward, pressing hard against the mattress edge; I moved the bristles, full of thick purple liquid, across her nail. It was all I could do not to kiss the white flesh and green veins of her instep.

Did she hear me groan? I thought I heard, up at the head of the bed, another light laugh. She twisted to the side, where a pile of 45 rpm records was stacked atop the spindle of her gramophone. She clicked it on. She had all the latest hits. As I stroked and restroked the nails of her toes I heard, first, *In the Cool, Cool, Cool of the Evening*; and then, *Come On-a-My House*; and then, *Your Cheating Heart*. From her end at the top of the bed, and from where I knelt at the foot of it, we both started singing, loudly, exaltingly, so that Patrizia could hear—hell, let the whole neighborhood hear—a ballad: "Oh, oh, oh! Kisses Sweeter than Wine!"

Mary had taken a roast beef from the stand-alone freezer that morning, and that night we had it, with string beans and potatoes, for dinner. We ate silently through the salad, though Lotte did her best to brighten the conversation. "I can't tell you boys how good it feels to be home with you eating Mary's cooking and not sleeping in a hotel bed. I certainly prefer my flowers to the Mayflower, ha, ha, ha! Even though it's dark out I feel comforted by the thought that they are in the garden. First thing tomorrow I am taking my scissors and making a big bouquet. Isn't it strange how though I was born in Atlantic City, New Jersey, I do not miss the East Coast in the least? Oh, I do not deny the charms of the Boardwalk and the jitneys and saltwater taffy; boys, we had a horse that would jump off a steel tower into a tank of water. I remember my father with his bicycle and his cigar collecting the rents from the Negro people. Oh, and sneaking crab-cakes into the house though they were not kosher. What else? My sisters! The three sisters, just like in Chekhov; but before you think I am completely dotty I am coming to my point, which is that when I return to California with its tropical flora and fauna—goodness, *cork* trees and the quail and the mountain lions, which we used to hear roar: well, to me in the oddest way it's like coming back to my childhood. I can't explain it. It's unnatural. Like the way I *much* prefer swimming in a pool of chlorine and never once go into the Atlantic or Pacific Oceans."

I thought, a little rudely, that there really wasn't much of a mystery. After all, it was only in California that her childhood fantasies, of being rich and a kind of princess, had come true.

At the smell of roast beef, Sammy came in and took up his station by Norman's chair. The strands of drool hung from his flews.

"Oh, don't!" said Lotte, as Norman threw him a piece of meat.

Then there was nothing but the click of the fork, the click of the knife. After a time Norman said, "Stanley called. He's got tickets for opening day. You guys want to go?"

"Is Paul Petit starting?" I asked, referring to the pitcher who had made such a stir as the first of the bonus babies.

"I think it'll be Johnny Lindell," Norman replied, "but I haven't seen the papers in a while. What's the outfield like?"

"Kelleher's being replaced by Carlos Beiner. Saffel's in center. This guy Ted Beard's in right."

"Stevens at first? Sandlock still catching?"

"Yes, but—"

"Oh, for Heaven's sake!" Lotte exclaimed. "The sky is falling down and we're going to talk about baseball? *Baseball!*"

"What would you prefer to discuss, Lotte? Saltwater taffy?"

Barton, with a milk ring around his mouth, said, "Are we going to have to move out of the house when the sky falls? Are Richard and Bartie going to be waifs?"

"Oh, Bartie," Lotte said. "I could bite my tongue. It's only a figure of speech."

"It's because you're Jews. I heard you say so. The sky is going to fall on you because you killed baby Jesus Christ."

"Why don't you just shut up, Bartie? You don't know anything about anything."

"I do so! You are Jacobies! That's why you are persecuted. The sky is going to fall on you and kill you."

"What the *hell* are you talking about? You crazy idiot—"

"Richard! Your language! Shame on you!"

"Well, listen to him. He should go to a crazy house or a crazy doctor."

Norman: "And you should go to your room. Right now. Move!"

"What about him? He thinks he's different than us. You're just the same as us, crazy Bartie."

"Not! I am not! I am Barton Wilson. Not Jacobi. All the Communists are going to burn in hell."

"I can't stand a minute more of this," said Lotte. "I'm going to scream."

"Stop it," said Norman, "the two of you."

"Make *him* stop," I cried. "Why won't he stop? Please make him be normal. I am tired of waiting and waiting for him to grow up."

"I *am* normal!" cried Bartie. "I believe in General MacArthur."

Then Lotte did scream, loudly. Bartie jumped from his chair and leaped toward Sammy; he covered the dog's ears with his hands.

Norman lifted a fist into the air. "Enough!" he shouted. Then he brought it down so hard on the table that, as in a magic trick, everything on it jumped half an inch in the air. "Goddamn it! Enough!"

Lotte spent the evening playing Schubert sonatas on the baby grand. Exiled to my bedroom, I heard the wrong notes. Later, waking, I heard her voice, then Norman's, arguing, even though they were at the other arm of the house. And this, at all hours: the thud-thud-thud-thump of Barton's head striking either his bedstead or the wall. In the morning we found our suits laid out for us, with white shirts and starched white collars. When I went downstairs I saw that Mary was dressed up as well; she had on a matching skirt and blouse, and the lamb's-wool sweater that Norman had given her for Christmas. A row of three suitcases, two small valises and a larger portmanteau, sat near the front door.

"What are those for?" I asked the maid. "They aren't Norman's. They aren't Lotte's."

"Those are your bags, yours and Mister Barton's. My clothes and Arthur's clothes are in that big suitcase. We are taking a car trip together all the way to the state of New Mexico; we are going to see those underground Carlsbad Caverns."

"What are you talking about? Who said so? Nobody asked us. What if we don't want to go? Don't we have rights?"

"None I know to speak of," Mary answered. "Long as you the little people, Miss Lotte, she makes the decisions."

"I am going to talk to her. I am going to wake her up. It's ridiculous, this beauty sleep. Where's Bartie? He'll never agree to go."

"You look out that front window where Arthur has the car in the drive. That boy has his foot on the gas pedal already."

I went into the dining room and pushed the curtains aside. There was the Buick, the top up, the engine off; Barton was in the driver's seat, twisting the steering wheel left and right. Arthur, in a brown suit, came downstairs and carried all three bags to the back of the car. The battle, I saw, had been lost. Nonetheless, I moved to the foyer and shouted up the long curve of the staircase. "You want to get rid of us! You're ashamed of us! Bartie was right! You're going to sell the house when we're gone!"

From the sleepers above, no answer. Mary came out with a hamper and her handbag. Docilely, I followed.

"Can't take that dog," Arthur said, from where he was rubbing a chamois over the already polished surface of the hood. "Don't allow no dogs in the motels or in the national monuments."

I saw that Sam had jumped into the rear and stuck his muzzle through the crack in the window, as if in anticipation of the breezes to come. "I'll take him back," I volunteered.

Sammy dug in; I had to haul him out by the collar and drag him to the portico and into the house. Arthur turned on the engine before I came out. I closed the front door behind me and started across the bricks.

"Richard."

That was Norman's voice. It came from overhead. I heard my

father's footsteps on the little balcony that jutted out from the room where all of those about to embark on this journey had watched the different sorts of wrestling matches two nights before. I stepped through the colonnade and squinted upward. I saw Norman's foreshortened head and torso.

"You'll have a hell of a trip," he told me. "The caverns are a natural wonder. You'll never see anything like them again."

"Yeah. Okay. But why don't you take us? Why Arthur and Mary? It's embarrassing."

"Some other time. There's a lot to deal with now."

"I guess I understand. You want us out of your hair."

"You're never in my hair, sweetheart. I'm sorry I didn't tell you: I'm glad you liked that silly show I put on. I shouldn't have done it. It's not fair to you. To any of you. You know the reason: it's the shaving mirror."

"I'm sorry too: I mean about Bartie. I feel bad. I heard him rocking. I said it out of exasperation."

"It breaks my heart, and it breaks Lotte's heart, when you talk to him that way. That's something I have to say to you. But I shouldn't be up here on a balcony. It's like I'm talking down to you. You know, like a pun. Rich, I'm proud of Bartie, the same as I am of you. Hell, I showed the pictures of the two of you in my wallet all over Washington. Even to Tavenner. You don't measure the love for your children. That would be like choosing between you. Barton is going to be fine. He needs time. Be patient. Please be patient. What I want more than anything is for you to be his friend. He has a pure heart. Remember that. You go on now. And don't worry. We aren't selling the house. It's paid for. You'll never have to leave San Remo Drive."

He blew a kiss toward where I was standing. He put his hands in the pockets of his bathrobe and stepped back. I saw, on his cheeks, at his jawline, a smudge, like charcoal, of a two-day beard.

3

In the morning traffic it took us a little over two hours to reach San Bernadino, and about three hours more to arrive in Barstow. Mary had fallen asleep almost at once, her chin, with its rows of frown lines, resting on her breast. Barton and I played our usual game: looking for out-of-state license plates and betting whether the numbers on them added up to odd or even. *Georgia* was as exotic as we got. Then my brother dozed off as well. What kept me awake were the signs for Route 66 that I saw at the intersections. This was the road the Joads had taken, heading westward, in *The Grapes of Wrath.* You couldn't see any Okies now, though there were plenty of open-backed trucks taking Mexicans up to the farms in the Central Valley.

We stopped to have a late lunch in Barstow, and to wait out the worst of that day's heat. Mary, digging into her hamper, refused to get out of the car. Arthur gave me five dollars; while Barton and I ate in the lunchroom, he filled the gas tank and bought a water bag, which hung dripping from the front bumper when we came back to the car. There was also a round tube, like an oversized thermos, attached to the passenger-side window.

"That machine going to condition the air," Arthur explained, while he scraped away the exoskeletons of the insects that had expired on the windshield. He let Bartie and me fish in a cooler filled with soda pop bottles up to their chins in frigid water. I took a Nehi strawberry and a Nehi orange, and my brother plucked up two Royal Crown Colas. Thus equipped, we set off into the Mohave Desert.

Do you know how heat can make the air above a radiator visible? As thick, somehow, as a syrup? That's what the road looked like, straight, black, unending, with little dust devils springing up on either side and— what to call them?—heat devils rising above the macadam. It was like looking through a pane of flawed glass. Between the road's occasional rises and dips a pool of water would shimmer and gleam. "It's just a mirage," I told Bartie, who had long since gone through both bottles of cola.

"It's not! Not!" he insisted, licking his parched lips. "Hurry up, Arthur! Go faster! It's an order!"

But that pond, and all the others, constantly receded, reforming beyond the next rise, like the waters that tormented Tantalus, Zeus's son.

We pushed on. The Buick's taut dark top concentrated the heat directly over our heads, so that it seemed we were caught between two burning black lids. Real drops of water, no mirage, dripped from the canister and spread across the glass beside me. It occurred to me to imitate Sammy—that is, to thrust my head into what I thought would be a reviving spray; but the minute I rolled down the window a hot blast, like a dragon's fiery tongue, forced its way into the automobile and began to lick the last drops of moisture from our bodies.

"Why you went and do a fool thing as that?" Mary said. The streaks of perspiration, long dried, left gullies in the dust on her skin.

Arthur pulled to the side of the road and got out of the car. He moved to the front and unhooked the wet burlap bag.

"Me first! Don't you drink! Uncle Ben isn't allowed!"

The servant handed over the sack. Straining with both hands, Barton lifted it and drank, not like a Spaniard with his wineskin, but with his mouth at the valve. "It's cold!" he exclaimed. "It's freezing!" He drank again, longer, the Adam's apple working beneath the flesh of his throat.

We watched. My tongue was so thick in my mouth I could barely say, "Hey! Come on! Don't drink it all!"

Grinning, he handed the pouch over the back of the seat. I instinctively raised it, then stopped. The heat of embarrassment was greater than that in the car. "Here, Mary," I said. "Ladies go first."

She clutched the bag; she closed her mouth around the nozzle. Streams of water spilled onto her blouse front. The rough canvas pushed her glasses askew on her forehead. At length she lowered the sack. "I appreciate the thoughtfulness," she said.

I drank my fill and handed the bag to Arthur, who was still standing outside the car. He took it and surprisingly poured the cool liquid into his palm. Then he drank from that shallow cup, refilled it, and sipping drank from it again. Wasn't there a story about this in the Bible? From Exodus? I couldn't remember, exactly. But I thought that the Lord killed the thirsty Israelites who plunged into the water and spared those who drank delicately from the palms of their hands.

"You want more, Mister Barton?"

My brother, a little pale I thought, shook his head no.

Arthur unsmilingly draped the bag over the bumper, so that the wind could cool it by evaporation once again. Then he settled in his seat and restarted the engine.

"My turn to drive! You promised! You said in the desert!"

Arthur kept his eyes straight ahead, unblinking, as if hypnotized by the repetition of the dashes in the center of the road.

Bartie protested. He struck his fist on the leather seat. Then, in frustration, he started to cry—at least I thought he was crying. His shoulders shook. He covered his mouth with his hands. But when he turned around I saw from the glint in his large eye and in his small one that he was laughing. Finally, he took his hands away and looking straight at me mouthed the words, *Nigger lips.*

At an unwavering fifty-seven miles an hour we made our way to Needles, and, on Front Street, pulled into the Grandeur Cafe. Arthur and Mary came inside; we sat in a booth and ate meatloaf for dinner. People did not stare so much as look twice, as if to make sure they had really seen a Negro couple.

The sun, when we returned to our car, was low in the sky. We had another hour's drive ahead of us, across the Colorado and into Arizona, where we had reservations at the Four Cacti Motel. As we approached the town of Kingston, Bartie cried, "I see them! Bartie saw them first!" Then we all did: the great green plants were clustered together like congregants, their arms raised to heaven in what might have been a prayer for rain.

Arthur and Mary had one room; Bartie and I had twin beds in another. I fell onto the mattress fully clothed. For a moment I watched the thin white curtains, on which the red of the setting sun was soon replaced by the red of a neon sign. I heard the sign's sizzle. I heard the tick of the Buick as it cooled. Then my eyes, and my ears too it seemed, dropped shut. What time it was when Bartie left his bed and climbed into mine I had no idea. I suppose the middle of the night. But he was there, one arm around me, and his mouth open on the pillow, when Mary knocked on our door with the first light of dawn.

We continued east, hour after hour, until the rising sun was no longer shining directly into our eyes. Bartie and I waved at the Indians, who sat under umbrellas and sold blankets and punch cards and jewelry at the side of the road. One time a brave stepped from the door of a wooden teepee and threw a can that bounced once and, spilling out liquid, struck the side of the car. Arthur went on for a mile and then stopped to inspect the fender; there wasn't a dent. But the poor Buick, with its false, gill-like portholes, looked to me like a fish expiring under the relentless sun.

On we went. With the hissing wind, the constant whine of the tires, the ever-mounting heat, it was impossible to remain awake for more than a few minutes at a time. At midmorning, dozing, I felt a slight bump and a swerve.

"What is it, Arthur?" I thought another Indian had struck us with a beer can; on looking back, however, I saw what looked like a piece of rope stretched across the road.

"You did it! You killed it! On purpose too!" Tears were streaming down Bartie's face.

Arthur kept his eyes on the road. "Ain't nothing to rile yourself with. That's but a common snake."

"Snakes have feelings!" Bartie wailed. "But you don't! You don't care! I hate this trip. Turn around. Take me home. It's an order."

"You hush up, Mister Barton," said Mary. "You got no reason to be carrying on."

"There is a reason! I know about snakes. They are cold-blooded, but Arthur is colder! They play fair. They give a warning. With rattles! He didn't even honk the horn! They shed their skin. It all comes off and they grow a new one. Ha! Ha! Ha! You! Arthur! I bet you wish you could shed yours!"

"Shut up, Bartie! I'll tell Norman you said that!"

My brother began to rock ominously against the back of his seat. "Take me home! Bartie gave an order! Take me home, slave!"

Then he put his thumb in his mouth, which at least stopped the flow of his terrible words. We drove on in silence. After a time Arthur said, "All right, Mister Barton, you put your foot here. You see? On the gas. Not too fast now. That's the ticket."

The car slowed as Barton, with a smile I could see from behind his head, moved next to the black man and thrust out his straight stick of a leg. We lurched forward, but soon settled back at the same speed we'd been making before.

"You doing real good," said Mary.

"It's true. Look, look, look: Bartie's a driver!"

"Now you take hold here, slow and easy. No need to tell Mister Norman this and no need to tell him anything else."

I think both Mary and I gasped; but Barton, twisting gymnastically, reached over with his right hand and seized the wheel. We went on straight as an arrow. All of us, Bartie included, pretended that we did not see the chauffeur's hand clutching the wheel at its nadir. A sound, a bit like a cat's purring, a bit like our engine's hum, came from the throat of my brother.

At the sign for Holbrook, Arthur took over and at the town itself we detoured north to the Painted Desert.

"Ain't got but ten minutes to see these sights," said the servant, as Bartie and I raced for the visitor center. There was an overlook that afforded a view of how the various minerals had stained the layers of sand. Mary came in to shoo us back to the car, but not before buying each of us a glass box whose contents were arranged in tiers of color. This time Barton climbed into the back. He sat close to Mary, turning the box in his hands, holding it up to the light, and then licking it, as if it were the spumoni we always ordered for dessert at the Swiss Chalet.

We remained on Route 66 into New Mexico and past Albuquerque; then, in late afternoon, we veered south, more or less along the course of the Pecos River. We had reservations at the Mescalero Motel, only a short drive from the monument, which we would visit first thing in the morning. It was already dusk by the time we reached Roswell, and pitch-black two hours later, when we pulled into Loving. The Muscalero had one large, red-tiled building and a series of cabins spread in a wide semi-circle. There was a small, lit swimming pool, a little putting green, and a horseshoe pit with iron stakes at either end. Arthur pulled up in front of the office, and we followed him inside. There, a tall, thin man with crutches told us there were no reservations for Jacobi.

"Must be a mistake," said Mary. "Miss Lotte gave me a number."

Arthur put his hand to his cheek. "No, there ain't no mistake."

"Can't we rent the rooms?" I asked the crippled man. "Do we have to have a reservation?"

"All full up," the clerk replied. "Full up since the start of the month."

"You're a liar," said Barton. "*Vacancy.* That's what the sign says. I'm a writer. I know every word."

"Looks like I forgot to turn the switch," said the man, doing so now; the word *No* flashed on in pink.

Arthur led us out the door. We turned back the way we'd come. There were no rooms in Otis and none at any of the motels in the town of Carlsbad. Our luck was no better at the only place in Lakewood, whose proprietor, already in a woolen nightcap, would not open the screen door. Finally, in Artesia, we found a vacancy at the Susanna Motel.

It had just a single building, long and low, with the roof sinking like a broken-down horse. There was only one room for the four of us, and it was at the end, closest to the highway. Barton and I claimed the bed—it was as swaybacked as the roof above us—furthest from the window. Arthur brought in the bags and then went back to the car. He wanted to fill it with gas, he said, and buy some sandwiches to make up for our missed dinner.

All we wanted was sleep. In the tiny bathroom, in the green-stained washbasin, Mary scrubbed our faces, which she hadn't done since the start of grade school; she hovered while we brushed our teeth. When we stepped back to the bedroom, Arthur had not returned. We got into pajamas. We got into bed. Mary turned off the unshaded light. She moved to the far side of her bed and sat, looking out the window. At midnight the floodlight went off outside the building. The headlights from the cars and trucks periodically swept across the black glass of the window, like a lighthouse beam. Mary made obscure gestures in the darkness; she was removing her clothes. She took off her sweater. She unbuttoned her blouse. Her skirt had a zipper. She stood to unzip it. She was wearing a white slip that, like the bones in a Halloween costume or the image in a fluoroscope, seemed to float and flit all on its own. She moved into the bathroom, then returned to her spot before the window.

Where is that man? I heard her say under her breath.

"Mary, is he lost, do you think?"

"My, oh my, I thought sure you asleep. No. He's stubborn. He's going to fill that tank or die striving. You go on to sleep, Mister Richard. Tomorrow we're seeing those caves."

I didn't sleep, not yet. I watched the ghost of the undergarment pace, sit, pace once again. Then I watched as, like a smoke puff, it began rising higher and even higher. I realized that Mary was taking off the piece of silk. Something clamped my shoulder. Barton's hand. I could tell he'd stopped breathing. The two of us, then, stared at her full breasts, the bulge of her belly, and the overlapping flesh folds at her waist and her thigh. A car came, followed by another. Her spectacles, of gold, shone; so did the cross of Jesus at her neck. Her body was like a black candle whose wax had melted. I held my breath too. I watched as she bent, so that her breasts hung swaying; off went her shoes. Then she reached up and spookily took off the top of her head. Behind me, Bartie gasped. He trembled, making the whole bed shudder. Then, simultaneously, we saw that she had removed what we always thought might be a wig. Her teeth came out next, into a glass of water. Then she wrapped her old plaid nightdress around her body and lay down on top of her bed. The three of us, I think, fell asleep.

When I woke I thought it was dawn. But the light that poured through the window came from across the roadway. A number of cars had gathered there, on the shoulder and beyond, and the headlights, crisscrossing, lit up the Susanna's facade. I heard music, or at any rate singing, along with shouts and curses and laughter. I rose to an elbow. Barton was already up, clutching his knees. "Shhh," he hissed, his fingers to his lips. "It's a lynch mob. I bet they've got Arthur. They started a fire. They're going to burn us down."

I sat bolt upright. My heart beat in my ears and in my throat. There was a fire, a bonfire, across the pavement. I could see silhouettes moving in a jumble before it. There were men in boots and cowboy hats. Some of them had burning pieces of wood in their hands. They waved the flaming torches. I heard, beneath the shouts and the song snatches, a steady moan. I knew it was Mary. She wasn't in her bed; she was sitting, dressed and bewigged, in the room's only chair. For a moment I struggled to work out what was real, this scene, this moment, and what—the image of the maid, naked, taking her head from her shoulders—was the dream.

"Where's Arthur?" I asked. "Isn't he back yet?"

She didn't answer. She continued to moan.

"I told you," said Bartie. "They've got him. They've got that nigger. They're going to string him up!"

I rolled off my side of the bed and moved to the window. I pressed, peering, against the glass. I was shocked to see that Barton was right: they did have Arthur. He was standing at the center of a group of men. His coat was off and each time he took a stumbling step it dragged behind him in the dust. The men, all white men, laughed and jeered. Then the old servant staggered; he fell to his knees. There was a whoop, a war whoop, like Indians in the movies.

I whirled around. "Mary, get the telephone. Call the police."

She did not move from the seat of her chair.

I ran to the phone. There was a low dial tone, which, no matter what numbers I dialed, did not alter its drone. Then I ran to the bathroom. The only window was small and high. I didn't think I could get through. Certainly Mary couldn't. But Barton, by standing on the toilet tank, might just be able to wiggle his way out and try to bring help.

"Bartie! Hey, Bartie!"

He didn't answer. I trotted back to the bedroom. The window was glowing with the reflection of sparks and flame. And not just the window. The door was open and Barton stood in it, the outline of his body lit by the fire. Before I could move he dashed across the sliver of court-yard and onto the lip of the highway.

"Let him go!" he shouted. "You bad people! Let him go! He belongs to Bartie!"

Then, as if the crazed men had heard him, the mob parted and Arthur lurched onto the black macadam. By one hand he was still drag-ging his jacket; in the other he waved a flaming stick. In the light of that brand I saw our Buick, parked at the other end of the motel. The chauf-feur weaved his way across the roadway, shedding sparks. He stopped in front of my brother. He grinned, his teeth a flash of white. Then, so that I could hear the sound from where I stood in the door jamb, he hiccuped. And immediately hiccuped again.

"Come in, Arthur," said Bartie.

The black man dropped the stick and stumbled forward. He braced himself in the frame of the doorway. I could smell his sweat, along with the unmistakable fumes of alcohol. Hiccuping still, he stepped inside and dropped onto the bed. Barton followed, closing the door. The celebration continued on the far side of the road.

"Look at this fool I went and married," said Mary. "Went to a party. Got hisself drunk."

4

The next morning we were among the first in line at the visitor center. Arthur, chagrined, bought the tickets. I read the brochures while we waited for the elevators. I told the others that not so long ago we'd have had to descend in a guano bucket. "*Guano,* that's bat doo-doo," I said.

Mary said, "I don't feature seeing no bats."

We went down to the Big Room and wandered among the illuminated formations, the Lion's Tail, the Sword of Damocles, and the rest.

"Looks just like Miss Lotte's glass chandelier," Mary said, pointing up at the collection of stalactites that hung, indeed like our dining room fixture, from the roof of the cavern.

After a half hour or so we gathered in the Hall of Giants. I began to feel lightheaded, perhaps from the strain of staring upward, the blood pooling at the back of my head; perhaps because I could not tell whether the enormous columns were stalactites that had grown down or stalagmites that had pushed up or a combination of both; or else it was the dinner we'd missed and the breakfast we'd gulped on the run. In any case, the towering pillars seemed to be doing a dance in the light from dozens of flashbulbs, and, at the same time, I thought I heard a voice saying my name: *Jacobi? The Jacobi party? Jacobi?*

It was a uniformed ranger. He walked up to Arthur. "I'm sorry, but you'll have to come to the surface."

My first thought was that Negroes were not allowed in the monument. But my brother knew better. He said, "It's Norman. It's an emergency about Norman. Bartie knows."

The ranger said, "I believe it is an emergency, yes."

When we arrived above ground Arthur and Mary left us outdoors while they went into the visitor center. I was amazed to see, leaning against the cab of a red-colored pickup, the man from the Muscalero Motel. When he saw Barton and me he sagged against the top of his crutches and lifted his hat. Mary was weeping when she came outside. Arthur, when we ran to him, kept his eyes down. "We got's to go home," he said. "You boys please to get to the car."

We drove the whole of that day and, though Arthur had not had much sleep, right through the night. The Buick, on the open road, hit seventy-five, then eighty, and stayed there. Mary never removed her handkerchief from her eyes. Neither she nor Arthur would tell us what had happened. We stopped for coffee. We stopped for soup that was too hot to eat. We pulled over so Arthur could take a half-hour's nap. Barton slept most of the time. Once he woke and said, not tearfully, but philosophically, "King George is dead. Norman is dead. All the kings will be dead."

We made a dash through the Mohave at first light and got to Sunset by midafternoon. Bartie began rocking as we followed the boulevard's twists and turns. I took his hand as we passed Mandeville Canyon and began the last climb to Riviera. We took the hairpin onto San Remo and drove to the house. There were no reporters, no neighbors, at the front of the lawn. We drove past the pillared facade and parked at the circle that surrounded the rustling pecan. Sammy came leaping and barking, as if nothing had happened. The Packard, I noticed, was not in the garage. Lotte was at the back door. She stood on tiptoe. She cried, "Boys! Here I am!"

She led the two of us up the staircase, left, and left again to her and Norman's bedroom. She lay down, dressed as she was, on top of the canopied bed. Barton stood by the window. I lay on the carpet, behind the chaise lounge. Lotte began by saying, "Did you get to see the caverns? Wasn't it a wonderful trip?"

Barton did not reply. I could not think of a word to say.

"Well, that was silly. I can't imagine why I said it. Of course it was not a wonderful trip. Now you are going to have to be big boys. All grown up. We are going to have to face this together. Norman went out in the Packard. He was going to Burbank, to clean out his office. Oh, if only Arthur had been here to drive! I can't help blaming myself for that! What happened, boys, Barton, Richard, is that he hit a tree. Perhaps he had a stroke. Or a heart attack. What does that matter? He hit a tree and was terribly hurt and he lingered for a time but at ten o'clock this morning I am so sorry to tell you your father died."

Now the tears spilled from me. Hidden by the furniture, I beat my fists on the green-colored carpet. "But he was a good man! He was too good to die!"

Barton said, "You are lying! Don't be a liar!"

"But Bartie darling, I told you the truth."

"No! You didn't! Bartie knows! It was suicide! Ha! Ha! Ha! Chop-suicide! Show Bartie! Show Bartie the note!"

"Oh, don't say that! I would tell you! I swear! There is no note. He didn't say a word. Oh, he said what he always said. *Here's my beautiful Lotte.* That was our catchphrase. Isn't that nice?"

My tears dried on the instant. I pushed my head out from behind the divan. I heard myself give a little laugh. "Well," I said, "now you can marry Pear Shape."

Two brand-new suits were ready for us the next morning, but we never put them on.

"I'm not, not, not going to the gravy-yard!" Barton shouted.

"And you, Richie?" Lotte asked. "I don't want to cause you too much pain."

"I'll stay with Bartie," I told her.

"Well, you can't be in the house alone. Arthur and Mary will be at the funeral. I'll see if poor Stanley will volunteer to take you. Oh, dear!

He'll hate to miss it. Everyone in Hollywood will be there. Even Jack."

Madeline came by after breakfast to say how sorry she was. Her father stood behind her in the portico, turning his hat in his hands. Stanley arrived not long after that. He drove us to see the scale model of Lindbergh's *Spirit of St. Louis* at the L.A. County Museum. The little plane hung above us on wires, its rubber wheels just above our upturned heads.

"Is it true? Was he lost in a fog? Lucky Lindy? Did he have to fly upside down?"

"That's the story, Richard. It's good to remember what one man can do. You don't give up. You persevere. Then you find your own way."

Did Norman give up? That's what I wanted to ask him. *Are you accusing him of not persevering?* But I saw how white his cheeks were, and the lines in them, more like Prune Face than Pear Shape, and I said, "This is great, thanks for taking us," instead.

We ate lunch at the Ontra Cafeteria and then drove down Wilshire to catch the afternoon showing of *The Lavender Hill Mob.* All around us people were laughing. Barton, as the plan to steal the gold ingots went awry, was squealing with delight. When Alec Guinness began to dash down the thousands of steps on the Eiffel Tower, I threw back my head and let out a peal of laughter too. How he clung to that valise! How much he wanted his golden prize! It was as if it were Norman's Oscar he had stolen, along with everybody else's Academy Awards. At the end of the picture, when the actor stood up from the table at which he'd been telling his tale, we were startled to see he was in handcuffs. We gasped as the policemen led him away.

"No! No! Run, mister! Mister, you won! Pear Shape! Help him to escape!"

We stayed in our seats when the lights came up. Bartie wouldn't stop sobbing. "Will they put him in jail? Poor mister! Why are they so mean to him? It's not fair! Not fair!"

"It's just the production code, Bartie." Stanley wiped my brother's tears with his thumbs. "I agree with you. It's stupid. It's not like true life. Movies are never like life. The rule is crime doesn't pay."

Stanley drove us all the way to Santa Monica Pier and treated us to dinner at Jack's-at-the-Beach. The sun was long down by the time we got home; but there was still a crowd at San Remo Drive. I ran up to my room. Bartie retreated to his. I lay on the bed for a time. Mary came in. She said, "You want to remember something. Miss Lotte, she sure loved Mister Norman. In front of all those peoples she jumped right into the grave."

Then she went out, closing the door behind her. But she could not shut out the sounds from the gathering below: the occasional laughter, the murmur of voices, and the tinkle of notes that rose from the baby grand.

TIJUANA

(1956–1960)

I

Lotte always gave us the worst news in the bedroom. That's where we heard that Norman, our father, had died; and that's where, four years later, Barton and I learned that we would have to sell the house on San Remo Drive. I suppose I moved back three decades later in order to undo the damage of that day. My wife and I sleep in that same bedroom, and my own two boys have the rooms that belonged to Barton and me, the ones that overlook the pool. Even Bartie—or at any rate the most productive part of Bartie—has moved in too. In the Eighties, when we bought back the house, I agreed to accept a Bekins van filled with his manuscript boxes and store them in the basement. Now and then I'm tempted to sneak down there and open one of the cartons. Who knows? Maybe, after all, Bartie had devoted his life to a masterpiece.

"Are you out of your mind?" Marcia will exclaim, whenever I happen to muse this way out loud. "They're the scribblings of the village idiot."

She's not happy that her cellar has been turned into a storage bin for Barton's opus. I know she'd prefer to use the space as a playroom for the twins, whose romping upstairs has begun to get on her nerves. I don't tell her how Bartie and I used to retreat down there during electrical storms. I'd worry about the furnace, a flame-spitting cauldron as big as the boiler we'd watched William Bendix labor over in *The Hairy Ape*. Would it explode if the house were hit by lightning? I kept my distance. But Bartie, in his bathrobe, would lie down on the coal dust, and by the light of the fire write out in block letters one of his tales.

JIN GETS A BITE

That, I remember, was the title of one of his stories. "*Jim*," I told him. "It's spelled with an *M*."

"*Jin!*" he retorted. "You don't know anything. Jingie-jangie-Jin!"

The real trouble started when he read the story out loud in front of his class: "*One day Jin went into the foret. It was dark. Jin saw a snake. He was frited. He ran away. Jin said I won't go to the foret again.*"

The students howled.

"That's stupid!"

"You liar!"

"Yeah! You said he got a bite!"

Bartie stood before his classmates, hands on his hips. "Well," he said, his blue eyes glittering with indignation, "he *could* have!"

At this there were hoots of derision. I suppose the listeners' response was aesthetic: the promise of high drama, a scene of horror, had not been fulfilled. They wanted their money back. But Bartie's vision had its aesthetic, too—except that, with its ambiguities, its reliance on the aleatory and happenstance, its postmodernism *en bref*, it was far ahead of its time. Even James' beast in the jungle leaves its mark by *not* giving a bite.

Mrs. Farullo, eagle-nosed and Brillo-haired, didn't get it. "I think, Barton, you had best change your title."

Bartie whirled. He leapt for her. Now the second graders had their hair-raising action: the author sank his teeth into the flesh of her arm and ground his way to the bone.

"He's so creative," said Lotte, upon hearing of his expulsion; alas, there were more to come, most of them connected to Barton's writing. One time Lotte and Norman had to get the eleven-year-old out of jail. That was because Bartie, in a *histoire à clefs*, described how a handsome, blond, blue-eyed youth and his dog, Sam, climbed through a window of Canyon Elementary School and burned half of Mrs. Milton's class to a crisp with a flamethrower and mowed down the rest with a machine gun. Mrs. Milton had her head chopped off by a machete. "How does that feel, Edith?" asked Bert, the hero. In the accompanying illustration, which Barton handed round to his schoolmates, Sam is licking up the red drops of blood that squirt from the teacher's naked torso, while her head, clearly recognizable, down to the dime-sized mole on the side of the chin, says, "You are a genus Bert! A true genus!" Spelling has never been Bartie's forte.

"Help!" he shouted to his parents from behind the bars of the cell he had begged the policemen to lock him up in. "They're going to electrocute me! *Bzzzz, bzzzzz, bzzzz*: with wires in my brain!"

"You're here for the night, Bartie," said Norman. "I can't make your bail."

"Please, God," I used to pray, down on my knees, and hands clasped like a Protestant. "Next year, when he's as old as I am, make Bartie like other people." The deity, however, remained unmoved; when the next year came, and every year after, Barton continued along his own peculiar path.

Norman wasn't entirely joking about the bail. His name had started to come up in testimony before the House Committee on Un-American Activities. Jack Warner put him on a list of subversives, and then, early in 1952, Elia Kazan claimed he had been something of a fellow traveler at the Group Theater. Even before Norman's sensational testimony in Washington later that year, his production company was folded into Hal Wallis' unit and his scripts began to be sent back for ever more extensive revisions. In 1953 Lee Cobb—whose violin the nine-year old Norman used to borrow for his weekly lessons—named him as a member of the Young Communist League; by then, with the finality of a thumb on a pendulum, Norman's heart had already stopped, and the car he had been driving, our prewar Packard, had run up over the curb and into the trunk of a tree.

Bartie, in my opinion, has been mourning ever since. I wasn't fooled when he told everyone his last name wasn't Jacobi, it was Wilson. Or when he affected dark glasses and a corncob pipe and stuck out his jaw like MacArthur. I suppose psychologists call this identification with the aggressor: better to become the enemy than his victim; but I think Bartie knew that Christians get resurrected and that the old soldier would keep his word and return. Unfortunately, the Republicans picked another general for their candidate, and when the newly widowed Lotte threw the last of her election-night parties—events which under Roosevelt had attracted every Democratic politician in the state, not to mention Republicans like Earl Warren—only six of her own friends showed up.

Bartie, still at Emerson Junior High, chose another hero. He'd sit scribbling at the back of the classroom and then, at the end of a history lesson, stand up and read aloud what he'd written: "On March 24, 1954, Mr. Stegelmeyer said that the Spanish conquistadors had deliberately used blankets with smallpox to infect the native population. To say this about Catholic people is much worse than what Herr Hitler said about Jews. Also, I have in my hand evidence that on February 3rd, 1954, he told us that the great Christopher Columbus killed the Indians on Hispanola or sent them back to Spain as his slaves. This is not what a patriot would say. It is Un-American activity. Mr. Stegelmeyer, you must answer: are you or are you not willing to take a loyalty oath?"

The teacher, who was probably trying to imagine the manner in which Bartie had spelled the word *conquistadors,* stood mute.

"I thought so!" cried his accuser. "You're a Communist! A dirty Red!" Barton managed to repeat this performance in all his classes, even music and physical education, before the Board of Education notified his family that he would no longer be welcome in its schools.

Lotte had long since fired our Japanese gardeners and Arthur and Mary, the butler and maid. She turned off the roaring furnace on all but the coldest winter nights. What money she had left for the string of Barton's tutors and psychiatrists disappeared when the self-proclaimed Frenchman she made the mistake of marrying looted the last of her accounts. Finally, during my final year at University High, she called us to her bedroom to announce that she had no choice but to put the San Remo house up for sale.

On Bartie's forehead, between his brows, a red welt began to throb. "It's your fault! You never should have married him! I knew he was a phony! You killed Sammy too!"

Lotte, taken aback, said, "It's not true, Barton. We gave him to a nice family in San Francisco."

"You put him to sleep! You loved his dog! Achille! The Nazi dog! You never loved Sammy!"

I saw from Lotte's expression, her averted eyes, the clamp of her teeth on her lip, that this time Senator McCarthy's accusation was true. Poor Sam!

Barton wasn't done. "It was first-degree murder!" he shouted. "And you lost all my money! You're the guilty one! I see things. I know things. They're in my head. You are the one who should go see the crazy doctor!"

He ran from the room. We heard him, Lotte and I, on the staircase. Then we heard the slam of the heavy front door.

My mother was lying on her divan. She pulled her robe, which had loosened, about her breasts. "It will be hard for Barton to leave the house," she said. "It's his childhood he's talking about, not the dog. And of course there are beautiful things here: the kilims, the china, the Soyer paintings. Oh, and the piano! My piano! I hate to give them up."

"Then don't. I'm no different than Bartie. I don't want to leave the house either."

"Do you prefer to stay here, Richard darling? Or to have your education at Yale?"

When I didn't reply she said, "The truth is that I won't miss it. Not at bottom. We weren't a family here. What did we do after dinner? I came to this room to read. Norman went to the library to work. Barton did his scribbling or rocked in his bed. You went to paint or watch the new Zenith. Arthur and Mary had a better life here than we did."

I turned toward the door.

"Don't worry about your brother," Lotte called after me. "He'll be back before it gets dark."

But there was no sign of him two hours after nightfall. Lotte paced the downstairs rooms, trailing cigarette smoke. She turned on all the house lights, as if Bartie were a mariner lost in the fog. "What are you waiting for?" she said to me. "Don't you care about your brother? You know what the canyon is like: there are mountain lions!"

I took a flashlight and backed the Buick out of the garage. Bartie's bike was there, its balloon tires flat and its front wheel and handlebars turned back against the frame, like an animal asleep. I drove around the neighborhood, stopping now and then to shout his name. We used to play in the lemon groves, a handful of which still remained among the new lawns and houses. I tramped through them, the flashlight beam flitting over the trunks and branches, as if we were once again at a game of hide-and-seek. No Bartie.

On the bluff above Sunset stood a row of cypresses. My gang of friends let Bartie gather the hard, round berries, the size of golf balls nearly, which we'd shoot with our Whamos onto the traffic below. "Bango! Bango! Bango!" he'd cry, as our ammunition clanged off the windshields and hoods. Now the acorn-shaped streetlamps illuminated the foliage, twisted like the trees of Van Gogh; Barton wasn't there. Nor was he at the rivulet of the country club, where he'd spend whole days diving in futility at the slippery toads. Finally I took the Buick back across Sunset and drove up Capri to Rustic Canyon. This is where the mountain lions were, and lynx, and bobcats. The dirt flew away in a plume behind my tires. The headlights lit the ghostly yucca. I stopped. Stars poured across the sky by the shovelful. I honked the horn. No response. Not even a coyote. I honked again. This time I heard—not in the canyon or up in the looming hills but in my own head—the memory of Bartie's laughter.

"Keep him quiet, for Christ's sake," Norman had said, out of character. But Bartie wouldn't be stilled. He was pointing at the screen in our living room, which Billy Wilder had set up to show us an early cut of *Sunset Boulevard.* "You're dead!" shouted Bartie, addressing the floating corpse of Bill Holden. "Shut up, shut up, shut up! You can't be talking!"

Somehow I managed to turn the car around on the rutted road. I raced back through the dust I'd kicked up on my way in. I was laughing too, and at the same time crying—laughing because Bartie had put his finger on the one flaw in the picture that Billy couldn't fix; crying because one of Lotte's economies had been to shut off the night-light of the pool, and I was certain now that Bartie, like the actor, was lying face down in it, but without the luxury of relating the unlucky life that had passed before his eyes.

I cut across the corner of the lawn, gouging it, and stopped at the top of the circle nestled in the L of the house. I ran through the arcade. I ducked into the pool shack and felt for the switch. The light came on haltingly, like milk making its way through iced coffee. Insects dotted the untended surface, and half a wasp's nest, and a flotilla of leaves from the eucalyptus; but wherever my brother was, it wasn't among those depths.

Lotte had fallen asleep on the sofa, a lipsticked cigarette in her hand. She sat upright, blinked, and saw it was I.

"Where's Bartie? Is he back?" I asked. She shook her head.

"Should we call the police?"

She shook it again; but early the next morning we did.

The detectives searched for two days in a desultory way; Bartie, after all, was almost seventeen and they knew that most runaways showed up sooner or later. I continued to drive around the neighborhood, returning once to the canyon all the way out to Camp Josepho; that's where in the Boy Scouts I'd helped stone a rattlesnake to death and, to Bartie's dismay, made a neckerchief-slide out of its skin. Lotte skimmed off the surface of the pool and began to swim laps. She stayed in for hours. At dusk I came out with a towel, but she swam on, determinedly, as if she meant to cross all the way to Catalina. The moon was up when she stopped. I could see her white cap and white teeth, chattering from the cold.

"He wouldn't stop crying," she said, treading water. "He cried and cried. I got a bottle of Cheracol. You remember Cheracol, Richard? It's got codeine in it. I ordered Mrs. Ortman to give it to him. I ordered her to give him the whole bottle. He was only a year old. I did it to him! This is my punishment."

She came dripping out of the pool. I put the towel around her. She leaned against me, her arms around my waist. Her breath, for all the chill of her, was hot against me. "I never picked him up. I never sang to him. I never read him a book. Oh, Richie! I used up my love on you." She was shivering. Her wet suit, her wet body, soaked me through. I could smell the chlorine in her hair and, from next door, the tang of lemons. She stood on tiptoe, stretching upward to kiss the soft flesh of my throat. Then she took the edge of the towel and wiped the spot. "I'll tell you the truth," she said, as she broke away toward the house. "You'd have both been better off if you'd been orphans."

On the afternoon of the next day the telephone rang. Lotte sprang from her chair and seized the receiver. "Thank God," she said, though I could tell it wasn't Bartie or the police. After a moment she handed the phone to me. "It's a monk," she said. "Or a yogi, or somebody. Barton's with them. At their temple downtown. Here. You take the directions."

The Vedanta Center turned out to be way up on Vine, north of Hollywood, north even of Franklin, up in the hills where the old-time actors had built their estates. *Yogi to the stars,* I thought, as I swung onto Santa Monica. But the compound, inside dusty walls, consisted of nothing more than a tumbledown stucco house and a small temple with three domes. In front was a little garden of pansies and geraniums, in which a stooped Bartie was pulling up weeds.

"Hey, Bro!" he called, jumping up to greet me. His face was beaming. He shook my hand, pumping it as Stanley must have Livingston's. "It's my lost Bro!" he shouted; I realized he was addressing the dark, robed man who was sitting cross-legged on the porch.

"I'm not lost, Bartie. You are." My brother gave his high-pitched laugh. Oddly, the tea-colored man on the porch laughed with him. He made a booming sound.

"No, no. Bartie's found. You're the lost one, Bro."

On the porch the swami waved his hand. It was a summons to

approach. "You are the brother of our new friend," he said. "You are very welcome."

"This is my guru," said Bartie. "He showed me the light."

The man put his palms together under his chin. He was fat as a Buddha and looked like the sculptures of the divinity I'd seen in the County Museum: the same thick lips, slanted eyes, and elongated ears. But he didn't have the jewel in his forehead. With a start I realized Bartie did; it was the welt that swelled with his emotions. Did the swami think nutty Bartie was some kind of god?

"You must understand," said the guru. "We are in ignorance. Each of us, Richard. All of being must be taught its true nature. Even the flowers—" Here he motioned toward a patch of what I thought might be daffodils. "They too may receive enlightenment." Bartie was leaning over the garden, the way I'd seen him when I first came in. But he wasn't rooting up the plants. Instead he moved his hands over them, around them, the way I'd once seen a musician playing the theremin by the manipulation of its electronic field.

The swami said, "Your brother is a devotee. He can guide them to the inner life."

Was I seeing things? Had I been hypnotized? The dull-brown weeds seemed to lie flat, abashed; while the golden-headed blossoms strained upright toward Bartie's hands, the way sunflowers yearned for the sun.

Bartie looked up, grinning. "Look, my Bro. They were also in a state of *avidya*. But now they're found."

It was dusk by the time we left the temple. The traffic was bumper-to-bumper. It took nearly an hour to reach the intersection of Wilshire and Santa Monica. The colored lights at the Electric Fountain were already playing around the Indian brave upon his pedestal. *Rainybow! Want the rainybow!* Bartie used to call out from the back of the Packard, whenever we'd get stuck there at the light. Up came the green-tinted water. Up came the rose.

"It's still pretty, don't you think?" I asked the silent disciple.

He laughed. He gave the swami's wave of the hand. "All these beauties, brother—they're just illusions. You see, you're lost under the veil of maya. That's why you're going to Yale. You're entranced by the baubles of this world. You've got to watch out. Watch your step, Bro! Things aren't what you think. Oh, you killed that snake! You bragged about it with your friends. But in your foolishness, big brother, you violated the rule of *ahimsa*. No, no, I shouldn't blame you. You didn't know the secret: that snake was one face of the goddess Kali."

The light changed. The cars inched forward. The light changed back, but I ran it; I wanted to get away from the fountain and its wind-blown mist. I sped up the clear stretch of Wilshire, with the golf club on either side. But Bartie's words kept gaily sailing out: "That was bad karma. You'll have to pay for your deeds in another life. You are tied to the wheel of suffering. You won't learn how to escape at Yale. All these pleasures, all your good fortune: they'll have to be paid for too. Wine! Women! Song! Those are the snares that await you. I know you've got your eye on Madeline. You desire her flesh. Go for it, Bro!" Here he laughed, a clear, bell-like, carefree laugh. It made me smile to hear it. Involuntarily I leaned toward the sound, as if I'd been one of his flowers. "But you won't be released from suffering and life. Oh, no! Mark these words. You are coming back. Again and again. You'll be reborn as a lizard or a chipmunk. Ha! Ha! Ha! You'll hop like a toad!"

I *did* have my eye on Madeline, and by that summer of 1956 I was doing my best to put my hands on her too. I had begun, years earlier, to paint a series of sketches of our neighbor—pastels and charcoals of her profile, her bare feet, the white swath of her back. She never thought twice, aged eleven, aged twelve, about pulling off her fuzzy sweaters or unbuttoning her blouse. She sat on the edge of my bed. The sunlight ricocheted from the pool in pulses, like a stream of billiard balls from a felt cushion, and got in among the hairs that lined her shoulders and forearms, and that lay in a dark furry patch at the nape of her neck. I tried, with a pencil point, to reproduce the fine line that shadowed her spine down to her bony buttocks. She was, in her hairiness, like an animal, a bear cub; but time like some mother grizzly licked her clean. I mean that as the years went by these vestigial traces of our ancestry were discarded, like the threads of her eyebrows that she began to pluck with tweezers one by one. Her pink eyeglasses disappeared too; contact lenses weren't fashionable in the Fifties, so that while I was reproducing the way sunbeams penetrated to the skin of her scalp, Madeline, squinting, saw me in a blur.

Summer afternoon. James, it was, who famously said those were the most beautiful words in the language. Listen to Bartie outside in the yard; he's shrieking with pleasure as he does his cannonballs into the pool. Sam, our spaniel, to illustrate the Doppler effect, yips running toward the house, yaps running away. Arthur, working on the Packard, guns the engine, and guns it again. Mary is humming something about Jesus while she dusts the furniture in the hall. Figs, the smell of figs, wafts into the room through the open window, along with that of chlorine, lemons, and eucalyptus. There is the slap and splash of Lotte doing her laps. That dazzle? Norman must be working on his tan with an aluminum reflector. If you hear voices that means it's Sunday, and the Fox and Lox Society, the actors and actresses and other movie people, are lounging on the flagstone or standing in groups on the grass. And here is Madeline: half naked, half turned away, her face all but hidden and the bone of her pelvis jutting out like the edge of a broken plate.

"Are you done yet, Richard? All done, Richard-boy?"

And all the while a fly, big as a grape, bumbles between the panes of glass.

The trouble was, the more Madeline became worth watching, the less she wished to be seen. By the start of high school she'd taken to posing with her chin on her hand as she recited her own unrhyming verses. Her skirts, by then, were down to her ankles. Finally, in that last summer before each of us was to leave for college—I to the East Coast, she to

Pomona—the portraits stopped altogether; but that's when the kissing began. Soon enough she risked giving me her tongue. In the movies she'd let me inch my fingers over the Orlon that covered her breasts. Once, she broke into tears. "I know what's going to happen. I know about those Vassar girls. I've read about the drinking and the dances. It's in Fitzgerald. And I've wanted you since I was nine years old!"

There seemed to be no place to take things further. Patrizia, the Italian maid, was forever on the lookout at Madeline's place, and Lotte was always at San Remo Drive, along with the realtor and a chain of prospective buyers. The biggest problem was having a saint on the premises. Madeline and I would lie, our legs entwined, on the hot tiles that surrounded the pool. From near the hedge we'd hear Bartie humming what might well have been the Hindu hit of that year, *Que Será, Será*. Under his care the figs, never before edible, grew plump, purple, and tender. All the flowers in the flower beds—the pansies, lilies, the bush with the rhododendrons—sprang back to life. Even the pepper pods on the pepper tree shone like tiny Christmas bulbs. I never woke at night to hear the repeated thud of Bartie rocking in bed, or the repeated bang of his head against the wall. In the morning he'd have already left for the Sunset bus that, with transfers, took him downtown to the temple.

Lotte blossomed too. Lead weights, chains of iron, had been lifted from her. One morning she came downstairs while I was leaning over the kitchen table, sipping at coffee and reading the *Times*. For no reason she launched into a speech. "For years and years I've been two people. I thought: well, Richard is the good side of me. So many talents, so many accomplishments. And poor Barton stood for all my weaknesses and my pride and my wantonness. That is over now. I thank God it is over. Don't you see how happy he is? His face is shining. He's filled with joy."

Then, as I've said, it was time for me to get on the airplane. I think it was a DC-6. We landed two or three times crossing the continent. Above the Rockies chunks of ice broke off the wing and crashed thunderously against the fuselage and tail. But all I could think of was how the night before Madeline had spread her legs over me and let me slide my hands into the slippery folds of her flesh; she'd dared to take me in her hand, however briefly, and say, "Richard-boy. Richard-boy. I'll still be here. I'll wait for you."

2

I arrived in New Haven with three tennis racquets, certain I'd walk onto the team. In the mid-Fifties, however, Yale was loaded with nationally ranked players; I quickly realized that while I could beat the Pumpkin and the Penguin and my other pals on the courts at La Cienega, I'd have to make my mark on campus in other ways. A month into the fall semester I handed Vincent Scully, who taught the famous History of Art 101, a portfolio of my charcoal sketches. That same week I found myself enrolled in graduate courses in the art school, where the ranking of the players—Joseph Albers, Hans Hofmann—was international.

Now I had all the models I'd ever dreamed of: housewives, faculty wives, actresses from the Drama School, nurses in training at Grace-New Haven. Breasts and backsides came raining down. Yet all my drawings ended up looking like Madeline—not the Madeline of adolescence, with bony plates beneath her skin like those of an arthropod, but the largely imaginary figure who had come, once, to my bed. Indeed I spent almost all my time compulsively recreating the precise sensations of that last night together: the sound of her heated breath by my ear; the rise of her nipple against the palm of my hand; the glimpse of the wet patch of hair beneath her underthings; the impression of her fingers as they in sequence closed around me and tugged; and the smell of the sweat, hers and mine, that pasted us together. It was as if I were dwelling still in the heat of a California September, oblivious to the increasing bitterness of the New England autumn, the New England winter to come.

I wrote Madeline letters, usually two a day. They were filled with descriptions of how I was going to suck and lick at her body, from her lower lip to her unpainted toe. Laughingly I reminded her of the way she'd stared at me cross-eyed after I'd reached into her throat with my tongue. I told her how I'd come in my sleep when she'd spread her legs beneath me and that in another dream I'd taken her from behind, as we'd seen Sammy, his penis as slick and red as a lollipop, trying to do to with our neighbor, Thomas Mann's, Doberman pinscher.

I spent hours at the post office station beneath Wright Hall, waiting for Madeline's envelopes to show up in the little window of my box. When one did, perhaps once a week, the dark-blue ink on light-blue paper talked about the plays she was acting in, or about Sartre and Kierkegaard and Nietzsche. Did I realize that after Sisyphus has lost his rock so near the mountain's summit, he makes a conscious decision to roll it back again? Did I understand that, at the end of Beckett's play, Vladimir *knows*—underlined in indigo—Godot will not arrive but that he wills himself to wait nonetheless? I wanted ecstasy; she'd become an existentialist.

Then, in November, one of the hockey players on my floor told me I had a phone call in the common room. I raced down the four flights and across the quadrangle. It was Madeline. She didn't bother to say hello. "Richard-boy, I want you inside me. Do you understand? I want you completely inside me."

We knew we'd have to wait until Thanksgiving. Just two days later another envelope, this time from Lotte, rested on the diagonal inside my box. It contained, instead of the plane tickets I'd expected, a note:

Dearest Richard,

I'm sorry to have to tell you I haven't been able to get a reasonable price for the house. Even *with* the furniture no one will come up to fifty thousand. Isn't that a shame? Do you remember the man who rang our bell and out of the blue offered us a quarter of a million dollars when your father was alive? I don't want to sell the Soyers. And when I think of that beautiful English credenza! It was made in the eighteenth century. Can you imagine what California was then? It was barely civilized when we moved here in the Thirties.

I am doing the best I can, darling. You know I want to see you. Barton has been talking about having his big brother back for weeks. If you could see him! We have been having the most intelligent conversations. I think he is going to end by converting me. It is, don't you think, this Buddhism or Hinduism, a peaceful religion. I am so grateful to his swami, who at last has done something for him after the years and expense of those doctors and those analysts. Betty said the other day when she was over that he was a joy to talk to and she hardly recognized him. Of course she asked about your work and said when you have some oils—do you? Then I won't *need* the Soyers!— she will be eager to hang them.

Don't you agree that in the circumstances the airline tickets would be an extravagance? I know you are disappointed. My heart is crushed too. It seems we have been apart forever. The bright side is your Christmas vacation is only a month away. That isn't so very long to wait.

And then she told me she loved me with all her heart.

The campus on Thanksgiving Day was deserted. I went alone to the Waldorf Cafeteria and, to rub it in, ordered the hot turkey sandwich. There was another turkey, made from paper, atop the coffee urn. Its brown and orange feathers were spread in a fan. I took two bites of meat hidden beneath the thick gravy. I do not think even Sisyphus could have willed himself to take a third.

I flew back to Los Angeles six days before Christmas. Packed in my luggage was the lingerie I'd bought for Madeline and, for Bartie, a briar pipe from the tobacconist across from the Shubert Theater. From the airport I took a cab not to 1341 San Remo but to Romany, and knocked on

Madeline's door. Her father told me that she was in Sacramento, representing Pomona in the state finals of a dramatic competition. Something by Tennessee Williams, though I was too stunned to recognize what.

I hauled my bags across the street to the garden-side entrance of our house. Everything was blooming, mid-December or not. Red dots filled the pepper trees, the ivy on the brick was green and glistening, and the tall pecan tree at the center of the circle was for one of the few times in its long history actually bearing pecans. What had Bartie wrought? Were the cork oaks going to start producing corks?

"Hey, Brother!" cried Barton, running over the lawn. He embraced me, crushing me to his chest. Then he stepped back. One eye, as always, was narrowed, the other wide. "Bartie thought about you. He thought about you every day."

"Hey, Bartie, you look great. Really. You're—I guess you're glowing."

"Yoo-hoo! Richard!" That was Lotte, waving from the arcade. She was wearing sunglasses and, because of the unseasonable heat, a two-piece outfit from summer. I waved back. "Oh, I can see from here," she called. "You have grown an inch."

We'd taken our meals in the kitchen for years—except for when, our one luxury, we went to the Swiss Chalet in Brentwood or a Chinese place in the Palisades on what used to be the maid's night out. But now Lotte had set up the china on the dining room table. Before we sat down, huddled at one end, she handed me—and my heart leaped to see it—a blue envelope. Postmarked Sacramento. Trembling, I turned my back to rip it open.

I couldn't bear to tell you, Richard-boy. Don't be sad. Don't be mad. Remember: only five more days.

No signature. No salutation.

My mother brought out the soup. She served a salad. As I ate I couldn't help glancing from my spot—she'd placed me at the head of the table—through the dining room, the foyer, and into the living room, with its black laquered Steinway and green rug, and the portrait of Lotte above the fireplace.

"Something is missing," I said.

"I know! Let me tell! Let me say! It's the tree! The Chrissy-mas tree!"

That was, now that I think of it, another custom we'd kept up—a huge Douglas fir, whose five-pointed star scraped our high ceiling. We trimmed it with popcorn strands and red, green, and silver balls, while Bartie threw handfuls of tinsel at the topmost branches. The gift boxes would pile up beneath it like ice blocks heaped by an ice breaker's prow. Barton and I would dance around them in a delirium of greed. Nothing could be touched, however, until Norman and Lotte descended the spiral staircase at the astonishing hour of 9 a.m.—and even then not a ribbon was pulled from the wrapping until Arthur and Mary had carefully undone the boxes that contained, for her, a sweater or a stole or even a little gray mink; and, for our butler, on at least one holiday, a solid-silver flask. Then Bartie and I would have at it, package after package, a soccer ball, a gyroscope, a first baseman's mitt, a copy of *Ivanhoe*, a copy of *The Kid from Lincolnsville,* a Slinky, a labyrinth game, a bag of marbles, a knife.

Lotte said, "I didn't have the heart for one this year, Richard, with you away. It is a bother. It is an expense. And I always felt guilty. You remember, when Grandpa Herman came. He couldn't pretend he wasn't upset. We're Jews after all. The more I find out about what happened during the war, the closer I feel to our own traditions. Oh, Barton: I don't mean that we don't admire the swami and his way of life."

She went out to the kitchen. Before she returned with the platter of roast chicken I reached behind me to retrieve the gifts from my bag.

"Here, Bartie," I said. "Happy Chanukah, Merry Christmas, and all that."

He opened the box. Immediately I saw his chin begin to quiver. A teardrop formed in one of his eyes.

"Why are you crying? Bartie? Don't you like it?"

Lotte pulled at my sleeve. "It's not allowed," she whispered. "He's following Prabhavananda. He can't drink, either. He has to keep—they call it purity of the body."

Bartie screwed his napkin into his eye. "Pretty," he said. "It's a pretty pipe."

I handed Lotte her present, an early RCA Victor "Long Play" recording. It was Rachmaninoff's Second Concerto, with William Steinberg and William Kapell. Lotte said, "Oh, isn't this more fun than sitting under that tree? I'd be picking up pine needles for weeks!"

"Should I put it on?" I asked her.

"That would be wonderful," she answered, while she started to cut through the skin of the chicken. "We can listen while we eat."

I went through the living room around to the bar, and threw open the doors to the Capehart. I put the record on the holder; the machine's long arms seized it and, as a spider picks up a morsel of meat for its dinner, turned it about before setting it upon the spindle. But the music, when it came out, was at triple speed.

"What's that *noise*?" Lotte called. I snatched off my gift and put on a Schubert sonata—seven two-sided discs that the Capehart could gyrate through in half an hour—and started back to dinner. On the way I saw, atop the piano, a photograph of Adlai Stevenson with his arm around my mother. I brought it into the dining room.

"Oh, *that!*" laughed Lotte. "The Ziffrins brought him by on the way to the fund-raiser at Gregory Peck's. It was right after you left for college. I think he was ashamed at not coming by during his first campaign. It was as if Norman was on the blacklist even after he'd died. I don't blame Adlai. I admire him for being brave enough to visit now. He stopped the whole motorcade in front of the house."

"Yeah," I said, "because he knew he didn't have a Chinaman's chance of beating that dope we're stuck with for another four years."

"Really, you're becoming so cynical. He wanted to make amends.

He knew how much Norman had done for him before his heart attack."

"He came back," Bartie said. "After Gregory Pick-Pack-Peck. I saw him. I heard him. All night long with Lotte."

"Because of the fog," our mother replied. "His flight was canceled. We had three days of it."

In the false candlelight of the chandelier I saw that she was blushing. I couldn't resist: "Old Adlai. So much for those rumors going around. I didn't think he had it in him."

"Don't be ridiculous," Lotte said. "I should slap your face."

"You are in the Kali Age." That was Barton's contribution. "Sex is your only means of pleasure."

"Knock it off, will you, Bartie? You don't have a clue."

He put down his knife. He put down his fork. "I've got a clue! I know all about that envelope in your pocket. I know about you and Madeline. You want to indulge. To wake the sleeping serpent of the kundalini. You know, f-f-f-ucking."

"Jesus, Barton, is that what they teach you at your temple? What happened to purity of the body?"

The smile he gave us was sad and sweet. "Such purity is not for the unenlightened. You must first understand that the true union is not between gross matter but between Shiva and Shakti, the cosmic consciousness and the cosmic energy."

"Okay. Got it. Pass the butter."

Once more the Buddha smiled. "I know you want to make a joke. But the joke, Bro, is on you. If only you could realize what you are missing during the *sadhana.* There is no thrashing in the dark and no sound of grunting, such as one hears from animals in the barnyard."

I threw down my napkin; I started to rise. But I sank down the moment he raised the palm of his hand.

"The enlightened ones bathe each other from head to toe. Their breath is sweetened with cardamom. A violet light fills the room. In its vase stands the scarlet hibiscus. *Devata blava siddhaya,* chant the lovers.

He looks upon her naked form and sees the Saphire Devi, the embodiment of bliss. He tranfers true knowledge to her by touching her heart, her head, her eyes, her throat, the lobes of the ears, the breasts, arms and navel, thighs, feet and yoni. She raises her legs and pulls her knees to her chest. Only then may the sex organs of man and woman, Shiva and Shakti, be brought into contact."

Barton was on my right, calmly speaking. I thought Lotte might cry out. I thought she might leave the table or break into tears. I never imagined, when I turned to my left, that she would be leaning forward, her elbows on the table, and that her face, cupped in her hands, would be inflamed.

"The lingham now enters the yoni, but without vulgar thrusting and agitation. The lovers are motionless, at peace, attentive to the currents of pleasure that pass between them and rise upward through the chakras to the thousand-petaled lotus at the top of the spine. This union of the gods lasts for thirty-two minutes. Thus do the enlightened ones achieve both purity of the body and liberation from it and from all material things."

He paused. Lotte picked up her glass of water and, with a tinkle of ice cubes, drank it down.

"Thirty-two minutes," I exclaimed. "Poor Adlai!"

There was no laughter. It grew quiet. I could hear, way off in the living room, the breathless ticking of the antique French clock.

"Look! Lookie! Look!" My brother had tipped his head back. He had the briar pipe clamped in his teeth and was speaking around the stem. "Bartie's a Yale man! Bartie's going to college!"

The five days went slowly by. I had a term paper to write. I was supposed to finish *Women in Love*. Instead, I got into sneakers and shorts and started playing tennis for the first time in months. Most of the old gang were already hanging around the courts at La Cienega. Many of them—Mosk, Fox, Werksman, the younger of the Coveneys—were also back from their first year of college. One day, after I'd beaten Mosk in straight sets, he announced that on the 28th a few of them were driving down to Tijuana and asked if I wanted to go along. "Come on, Duck," he urged. "Don't you think it's about time?" I was under no illusions about the reason for this trip. I told the Penguin—we all had such nicknames; mine derived from the fact that I had a wide mouth and *Donald* for a middle name— that I'd think about it. But I knew that Madeline would be back on Christmas Eve and that I'd have no need to take part in their ritual: the defloration of the freshman.

The night before Christmas duly arrived. Lotte was off at a party that Betty was throwing for the first of her abstract expressionists. Bartie hadn't returned from his Vedanta temple. The knockwurst that Lotte had left simmering for him atop the stove had split open and filled the pan with a kind of milk. The desert wind rustled through the pecan tree, rattling the nuts in their shells. On San Remo the streetlights were on. Madeline's father had driven her back from Union Station late that afternoon. From the window above our garage I'd watched her get out of the car. I didn't telephone. I didn't go over. I didn't even turn on the lights to let her know I was home. I knew she'd come through the garden gate some time that evening; and sure enough, at a little past nine, she did, walking carefully along the gravel path between the yellow and purple-headed pansies. I opened the back door, and she stepped into the light.

"Hi, Richard-boy," she said. Her hair, I saw at once, had been cropped to the line of her jaw and chin. Her throat, which dove into the V of her short-sleeved blouse, was tanned, the shade of my sienna-brown pencil. She seized my hand and squeezed it between both of her own. I stepped against her, so that she could feel me against her hip.

"Come up. I brought you a present."

I let her go first, taking the curve of the staircase. Her little dark skirt tick-tocked against the back of her knees. Both of her stockings, a heartrending white, had collapsed around the tops of her shoes. In my room I plucked the package from the bedspread. "I hope you like it," I said. "From Macy's in New York. You know, Macy's and Gimbels.

They're on the same block, right across the street."

She opened the box. She lifted the lavender panties and let them hang from her finger. "Ooh, la la! Brigitte Bardot! *Et Dieu a créa la femme!*"

"Want to try them on? To see if they fit?"

I swear I saw her reflexively lick her lips. I moved behind her and, through my jeans, fit myself between her buttocks. Reaching, I slid my hand into her blouse and worked the buttons.

"Oh, you wait, Richard-boy. You wait. I'll put them on." She stepped aside, into the bathroom that separated Barton's room from mine. While she was gone I ripped off the bedding and hopped out of my shoes. I tore my shirt over my head and let my pants drop to the floor. Then I fell back onto the mattress. I needn't have hurried. A minute went by. And then another.

"Hey! You okay? Madeline?" As Sartre would put it, *Pas de réponse.* I waited a third moment, actually counting off the seconds; then I got off the bed and knocked on the bathroom door. Still no answer. With a feeling of dread known to all existentialists, I knocked again. But I knew that she had gone. For a crazed instant I felt the top of my head start to burn, as if cuckold's horns, or Jews' horns, were sprouting from it. I hurled myself against the door, which comically flew open. She hadn't flown back to Romany Drive. She was standing on the floor tiles, with her old lingerie crumpled at her feet and the new silk panties—cut to reveal her haunches and the prickly skin at her groin—still dangling from a finger. She put her hands over her naked breasts.

"Oh, darling Richard," she said. "We've made a mistake."

I stepped into the room. "What do you mean? Don't you remember your phone call? Don't you remember your letter?"

She only stared at the tile.

"What's going on here? Huh? What's going on?" In three steps I was beside her. I ripped her hands away and put my own over her breasts. "It wasn't a mistake in September, was it? You let me then. You wanted me then. What's happened? Tell me. Did you meet somebody in Sacramento? Some actor? Some stage designer?"

"You know I didn't. You know there's only you."

"Then why don't you kiss me?" I kissed her, her lips, her neck, the tips of her shoulders. I ran my tongue over her nipples. She remained as still as a statue. Her skin was like marble under my hands. At last she looked up. She handed me the underwear, with the Macy's tag still attached.

"I guess these are the wrong color," she said.

I looked away as she pulled on her own cotton panties and reattached her brassiere. She hiked her skirt around her waist. She buttoned her blouse and stepped into her shoes. The door to Bartie's room was closed. I stepped aside like a gentleman to let her walk through mine. Then she turned down the corridor that led to the stairs. She stopped halfway down them and looked back at where I was leaning over the bannister. "It's getting chilly," she said. "Put your clothes on. I don't want my Richard-boy to catch cold."

The Buick drove into the garage well after midnight. I checked my glowing clock. 1:21 in the morning. The engine fell silent. The door slammed shut. My mother's high heels clacked on the drive. The back door opened and shut. A moment of quiet. Then I heard her in the hallway, just outside. She hadn't come into my bedroom, not at night, in the four years since Norman had died. But she came in now, her silk dress like a wind. I feigned sleep. I prayed that her smells, the alcohol, the perfume, the tang of dry perspiration, would overwhelm my own. She sat on the side of the bed.

"Richard? It's too dark to see. Are you awake? Are you alone?" Her voice, unmistakably, was slurred. "Poor boy. I thought Madeline might be with you. That's why I stayed so late at Betty's. Oh, and a man was stalking me! That wolf of a painter! Don't you think I've had enough to do with *them?* René and now Maxim! You are the only artist in my life. Would you believe it? All the help had gone to sleep and Betty and I were doing the dishes. But the man wouldn't go home. He said, 'Maxim will dry them spotless for you.' Ha! Ha! Ha! *Spotless!* Oh, Richie? Are you very disappointed? Didn't she let you hold her in your arms. I was so happy for you."

She leaned toward me. She kissed, through my matted hair, the top of my head. I groaned, as if I were having a dream, and rolled away; the bottle of hand lotion, stolen from her cabinet, ground against my leg. Whom did Bartie pray to? Krishna, the all-powerful? Who lifted elephants on the palm of his hand; who with an exhalation toppled the Himalayas. *Oh, Krishna! Remove her! Swallow her! Plunge her into the Arabian Sea!*

"The phony Frenchman. Now the mad Russian. Goodness, he threatened to kill himself if I wouldn't kiss him. He said, 'I go to studio and eat my paints.' I shouldn't have. Kissed him. That would have been my contribution to art. You should see his swirls and squiggles. They've got Betty completely bamboozled. The way Norman did. Ha! Ha! Ha! You remember?"

I did. He and Stanley got an old canvas and rubbed in the pigment with their feet. Then they bought a fancy frame and a bronze name tag. They brought it over to the gallery themselves. *Nazis in Norway*, by Jan Schmeer.

My mother leaned over me. I could smell the wine on her breath. "It wasn't much of a kiss. Not on the lips. But he said it brought the beast out in him. The beast! And him with a dishtowel! Oh, I had a lovely evening! But you! You're so censorious. You are a censorious son. You think everything is easy for me because it's all been easy for you. I don't have anything left, dear Richard, of my charms. I've got to pinch their cheeks. Oh, God: I laugh at their remarks. I'm the pixie, everyone's darling. Yes, yes, yes: he wanted more than a kiss. He wasn't hanging around for his health. You know what saved me? The knowledge that in two more weeks I will be at UCLA. I've been accepted! You aren't the only one with a letter. I've got mine right here in my handbag. I am *much* too tipsy to find it. We'll both be in college together. Yes, smarty, I am getting my MS. And so I thought: well, a brand new social worker doesn't spend her time with Rasputin rolling in the hay. I am going to help people. Why does that thought make me cry? Oh, dear: tears. Children. Damaged children. Lotte's specialty."

The irony of that made me want to laugh out loud. Not to mention the memory of Betty exclaiming over the plastic qualities of the great Jan Schmeer. But it wasn't laughter I fought to smother in my breast. It was a rising tide of misery.

"I shouldn't be crying. If I'd gone home with Maxim—oh, I know I'd regret it. So now I will resign myself to a lonely life. Are you lonely, too, my dear Richard? Without your Madeline? We'll have to find ways to satisfy ourselves. Do you know what I mean? I bet you do! What's been going on here, my little man? What's my little man been doing under the covers—?"

Drunkenly, she lay down beside me. I felt her hand fumble beneath the blanket. It crawled over the sheet. I felt my heart stop, then start with a tremendous thud.

"Oh!" gasped Lotte, sitting up straight. The thud sounded again, but not from the crash of my heart against my rib cage. The concussion came from Bartie's room. We hadn't heard it for so long that we'd almost persuaded ourselves, Lotte and I, that we never would again.

Crack!

She was on her feet now, stumbling through the dark toward the bathroom.

Crack!

I could feel the shock wave, as if an earthquake were rocking my bed. It wasn't an earthquake. It was the back of Bartie's head striking his bedroom wall.

Lotte switched on the bathroom light. I plunged ahead, wrapping a towel around me, and then threw open the door. My brother was propped on his mattress. He was fully clothed. Before our eyes he smashed his head backward. There was already a small circle of blood on the wall. Lotte rushed forward. "Oh, Bartie! Stop! I beg you to stop."

I stepped into the room, which smelled of incense. A painting of an eight-armed goddess was propped on his chest of drawers. "Hi, Bartie," I said, struggling to keep my voice even. "I didn't hear you come in."

"I just got here. I walked. I walked all the way."

Lotte said, "But why? Why did you walk? In the middle of the night. Something happened. Tell me what happened."

Bartie ceased rocking. He broke into a smile. Then he said, "Oh, nothing happened. Nothing important. It was only on the earthly plane."

"Please, Barton. Won't you stop that talk?" Lotte threw herself on him. She held him fast. "We *live* on the earthly plane. Look at your poor head. It's made from flesh and blood."

I cinched the towel about me. "What is it, Bartie? Why are you so late? Why didn't you take the Sunset bus?"

He looked at me, his eyes wet and gleaming; then he said, matter of factly, "They weren't running. It was too late. The swami's soul left his body."

Lotte let out a groan, low and piteous. "Oh, no. Oh, Bartie. What are you saying?"

"We were waiting for him to speak to us. He sat on the ground. Like this, you know." Bartie drew himself up, with his crossed legs beneath him and his circled hands on his knees. "But before he could open his mouth I saw it fly away. His soul. It was a little person, just the size of a thumb. Bartie saw it. Only Bartie. Then something came out of his ear. We all saw that. Something wet. Like water. He fell over. He was just an empty vessel."

"No, no, no!" cried Lotte. "Poor Bartie. Your swami. He loved you. Oh, unlucky Bartie! In front of your eyes."

I said, "Bartie, listen. Are you sure? Maybe he just fainted. Maybe it was, you know, a Hindu trance."

"Oh, he was dead. Dead as a doornail. The ambulance people said so. The doctor said so. They put him on a stretcher. They drove him away. Lotte, why are you crying? Brother, you're crying too. That was just the husk without the kernel. The Buddha told his disciples that he could remember five hundred and fifty-five of his earlier lives. The swami told us of his past lives too. To the enlightened, the storehouse of memory is thrown open. You should be happy for the swami. Now he is released from bondage. He is hanging like a dewdrop upon the web of Brahma."

Here Barton, catching us by surprise, hurled his head once more against the wall. I sprang forward. I took him in my arms. Lotte was sobbing. I held him, sobbing too.

"*Unlucky Bartie,*" my brother said. "Where did he come from? Bartie tries. He tries and tries. He can't remember one of his lives."

3

We set out for Tijuana, the Penguin, Pumpkin, Cow, and I, early on the morning of the 28th. We had a passenger, squeezed into the corner of the back seat, sucking his thumb. I didn't dare tell the others that Barton would be coming along. Instead I volunteered the Buick and picked up the gang at La Cienega. We told our parents that we were going to a tennis tournament in San Diego over the weekend. That hadn't gone down well with Lotte.

"How *dare* you think of abandoning your brother now? For a *tennis* tournament? Look at him. He's practically catatonic. It is out of the question."

I couldn't tell her what my own needs were, so the compromise was that Bartie would join us. On the appointed morning I waved my racquet conspicuously, jumped into the driver's seat, and drove off to the courts. When the others saw Barton, huddled against the fake-leather cushions, they stopped in their tracks. Before anyone could say anything, however, I shouted, "Get in, get in. Bartie's coming with us to San Diego."

Where Bartie himself thought he was going I didn't know. By the time we'd reached Long Beach and the bobbing derricks at Signal Hill, it had grown as hot as a day in June. I put down the black top. Then the road cleared, and we moved southward along the Pacific Coast Highway past Huntington Harbor and Huntington Beach. My brother leaned over the side of the car the way a dog does. His blond curls tossed and rippled. He was staring out over the hazy ocean toward what looked like an impressionist version of Catalina. Grandpa Herman, on that same ecumenical visit, had taken the two of us out to the island. I shouted backward, into the wind, "Remember, Bartie? That glass-bottom boat? When we saw the pretty fishes?"

He didn't answer. The rest of the virgins kept their silence too. We sped on past Newport Beach and Corona del Mar. In those days the farmland—cotton, I thought, lettuce, artichokes, the occasional field of garlic—stretched all the way to the Santa Ana Mountains on our left. Finally, as we swung round Dana Point, Barton pulled his head out of the breeze and said, "Vichy-wishy-soisse." Then, instead of returning his wet, callused finger to his mouth, he used it to give the thumbs-up sign. I understood then that he must have thought we were going not just to San Diego but to the Coronado Hotel, where Norman used to take us every summer. To Bartie it was a castle, with red-roofed turrets and the whole of the sea for a moat. He was fond of the soup. In the dining room, his mouth painted with thick cream, he'd cry out to the orchestra on the balcony above: "*Porgy! Porgy!*" And, as if he were indeed a little king, the obedient musicians would go through their rendition of *Summertime, Bess, You Is My Woman Now,* and what strikes me now as the oddly Vedanta-like *I Got Plenty of Nothin'.*

"Jesus Christ, Duck," hissed the sharp-beaked Penguin. From his seat beside me he leaned close, pulling at my sleeve. "You must have lost your mind. Come on. Tell us. What the hell are we going to do with him now?"

That indeed was the question. It seemed the others had been mulling it too. The big, bland-faced Cow leaned forward from the back seat. "We can't drag him with us. Not through the streets. Not into the bars."

"He's too young," piped up the Pumpkin, round-headed, round-bodied, and with a jack-o'-lantern's chipped tooth to boot. "Look at him with that curly mop. He looks like a baby. He could pass for a ten year old."

"What about the girls?" asked the Penguin. "They'll just laugh when they see him."

Cow: "Who knows how he's going to behave? One minute he's quiet; the next minute he's throwing a fit. It could be an international incident."

Pumpkin: "Right. He starts howling or has a vision or bites somebody and we'll be the ones inside a Mexican jail."

Duck: "Shut up, will you? Just shut up. Do you think he doesn't have ears? That he's made of stone?"

We all glanced over to where he sat, motionless and blank-eyed, his hair collecting the light in a halo that suggested the real reason for our unease: the silent saint who rebukes the determined sinners.

In the end we swung inland to Chula Vista and pulled into a motel. The idea was to leave Barton there while the rest of us, so went the story, played our matches under the lights. "It's a private club," the Penguin explained. "Only members allowed." We brought in sandwiches and cans of 7-Up and Dr. Pepper. We turned on the TV. If Bartie knew this was not the Hotel del Coronado, he didn't seem to mind. He watched, in seeming fascination, as the head of a hatted man kept rising into his padded shoulders, because of a flaw in the vertical hold. The rest of us gathered in the courtyard outside. The sun still beat down through the haze. Trucks—a line of eighteen-wheelers, each filled with lowing cattle—rolled by along the strip of highway. We made a few nervous remarks about the Cow being led to the slaughter. Then the Penguin said, "Okay, what are we waiting for? We might as well get this over."

"Oh, no," said the Pumpkin. "We're waiting for waiting's sake."

Duck: "What's that supposed to mean? Aren't we down here to have fun? Let's get going."

"Fun? Fun is a corollary. We're here for sex."

Cow: "So?"

Pumpkin: "I've thought about it. I've figured it out. What is sex but tension and release? I am describing the formula for the only known source of human pleasure. It's your turn to think about it. Try to give me another example."

I did think about it. I said, "What about beauty?"

"Get serious, Duck."

"I *am* serious. What about the pleasure you feel when you see something beautiful? Or hear a symphony, say?"

"Which wins—the most beautiful thing you ever saw: a Rembrandt, a flower, a sunset? Or a good shit? Give your opinion and not what they told you to say at Yale."

The Cow broke in. "The good shit."

They all turned to me, the artist, the idealist, who said, "Hands down."

"That's right. Because of simple physical laws—in this case the pressure on the colon and the sphincter. The greater the tension the greater the release. Ergo, the greater the pleasure."

"What are you saying? We should all get constipated?"

"Spare us your wit, Duck. Most people most of the time settle for a little pleasure because they can take only a little pain. But we're in a once in a lifetime situation here. We can never duplicate this day. So let's stick to the plan. Tonight is only to increase the tension. A few drinks, okay? Maybe a sex show—I hear they've got them with a woman and a burro. Or anyhow a flick with lots of blondes. Then Long Bar. The important thing there is to sit next to the runway. These Mexican chicks will drop their panties right on your head. They let you smell the juice on their hands."

The Cow said, "Do you believe that?"

The Pumpkin brought the tips of his fingers to his nose. "Oh, baby! Oh, baby! Ambrosia!"

"All right. Okay," said the Penguin. "It's our golden moment. It's the happiest day in our lives. Let's get the show on the road." Then he stomped off, in what seemed a fury, toward the parked car.

The Pumpkin rose from where he'd been squatting. "Just remember, tonight's only the build-up. We'll get hot. We'll get boiling. Then on the next night the tension is released. Keep your heads. Be strong. The frustration will pay off in all-time thrills."

We got into the car, two in front, two in the rear. I put the top up and latched it down. Then, as I began to back out of our spot, I heard a moan, a bellow. All I could think of was one of the animals on the cattle trucks—its throat had been cut, its life was running out. But the Penguin said, "It's your brother."

I looked back toward the motel. Bartie's face was pressed against the glass. His howling mouth was open.

"Pull out," said the Cow.

"He'll be all right," said the Pumpkin. "He'll be fine once we're out of sight."

But I was already out of the car. I ran to the room and struggled to get the key into the door. When it opened, Bartie tumbled into my arms.

"Why are you leaving me? I don't want to be alone. Take me with you."

Pumpkin and Cow made room in the back. I pulled out into the busy roadway and turned at the sign that pointed toward the border. The four freshmen didn't say a word. We left it to Barton to keep up the chatter.

"I know where you're going. I know all about it. It's to get a little ass, right? You couldn't fool Bartie. You tried but you couldn't. Some of that nooky. That was the secret plan. You want to kiss their faces. You want to take off their clothes. Ooooh! Big breasts! Big boobies! Real titties! Bartie knows about cunt. Hairy cunt and hairy balls. It smells like fishes. Bartie's going too. Lucky Bartie! He's a red-blooded American! He wants to humpty hump one of those Mexican girls!"

The weather turned at the border. The high haze gave way to thick, dirt-colored clouds that hung over what in those days were brown and green hills. Now and then the setting sun would radiate upwards, like spikes on a crown, or light up the odd acre in the distance. Four or five fat raindrops struck the Buick's windshield, and silent lightning raced horizontally among the clouds. Now even Bartie fell silent before the ominous landscape, in whose valleys and on whose hillsides the town of Tijuana lay sprawled.

My brother and I had been to Baja California before, on family excursions from our famed hotel. I still have a photograph of the four of us— Lotte and Norman are smiling in the back of a cart and Bartie and I are on top of a donkey that had been painted to look like a zebra. The backdrop is fake cacti and a banana tree. All but me are wearing comical sombreros; Bartie's is labeled "Cisco Kid." We'd never fail to watch jai alai, of which Tijuana seemed to be the Cooperstown, and stroll down the main street, which was really no different than Olvera Street in downtown L.A., a place where I bought a skull-shaped brass ring that left a green stain on my finger, sucked on dripping sugar cane, and brought home jumping beans that hopped about until the living worms within finally died.

On this occasion we parked outside of town and made our way along the central arcade. Plan Pumpkin called for caution: drinks, a movie, followed by stage-side seats at Long Bar. At first we held to it: when the señoritas, who lingered in the negative spaces between the arches, called out to us, we'd say such things as "You are very charming, my dear, but not on this fine evening." Then we'd laugh and elbow each other and buy another cold bottle of beer. Things went awry when the clouds opened up and the rain fell so hard that the mud on the road ricocheted around us like small-arms fire. We ran across the intersection and beneath the yellow and red neon tubes that marked the entrance of what turned out to be Long Bar itself.

Half of humanity seemed to be crammed into the steaming room. Everyone was packed shoulder to shoulder, shouting, screaming, laughing. Two bands played at top volume. The runway, tantalizing, unapproachable, might as well have been on the far side of the moon. We stood speechless, buffeted about in random directions like molecules suspended in a gas. "Look! Over there!" That was the Pumpkin. He'd spotted a table and was already moving like a bowling ball through the tenpins of the crowd. We followed him and grabbed up the spaces. Immediately a waitress came over and asked us if we wanted margaritas. "Yes, yes," said the Penguin. "Margaritas."

"Except for him," I told her, indicating Bartie. "Can you bring him a grenadine?"

"This is great," said the Cow. "We got a table at Long Bar."

"Yeah, but we can't see anything. What's the point?"

The Penguin was right. The crowd pressed close on every side of our table. Now and then, through the curling smoke, we could catch a glimpse of the empty stage. The din made me want to clap my hands to my ears. A thousand people, it seemed, were shouting at once, and the bands, with their trumpets and trombones, were in a contest to determine which could make the most noise. The waitress returned with our drinks. She leaned well over the table, so that her breasts swung freely before our eyes.

"Jesus! Did you see that?" exclaimed the Pumpkin. He took a gulp from his salt-rimmed glass. "Let's order again. I heard you're allowed to touch whatever you want."

Bartie, I saw, had a margarita too. He put a finger into the liquid and licked it.

Just then the music stopped and the lights went out. Cigar ends and cigarette tips twinkled about us. A whoop went up from the crowd. The whole room, as if in an undertow, swayed toward the far-off stage.

"It's the show," cried the Penguin. "And we can't see!"

Now three or four green-tinged spotlights poked through the darkness. A shout went up, a roar really, and the bands once more started to play. The Cow got up. He stood on his chair. The rest of us did the same. Three girls were on the runway. They walked up and down, gaily swatting aside the hands that reached for them. Then, between dance steps, they began to take off each other's clothes. The skirts. The woolly scarves. The flowery blouses.

"Oh my God," said the Penguin. "Do you think there's going to be a burro?"

The girls skipped about. The one in the middle turned her back to us; when she turned back she was not wearing her brassiere. The crowd cried out in Spanish. They whistled with their fingers in their mouths. The two other girls did what looked like a Scottish dance, hooking arms with each other, and then removed their halters as well. Then they leaned over in a line and moved their shoulders, so that their breasts tumbled about. They turned around and did the same thing with their buttocks. Even from our distant vantage we could see the lines of perspiration running down their bodies and flying off into the air. Now the two outside girls lay down and began to kick their legs, as if riding invisible bicycles. The girl in the middle remained upright. She clutched her breasts and looked about the room. Wherever her eyes happened to alight the men would cry, "*¡Oyeme, mirame, tesoro, bonita! ¡Soy el machote que buscas!*"

In time she pointed her long arm and red-painted finger at our table. "What?" said the Cow. "What is it? Do you mean me?"

She shook her head, so that her black hair flew to either side. My heart lurched wildly. I pointed to my chest, which seemed barely large enough to contain it. "Me? You want me?"

"Step aside, Duck," said the Pumpkin. He flashed the señorita his snaggle-toothed smile.

"*¡Pero no, estupidos! ¡El niño! Si! ¡El Guerito!* The baby. *¡Si! ¡Si!* With hair that's gold!"

For a second there was a hush. Then the crowd burst into cheers. Hands reached out on every side. They grabbed at Barton. They pulled him from his chair. He was smiling. His head bobbed loosely about. Was he drunk? From a few drops of tequila? Then the crowd lifted him high. From there, suspended before us, he called out. "She chose Bartie. She didn't choose you! She wants me!"

Now the crowd began to pass him from hand to hand. He moved through the smoke and the spangled atmosphere the way Krishna allows himself to be transported through the wonder-struck clouds. In half a minute he had reached the stage. The girls surrounded him, touching him, patting him. They put their hands to their mouths. They pointed at his crotch. They oohed and aahed. Bartie stood silently grinning. My friends were choking with laughter. They held each other upright, lest their hilarity bring them to the ground. Suddenly the music stopped, save for a roll of the drums. Two of the dancers put their hands on Bartie's shoulders and pushed him to his knees. I felt about me a growing heaviness. It weighed on me with such force that my own legs almost gave way. On the stage the señorita moved before Bartie. She hooked her thumbs in her panties and pulled them down. Then, standing open-legged, she seized the back of my brother's head and drew him forward, until his face was buried in the darkness of her crotch.

The crowd hooted and yelled. The two bands played a wild mariachi. My friends were doubled with laughter. Tears of merriment rolled from their eyes. I saw Bartie's blond head twisting and thrusting. The load that oppressed me grew heavier still. It forced me to bend my head low. It brought me to my haunches. Finally I sank under the burden to the sawdust that was strewn on the floor. What passed through my mind were not the sayings of the Buddha or those of a sage from my own tradition; what I heard were the words of the prophet whose birth we had so often celebrated at the foot of our tinseled tree. What fate awaited those who offended the little ones? Better that a millstone be hung round their necks and that they be cast into the sea.

The rain had stopped by the time the five of us came out of the bar. What fell about us was no more than a mist. The Penguin trudged through the puddles that lay in the road and began to negotiate with the driver of one of the town's fabled "Blue" cabs.

"What? Three-fifty?" he shouted, with a flap of his arms. "For a stupid flick?"

"*Si.* You wan' gorls you pay ten dollar more."

"No girls, no girls," interjected the Pumpkin. "Stick to the plan."

The cautious Penguin: "How much for just a ride out there? One way? You going to charge an arm and a leg?"

"One dollar fifty cents," said the driver.

"Each?" queried the Duck.

The Mexican grinned and threw open the back door of his Dodge, which was white with a blue top and a blue stripe down the side. "You pay five dollar altogether. Special good deal."

"Okay," said the Pumpkin, getting into the front. "But no nooky."

Cow, Penguin, and Duck slid into the rear. Bartie stood on the curb, wringing his hands. I pulled down the little round jump seat. "Look, Bartie," I said. "A special chair. Just for you."

The car lurched forward, splashed through several turns, and then headed off onto an unlit, unpaved road. We started a steady climb.

"Jesus," said the Penguin, peering out into the dark foothills. "I don't like this."

"*Si!* You like! You going to like!" The driver batted the steering wheel with the flat of his hands, as if keeping time to an unheard song.

The Cow's broad brow was furrowed. "There's nothing out here. There's no houses. No lights. I don't think we're even following a road."

"Anything could happen. There could be bandits. Killers with knives."

"Relax, Penguin. You act like you've never gone to the movies be—"

The words died on the Pumpkin's lips. Without warning the taxi lurched rightward and careened up a rocky ravine. Our heads hit the ceiling. Then our rumps slammed down onto the exhausted springs. Suddenly the Dodge was at the top of an embankment; it hung there motionless, its headlights casting cross-eyed beams into the black of the sky. Then we crashed down and began pitching across a rutted field. Ahead, in the darkness, was a cluster of what looked like tar paper shacks.

The driver, with his balled up fist, hit the horn. Instantly the little settlement came ablaze. Strands of light bulbs stretched winking between the huts, like the popcorn we used to tie on a string. Scores of figures, dark as bats, ran out to welcome us.

"Look," said Bartie, leaning from the window. "I see lots of girls."

And so did we all. They surrounded us, giggling, linking their arms through our own. We could see more señoritas waiting inside the door of the largest of the tar-covered shacks. To that portal, as if into the gaping maw of hell, we waded. The interior was lit by shaded lamps. Everywhere we looked—on chairs, on sofas, even on the planks of the floor—the dark-haired women lounged, legs crossed, sandals dangling from sandal straps." Look at him! That one for me," cried a plump, pretty woman, glancing disturbingly in my direction.

"Calm down, Duck," muttered the Penguin from the side of his mouth. "She's not talking about you."

"She's crazy about *you*, is that it? Lost her heart to the gentleman in the tux?"

"*Quack! Quack! Quack!*"

At that sound a ripple of interest passed through the gathered ladies. They began, with their puckered lips, to make sucking sounds.

Pumpkin: "Never mind. Ignore everything. We're here to see movies."

The driver of the taxi stepped forward. "*Si.* You wan' movie, you come with me. Come, come, come."

He beckoned us after him through the parlor to a small windowless room that contained nothing but a row of chairs and, on a round table, an 8-mm projector. We took our seats. The light bulb overhead went off; the one inside the projector came on. Simultaneously a woman—she might have been forty, with coal-dark hair and surprisingly light skin— appeared within a rectangle of light on the wall. We watched as she paced to and fro beside the frame of her double bed; she stamped her high heels and gazed at the bedroom door, which finally opened.

"*Now* we get the burro," came the Cow's voice from the dark.

But it was only a man, thin, middle-aged, with what is called a pen- cil moustache. He stood without expression as the actress unzipped his fly and took his spineless member in her hand. The film snapped. When the cab driver repaired it, the woman was in bed, attempting the feat of forcing her own breast into her mouth. This time the film simply refused to move forward; it hung on its sprocket and started to burn. The projectionist rapped the machine with his knuckles. Now the actor lay feet forward in bed, while his paramour sat astride his belly facing the camera. The gentleman's member stretched up and back, ending in what was for each of us the first sight of a working vagina.

This time the film slipped off the gears altogether and began to pool first on the table and then on the floor. We waited in a silence broken only by the whirring of the hapless Bell & Howell and the more distant chug of the hidden generator that must have supplied this outpost with its electricity. In time, in black and white, three or four or five men and women were crowded together upon the bed. A lady peeled a banana, pushed it between her thighs, and then took a bite. Another woman held a penis like a telephone receiver to her ear. A couple copulated doggie-style at one end of the mattress.

Of course the film jammed once again on its sprockets. No one in the audience uttered a complaint. Not even the Penguin demanded his money back. No, we strained forward, eager to take in what was offered of the tangled bodies and body parts. It was as if we realized that this uncertain light passing through a tattered slip of celluloid; the parade of images, derailed, halting, blurred in focus; the dance of frail shadows and motes—that the entire spectacle represented nothing other than the repressed unconscious of each of us as it wended its way through myriad defenses toward full exposure.

Behind us the door flew open. Four living ladies ran into our half-lit room. One went straight for the dumbstruck Pumpkin and began to squirm on his lap. A redhead threw her arms about the Penguin's neck and, between fits of coughing, blew in his ear. "This one, the minute I see him—" a little brunette was saying, as she threw her arms about the neck of the Cow, "I know this one for me!" And the Duck? He was approached by a woman who seemed to be about the same age as the actress on the wall. She sat on my knees, unbuttoned my brown suede jacket, and ran the palm of her hand over my chest. "What kind of job you want?" she inquired. "I do any job on you."

For a brief span everything save for the soft cough of the redhead and the buzz of the machine was still. Suddenly one of us—of all people it was the Pumpkin—got to his feet.

"Hey! What are you doing? What happened to the tension? You're ruining the plan."

But he only stood there, his mouth hanging open, his chipped tooth reflecting the light. Then, arm in arm with his señorita, he disappeared through a door on the opposite side of the room.

I know now that the Pumpkin was not merely moving into a corridor lined with plywood cubicles, but taking a journey in two contrary directions. The first of course was forward, from innocence into the life of the adult—that is, from the light that plays about childhood into the shadow that is always associated with the union of the sexes: desuetude, obsolescence, aging, decay. But he was also traveling backward into that Eden of infancy where there is no gap between wish and fulfillment, a place without repression or history or culture, and where the mere glimpse of what is desired—a white breast on a white wall, dark hair, high-heeled shoes—is followed, as in a nursery rhyme, by that desire coming true.

"I guess this is it," said the Penguin.

"I guess," said the Cow.

Then we all rose and walked off, each to his little cell. In it was a mattress, a condom, a roll of toilet paper, and of course an eager whore. Mine wanted to charge me an extra five dollars to take off her clothes. But there was no charge to throw her dress backwards, away from her hips, and against that dark backdrop to spread her pale legs. When I reached to grasp the meatiness at her thigh she said, "*Loco*, you *loco*, you." Then she stretched her arms, also pale, upward, and drew me down.

From the cubicle on the left came an insistent thumping. From that on the right, a no less rhythmic deep-throated cough. My mistress lifted a finger and put it to my mouth, where there were two shining braces on my lower teeth. "Oooh," she said, "pretty!"

In let us say a quarter of an hour the four of us met once again in the parlor.

"Duck! Duck!" cried the Pumpkin. "I'm itching! It's an itch! I've got the crabs!"

"What about me?" interrupted the Penguin. "I've got TB!"

The Cow: "Jesus! Jesus Christ! I think the rubber broke!"

What I said, with a sudden intake of breath, was, "Wait! Wait a minute! Where's Bartie?"

We looked around. The room was, as before, filled with women, together with a handful of good-natured pimps, and our own smiling cabby. But my brother was nowhere to be seen. We dashed to the second room, where the light from the projector hung in a blank upon the wall. No Bartie.

"Duck! Don't dawdle! We've got to get out of here!"

"I've got to get home and wash my dick!"

Suddenly, from the nearby corridor, we heard a scream. "*Eeee-oh! Eeeee!*"

We ran into the hallway. From the furthest cubicle a woman's voice rang out again. "*¡Ayeee! ¡Caramba! ¡Hijole, que macho hombre!*" There was a thump. There was a crash. We all heard the steady panting.

"Gosh," said the Penguin.

"I don't believe it," said the Cow.

The Pumpkin: "He's just a kid."

The four of us, at the repeated sounds of what I supposed to be the union of cosmic consciousness and cosmic energy, stood spent against the rough boards of the wall. We heard, from the male, a low, guttural growl, and a groan; and from the female, a final, earsplitting shriek. A moment later, with her hair in a tangle and one breast hanging loose from the fold of her robe, a woman emerged from the chamber and ran by us, weeping. Then, after a brief spell, a tall man with freckled skin and a red moustache came out as well. As he walked by us he put on his ten-gallon hat.

We soon found Barton. He wasn't in the cubicles. He wasn't in any of the huts. He was outdoors, crouching in the mist. He had made a kind of channel from the high ground to the low, so that a large puddle of water ran down toward the little plot of ground that he'd dug up at the side of the shack. A group of women stood around him, holding flowers in flower pots. One by one he took them and, still in their clay vessels, planted them in the loosened soil. More women came up, and then some of the men. The light from an open window fell on Bartie's hair. In just moments he had arranged all of the flowers in the ground and patted the earth smooth around them. Each of the blossoms was red: a drooping geranium, perhaps; a half-withered carnation; a poinsettia.

Bartie glanced up. "Hi, Bro!" he declared, upon seeing me. "Hi, fellows! Do you want to watch?"

So saying, he dug through the earthen wall surrounding his plot, and the water flowed grudgingly through the little aqueduct and swirled around the planted stems. Each plant, drinking in the recent rain, seemed to shudder; and then, as one can see in a film in which the light has been allowed to move past the shutter after moments or even hours instead of many times each second, the flowers, which had been bowed, lifted the flaming red petals of their heads.

We did not spend the night in Chula Vista. We stopped at the motel only long enough to gather our clothes. Then we drove back along the seashore the way we had come. We decided to tell our parents that we were so disheartened by our performance in the tournament that we wanted to return at once to our homes. It was almost three in the morning by the time we reached Santa Monica. In the darkness the rows of palm trees looked frayed and exploded, like trick cigars.

I turned inland and dropped each of my friends at the front of his house. No one said a word to anyone else. Then I turned westward, to Wilshire, San Vicente, north on 26th Street, and up Sunset to San Remo Drive. All the lights were off in the house. I left the car in the open, under the tall pecan. Was the sky brightening? Over the mountains to the east? I pulled out the brick that hid the key to the back door. We went in, involuntarily slamming the screen behind us. Lotte was at the top of the stairs. "Who is it?" she asked in a frightened voice. Then she flicked on the sconces. She was wearing a robe. White cold cream made her look like a ghost. "Oh, Richard! Oh, Bartie! It's you!"

"We went to a motel, Lotte! A real motel!" Bartie, quite eager, began. "There were trucks outside! I watched TV! Then we went out. We drove and drove in the car."

He paused. I stood, my heart in my mouth. I felt that my brother held the whole of my existence in his hands.

"Richard played in a tennis tournament. He lost. Ha! Ha! Ha! He was the loser! Cross my heart! Ha! Ha! Ha! Hope to die!"

4

I went back to New Haven shortly after the start of the year. The house on San Remo, with all its furnishings, was sold before I returned for the summer. The three of us squeezed into a single suite at a place in Westwood called the Ashley Arms. We ate in Chinese restaurants or a little fish shack near the beach. I had a bed. Barton took the couch. He wrote all day long. It was a saga about how all of Los Angeles was about to fall into a crack in the earth or be swallowed by a poisonous fog. As he explained it, we were already lost in a thick miasma.

"These Angelenos! They can't see their hands in front of their faces. All they want is to roll down the window at the drive-in. The waitress will bring them their hamburgers. Hamburgers, Bro! Made from the meat of cows. They want to see those waitresses wriggle their asses. And their tits are falling onto their trays. It's the Kali Age. That's all they can think about."

On weekends he'd go to the Vedanta temple. I think the famed Prabhavananda tried to take him under his wing. Once he called me on the telephone and said, "Your brother was put on this earth to be a disciple. Please try to understand his deepest thoughts." But Bartie kept those thoughts mostly to himself, scribbling day and night. Lotte told me that sometimes, rising early for her classes at UCLA, she'd see him seated in a meditative posture, facing Glenrock Avenue—that is, in the direction of the morning sun.

"He looks so peaceful then," she'd say. I didn't tell her about the muscles he was contracting; or the breath that he expelled from his lungs; or that he was affirming the sensation, as it moved through his spine toward his golden head, of kundalini, the uncoiling serpent of desire.

I did not return to San Remo Drive until after I graduated from college and was preparing to spend two years of further study abroad. That August I packed my easel into the trunk of the Buick and parked across the street from 1341. I set up the tripod on the edge of the lawn. I managed with my pastels to sketch in the cork tree off to the left, and the row of mighty pillars, with the red brick behind. Only a Chinese artist, or a Zen master from Japan, could capture in a single unbroken stroke the rise and flutter of the silken curtain. I poked in the leaves and the peppers on the pepper tree. I was working on the blue, cloud-spotted sky when a car drew up behind me.

"Richard! Richard-boy!"

Madeline. I had not seen her for almost four years. She jumped from the driver's seat and kissed me. She clapped her hands at the sight of the painting. "Oh! It makes me want to cry!" She clapped her hands again. "It's so beautiful! Oh, that window! I know what's behind it. It's your whole life!"

There now fell what anyone would recognize as an awkward silence. I entertained at the speed of light the fantasy that she was about to invite me around the corner to Romany Drive; that, in her bedroom this time, she'd pose for her portrait. A nude, of course. She would face me, boldly, a bit lewdly perhaps, with her legs partly open. I looked at her dark eyes beneath her dark brows. I believed I could read the thoughts that she too was having.

Then, from within the house, a stranger began to play the piano. Not Schubert. Not Rachmaninoff. No selection from *Porgy and Bess*. Just a child banging away at chopsticks. There was a girlish laugh. And a second laugh. Then the lid of the piano—our piano, Lotte's piano—slammed down. Two heads, heads of young girls, peeked through the open window. A towhead. A carrottop. They grinned. They waved.

"Do it," said Madeline.

So with my chalk pieces, a canary yellow, a Naples red, I sketched in the children behind the blowing curtain.

NEGROES

(1948)

I

In 1948 Halloween fell on a Sunday night. Just after dinner I put on my costume—a Sufi, I guess, or a Sikh, complete with scimitar and turban—and my brother, Bartie, struggled into the same dancing skeleton he wore every year. "My *God!*" cried Lotte, seeing her younger son's wrist bones and ankles protruding from those that had been applied with fluorescent paint. "How you scared me!"

"Ha! Ha! Ha!" laughed Bartie, taking his thumb from his mouth.

Norman waved to us and then turned back to the telephone. "B-E-R-N-A-L-A—" he intoned, spelling out the word for the Western Union operator. I can't swear to it, but I think Tony Curtis had just gotten married, and this was to be a message of congratulation. "That's right. *Bernala Don't Get a Hernala.*"

Mary, the maid, set down a basket she'd filled with Sees candies and prune taffy from Blum's. "You keep your eye on Mister Barton, you hear?"

I nodded and ushered Bartie outside to meet our friends. Gordon, Tim, Warren, and Ned had already gathered on the lawn in front of Madeline's house. Madeline came out, dressed as a ballerina, or maybe Glinda of Oz; and an old LaSalle pulled up, out of the back of which jumped a lion and tiger, the Coveney boys. Sandy, a screenwriter's son, was the last to arrive. Shortly after the war the Riviera neighborhood began to fill up with movie people, though, as might be apparent from the names of my companions, few of them were Jewish. In truth I thought of myself as nothing more than a vague deist, a worshiper equally of the wonders of Nature and the memory of FDR. But Barton, on Halloween night, was about to pull that wool from my eyes.

Not every house we approached belonged to a celebrity, of course, but the four I am going to tell you about did. The one closest by belonged to Marion C. Cooper. Each year the old Chinese servant asked us in for a showing of *King Kong* that we never stayed to see; that year the prize he gave us was a metal top that shot out stinging sparks.

"Where to next?" asked Sandy.

For a moment we stood, undecided. "It's too hot to go anywhere," said Tim, from beneath his Western bandana.

"I'm r-r-r-roasting," said one of the Coveneys, making a joke of it. My own head, inside the bands of my turban, felt aboil. Hard to think, in the blast of these desert winds, that the next day would be November.

Ned took out his slingshot and sent off a few stones toward a nest of hated blue jays. Gordon did the same. Suddenly the streetlights came on, spreading an odd, thick, greenish glow. Madeline leaned near me and pointed toward the acorn-shaped lamps. "Like Van Gogh," she said. I knew at once she meant the billiard table in Norman's book of famous paintings.

"Okay," said Warren, as if he were commanding a patrol in the army. "Let's go up San Remo."

I knew most of the people on that street because I had spent a few weeks earlier that summer canvassing its houses in the hopeless cause of Harry Truman. After a block and a half we came to a two-story, Spanish-style place.

"Trick or treat," Gordon said to the tall man with close-cropped hair who answered the door.

"Ah! Ah, yes. I have forgotten this. I am so sorry. We have, to eat, but little in the house."

"Candy! Candy!" cried Bartie. He hopped up and down in a dance macabre. "Boo! Boo! Boo!"

"Don't worry about Bartie, Mister Mann." I'd recognized the famous writer, not from the newspapers or his book jackets but from the time he'd been a guest at our house. "He's my brother."

Bartie was still gyrating about. "Watch out! Watch out! I can make a curse."

"Yes?" said Mann. I could see he did not recognize either one of us. "Your brother?"

"He's in disguise," I foolishly stated. "For Halloween. I'm Richard. From down the street. 1341. The Jacobies."

"Ah. I understand. You are the son of the charming Lotte."

I remembered clearly enough the moment my mother asked her guest, until then somewhat aloof, where he would like to sit for dinner.

From my perch on the staircase I saw him bow, smile, and take her hand. "It does not matter to me in the least," he declared, "as long as it is at the side of my delightful hostess." Now, and suddenly, a huge snarling dog came hurtling toward us from the interior of Mann's house. "Paco! *Nein!*" cried the writer, and slammed the door shut.

We regrouped on the far side of the street. "He's a Nazi," said Sandy. "We've got to get him."

"That's a kraut dog," said Pat, the younger of the Coveneys. His brother, the lion, said, "Right. I've seen those dogs in the movies. They train them to attack."

"So what do we do?" asked Ned. "Do we soap his windows?"

"I'm not going near that Nazi's house." The speaker was Warren. "Did you get a look at him? That's a mad dog. There was spit coming from his mouth."

Gordon said, "See his car in the driveway? That crummy Chevy? He drives a Chevy, I bet, because he's a spy. We're going to puncture his tires."

"Yeah," said Tim. "He's a spy. We'll let all the air out."

The lion and tiger cried, "It's our duty!"

In the darkness, the band started forward, toward the rear of the little coupe. But Bartie held up his glowing bones, the radius and ulna of his arms. He was the youngest by far—a sort of mascot, or a Shakespearean fool. His laugh stopped everyone in his tracks. "Terrible things will happen! Awful things! Watch out for your family!" Here Barton waggled his chalk-white skull mask. "Death!" he intoned. "Death to your children! Death to everyone!"

My sack, a shopping bag from Ralph's, was already full of toys and half-melting chocolate. Still, Barton and I pushed on with the others to the top of San Remo, where we knew Gregory Peck would be handing out fruit and gingerbread men. I was the last in line. "It doesn't look good for the president," he told me, one adult to another.

I dropped his apple into my bag, and nodded. "What's wrong with people? Didn't we fight the war for the values of the Democratic Party? How can we give away what we won?"

"Think of a pendulum," Peck said. "That's how politics works in this country. It swings left and it swings right. But every time it swings to the left, it moves a little farther."

I caught up to my friends at D'Este, and we plodded on, silent and exhausted, until we reached the brown stucco house of Joseph Cotton. His reputation, at least among our set, was worse than that of the blue jays, and they were rumored to eat their young. Each year in the fall his place was deserted. The poor man was probably on tour or location, or simply traveling abroad; but we took his absence, the locked green shutters and uncut grass, the thud of the horseshoe-shaped knocker, the echo of the unanswered bell, as a deliberate attempt to cheat us of our rewards. Ned had already taken out his Whamo. He shot off a handful of gravel that whistled through the ivy that covered the porch. "We'll give him a whiff of the grape!" he exclaimed, borrowing language he'd heard in the movies.

Sandy, his forehead X'd over with a Frankenstein scar, was pulling at the wooden slats of the shutters. Tim helped him rip one of the panels away. Then they rubbed the window glass with a mixture of spittle and soap.

I barely noted the mischief. My inner gaze was fixed on my history lesson. Was it true, what the actor had said? During the war I'd moved red flags to mark the progress of the Soviet Army. How thrilling the day those flags joined the blue ones of the Americans at a river in Berlin. Now the people's army had blockaded that same city, and its former allies were forced to bring in food and clothing by air. Not only that, someone had assassinated Mahatma Gandhi. The unspeakable Chiang Kai-Shek had just been confirmed as the leader of China. Worst of all, that no-good

Taft-Hartley Act, that's what Harry Truman had called it, had been passed by a Republican Congress. Working men and working women couldn't even strike for a living wage. What had the sacrifice of so many been for? The blood! The suffering! And now Truman himself was about to go down to defeat. When would the pendulum swing back? Could it go any more to the right? What about Jackie Robinson? That had to mean something. Could it be that Americans were beginning to accept what was written in the Declaration of Independence: that all men were created equal?

At that point in my ruminations I heard Barton's cry: "I do so dare! I do!"

The Coveneys were baiting him. "No you don't! You're just a baby!"

"I'm not a baby! You take that back!"

"Yes you are." That was Gordon. "Only babies won't take a dare."

Suddenly, with a whoop like an Indian, Bartie was running across the unmowed grass in front of the Cotton house. The whole gang watched as he fell upon the lawn jockey that stood at the bottom of the front door steps. "Kike! Kike! Kike!" Bartie screamed. He beat at the little black face and the little red cap.

"What are you doing?" Madeline shouted. "You shouldn't say that."

But Bartie was a wild man. He ripped at the statue, tugging at it, trying to topple it from its base. "Kike! Kike! Kike!" he kept repeating. "Dirty kike! Damn dirty kike!"

"Shut up!" cried Sandy. "He isn't a kike."

"Is too! Is too!" screamed Bartie through the mouth of his paper skull.

"Can't you see?" asked Warren, in a tone that was almost pleading. "He's black. That means he's a nigger."

Tim: "Right! That's right. He's a nigger!"

Ned: "Stop calling him a kike."

Then Gordon said, "*You're* a kike! That's what you are, Bartie. A kike."

Barton stopped kicking at the shins of the jockey. Now he started to wail. "No, I'm not! I'm not! Not!"

"Then what are you?" demanded Pat.

"I'm not a kike!"

I stepped onto the lawn. "Leave him alone, will you? Come on, Bartie. We're going home."

"Sure, you protect him," said Gordon. "Because you're one too."

"One what?" I asked.

"A kike."

"That's right," said Sandy. "Just like your brother."

"I am not any such thing," I protested. "I'm not and he's not."

"Oh, yeah? Then what *are* you?"

Out of a moment's confusion I did not reply. Gregory Peck had come down to our place some months before and we'd all watched his latest film, *Gentlemen's Agreement,* on Norman's 16 mm projector. Perhaps it was the lateness of the hour, but the film had left me bewildered: was the actor a kike or wasn't he? Why had Lotte gotten so upset when the main character gave a speech about how a simple remark on the street could end up in—what, exactly? Beatings? Prison? Death? I had seen newsreels of bulldozers and mounds of corpses. Was Lotte thinking of that? Was that why she was in tears?

"Well," I at last responded. "What are *you*?"

"I'm a Catholic," said Tim.

"I'm a Catholic, too," said one of the Coveneys.

His brother said, "We go to church. Where do you go?"

Warren said, "I know what I am. I'm a Protestant."

"So," said Gordon. "Tell us, Jacobi. What are you?"

"Not a kike," I answered.

"Religion changer!" That was Ned. I saw he was loading his slingshot with pebbles from the driveway.

"Bartie, over here!" For once, my brother obeyed. He came running to my feet.

"He changed his religion!" cried Gordon.

I took up my bag of treats in one hand and Bartie's in the other.

"Religion changer! Religion changer!" Everyone was chanting the words.

"Run, Bartie!" I commanded.

He took off at once, down the center of Romany Drive. The pebbles from the slingshots sprayed around him. Those without weapons were throwing sticks and branches. Warren had hold of a rock.

Madeline yanked at my arm. "Don't stand there!" she cried. "Go home!"

I did, ducking, while a single stone sailed past my shoulder and a clod of dirt broke into pieces against my back.

Was that long night now done? Not quite. I turned into our side gate on Romany, but Bartie was nowhere in sight. I walked through the unlit garden, among the purple and yellow bent-necked pansies. The streaks on those flowers, their markings, looked like the dark tear spots under a spaniel's eyes.

There was the outline of the pecan tree; there sat the new Buick, its chrome grill grinning. I went through the arcade into the back yard. The green grass was black. But the lit pool was gleaming. Bartie was standing waist-deep inside it. The illuminated liquid refracted his leg bones, making him look like a cripple. He was scooping up the water in both hands and pouring it onto the curving stones at the edge of the pool.

"Hey, Bartie," I called. "I've got something for you." I rummaged in one of the paper sacks and took out a long, narrow bar of candy. "Peter Paul's Mounds."

He gave me a bucktoothed grin. "Coco-loco nut," he answered, pointing to himself.

For a moment I watched him continue his wading. I knew what he was doing: the insects, the beetles, the bugs came out at night, attracted by the shimmer on the surface of the pool. He was saving the drowning creatures. He was giving them a new life. Then, over my shoulder, I saw Madeline under the arch of the arcade. She moved halfway across the grass and came to a halt. I went up to her.

"What is it?" I asked. "What do you want?"

"I want to kiss you," she said; and before I could answer she leaned forward and put her half-open mouth on mine. Her arm went around my waist. Her knees, which were trembling, brushed against me.

"Hey! I see Richard! He's got a boner!"

The voice, Timmy's, came from the lemon grove at the back of the yard. I whirled. I saw dark shapes darting from tree to tree.

"A boner! A boner!"

"What are they talking about?" I asked Madeline. "What do they mean?"

But the girl was already hurrying back through the passageway and out of the garden.

Now I could see, like so many lemons among the branches of the grove, the pale, white faces. They were laughing, my friends, and rubbing their hands at their crotches.

Suddenly there was a splashing sound. Bartie had hauled himself out of the water. For a moment he stood dripping. Then he reached up and removed the mask from in front of his face. He might just as well have displayed his own skull underneath. The boys in the lemon grove drew back, gasping, and in the next moment each one of them had vanished. I knew what they were afraid of: one of Bartie's curses. It was as if they had some premonition of what we would all come to know within the next year: that Thomas Mann would lose Heinrich, his famous brother; and that, just as Bartie had predicted, his son would kill himself in a fit of despair.

2

The next morning I was awakened by a chiming that seemed to come from the walls, the floors, even the ceilings of our large, L-shaped house. For a time I lay in bed, listening to the near-musical sound. In the bathroom the effect was louder, more like the clash of cymbals. A cigarette, I saw, was floating in the toilet bowl. I knew it had to be either my mother's Chesterfield or a Lucky Strike that had been discarded by Arthur, our butler and chauffeur. In any case I directed a stream of urine onto the half-smoked butt. Like a Japanese destroyer, a battleship even, it dodged and darted; but there was no escaping the attack from above. In only seconds the target burst apart, sending myriad brown flecks across the turbulent surface. When I attempted to put the drowning sailors out of their misery, however, nothing happened. I pulled the lever again. The toilet did not flush. I turned the sink's faucet. No water came out. Only then did it dawn on me that these sounds, seemingly nowhere and everywhere, came from all the hidden pipes in the house.

I went down the back staircase to the kitchen, where the noise in the pipes was louder—a harsh, insistent clang. The dishes rattled inside their cabinets from the percussion. My breakfast, with a glass of orange juice, was on the table. I preferred a drink from the Arrowhead cooler.

"That there is the only running water," said Mary. She dabbed at the lines of perspiration that ran from what I always thought was a wig, past the frame of her wire glasses. "And this day so hot."

I heaped my eggs on a wedge of toast. "Why is there no water? What is that banging?"

"It's those mens," said the maid. "The city mens. They intend to hook us to the sewer."

Bartie came in, clutching his sketchpad. "Hewey and Dewey and Louie," he said, or rather quacked, in imitation of the cartoon ducks. Then, to torment me: "Dewey! Dewey! Dewey!"

I covered my ears and read the paper that was spread between my elbows. Truman behind in California; Truman behind in New York; Republicans expected to increase their seats in both houses of that *no-good, do-nothing Congress*. Maybe democracy hadn't been worth the fight, that's the gloomy thought that assailed me. The fat cats owned all the newspapers, the way the Chandlers owned the L.A. *Times*. It was too easy to fool the people. Plato, the Greek philosopher, had the answer: a Philosopher King.

Arthur leaned into the kitchen. "You boys had best hurry if you mean to catch that school bus."

I jumped up, stuffing the newspaper—Lotte and Norman would not wake until twelve, at which time a later edition would be waiting, hotel-style, at their bedroom door—into my bag of books. Bartie did not stir. His head was bent inches from the table. He kept throwing down one of his colored pencils and picking up another. He squinted, his tongue out.

"Hey, come on, Rembrandt," I yelled.

But Barton leaned closer to his pad, his cheek nearly brushing the paper. "I'm painting!" he said, pushing so hard on the brown-colored pencil that the lead snapped in two. He held up the unfinished drawing, a portrait in a style I now know to be not that of Rembrandt but, with its swirling lines, the colors piled upon colors, the distorted features of its subject, Soutine. "See? Do you see? Those are her glasses! That's the cross on her neck! See? It's Mary!"

The bus stop for Canyon Elementary was on Sunset, where Bartie was not allowed to go alone. I waited for him on our front lawn, breaking off piece after piece of the cork tree's rubbery bark. Where were the November rains? The heat beat down through the branches and leaves, seeming to shrivel them before my eyes. Each leaf, in curling, ticked, as if a foot were stepping upon it.

Bartie burst through the front door and ran toward me from beneath the pillared portico. At the same time a huge black man came around the corner of the house. He wore tight, coal-colored pants and a white T-shirt so soaked through with sweat that it seemed to be part of his skin. I watched, astonished, as he stretched his arms from pillar, almost, to pillar. He was like the famous drawing of Da Vinci's naked man, or the darker figure of Samson who, gripping our columns, threatened to pull the large house of bricks down upon him.

For the first few years after the war our school was on half-session, which meant we would arrive home in time for a late lunch. I spent the whole of the morning asking permission to go to the water fountain in the outside hall. Yet no sooner had I slackened the thirst that assailed me—it was as if my mouth and throat were stuffed with saltines—than I raised my hand for another drink. This affliction reached its peak during the geography lesson, a little before noon. Madeline was saying something I only half-heard: *What if the globe were a balloon?* She meant the large blue sphere that stood in its wooden holder at the front of the classroom. *What if we let the air out? Then wouldn't South America fit exactly into the hollow of Africa?*

The boys sent up a howl. "A balloon!" they shouted. "She thinks the world is full of air!"

"Well, is it just a coincidence?" asked Madeline, holding her ground. "Maybe once, a long time ago, the earth *was* smaller. Or else, maybe the continents were all joined together. Then they drifted apart."

There was, at this, a series of catcalls that the teacher, Mrs. Statik, was powerless to quell.

Meanwhile, Roger, who lived close by in the canyon, slipped me a fresh piece of paper. It was covered with inkblots—rather, with a series of black humps that might have been filled-in croquet hoops or the dark mouths of tunnels, had not each of the semicircles been slightly bifurcated at the top. I studied the rebus, turning it this way and that.

"I give up," I said.

Roger snatched back the drawing and waved it before me. "MOLASSES!" he cried. "Get it? Mole-asses!"

But Tim was on his feet. He was red-faced. He was pointing his finger at Madeline. "You dummy! You idiot! If what you said was true, America would be full of niggers!"

As soon as he said that I thought of the huge Negro I'd seen that morning. His ancestors hadn't walked to this country over a land bridge from Africa. They had been brought here in chains. Now he was forced to labor in the dark, airless dungeon beneath our house. Was he still there? Working in those inhuman conditions? He was no better off than a slave! Once again the sensation of thirst overcame me. But I didn't raise my hand for permission to go to the icy cooler. Nor did I pay any attention to the rest of that class, or any of those that followed. All I wanted was for the school day to end. I wanted to see the black giant again.

The bus left us off at the empty lot on the corner of Sunset and Capri. Bartie dawdled, chewing on the wild fennel that grew there in purplish clumps. "Do me a favor?" I asked Madeline, as I moved off toward San Remo. "Bring Bartie to play at your house, okay?"

She nodded. I waited for the traffic to clear, then crossed the boulevard at a trot. On the far side I paused, cupping my hands to my mouth. "I didn't laugh at your idea," I shouted. "It's true! That's why all men are brothers!"

Then I started to run. My heart banged in my chest. My book bag, and the sharp points of the books inside, struck repeatedly against my ribs. Long before I reached our corner I was listening for the telltale clang of a hammer, a saw, a wrench against the metal pipes. But the house, as I approached it, was silent. I raced across the lawn, where the Japanese gardener, on his knees, was clipping at the fringe. *Snipping, snapping*: not the sounds I had hoped to hear. I ran into the house, into the dining room, and slammed through the swinging door that led to the kitchen. Lotte was there, with Mary, trimming flowers at the sink.

"The water!" I cried. "It's on!"

"It went on a half hour ago," my mother said. "Can you imagine the nerve? Look at these circles under my eyes. I couldn't sleep with the banging. Do they really have to begin at the crack of dawn? Thank God they're quiet now."

I was aghast. "What does that mean? Does it mean they're dead? From the heat?"

Lotte glanced down, toward her handfuls of gladioli. "No, no," she laughed. "They're fine. Where's Barton? Isn't he with you? And there you are, my big boy, and I haven't had a kiss."

Mary indicated the table, where my place was set. "You sit down now. I made you the tuna fish."

I didn't sit down; I didn't give my mother a kiss. I dropped my book bag and ran through the hallway out to where the driveway made a circle between the two arms of the house. I saw at once that the Packard was gone, which meant that Norman had already left for the studio. I trotted over to the wing around which the black man had come that morning. There was the opening, like the mouth of an animal's burrow, that led to the crawl space below. Without a moment's thought I lowered myself into the earth.

It was dark, with only a few stray beams of light filtering through the narrow band of lattice work behind me. Already I was stooping; to move forward, into the blackness, I would have to crawl. I did, on my hands and knees; soon enough the last ray of light disappeared. In spite of the darkness, the perpetual shade, the air seemed hotter here than it had been in the direct light of the sun. The ground, wherever I touched it, felt warm, a reminder from geography class that the core of the earth was actually composed of burning, liquid rock. I halted, wondering if I would be able to find my way back over the dark half-acre. Only then did I think of actual danger: snakes, for instance, or coyotes, or the mountain lions that ranged through nearby Rustic Canyon. Even the bite of a black widow spider could kill a man.

I looked back, over my shoulder. It was as dark there as night. Then I saw, well ahead, between a row of pilings, a faint yellow glow. Had I become disoriented? Gone round in a circle? I moved toward the light, which I soon realized came from the bulb of a lamp whose cord was hung over a metal pipe. What it revealed was the worst of my fears. Two dead men lay sprawled: the enormous Negro I had seen that morning, and a second man, smaller, older, lighter-skinned, with a moustache over his open mouth. The giant was on his side, his palm open; the slighter man lay on his back, one arm caught beneath him, the other flung over his companion's hip. I froze. It was as if I were gazing into the galley of a slave ship, a sloop whose human cargo had expired from exhaustion, asphyxiation, the lack of a drop to drink. "Hey!" I called, inching closer. "Hey! Hey! Hey!"

The smaller man, not all that much larger than I was, lifted his head. "Who's that?"

"It's me. Richard. I live here."

"What are you doing down under the house?"

"I didn't hear anything. I think I wanted to see if you were all right."

"That was your momma I saw? Picking flowers out of the garden?"

"Yes. Lotte. She does that every day."

"Well, she got a lot to choose from."

Now the other man, shiny as a lacquered box, drew his legs up to his chest and stretched them out again. His eyes snapped open. I saw that the whites were actually a shade of yellow.

"This is Richard. Says he is the gentleman of the house."

The man nodded, just slightly, his head. His mouth, with its thick lips, seemed to hang perpetually open. The smaller man did the talking:

"How come you ain't in your school?"

"Because it's half session. It's been that way since the war."

"Martin, here," said the same fellow, "was in that war."

"Really? Were you in the army? Were you in the navy?"

The man looked over my head. "Army," he said.

"What do they teach you? In that half-day school?"

"Lots of things. Ordinary things. Multiplication. The story of the Mayflower. I had to learn to play the violin. Last week I did a report on the Boston Massacre. There were only five people who were actually killed, but they call it a massacre anyway. The very first to fall was Crispus Attucks. His story is really interesting. He was a freed slave, you know, and he worked as a seaman for twenty years. When Samuel Adams called on the dock workers to protest against the British, Crispus was the first on the line. Some of the Americans had only sticks! Some had only snowballs! I said in my report that not enough people today know that a Negro was the first person to die for our freedom."

I paused. I could feel my cheeks starting to burn. It dawned on me that these men had not heard of the patriot, either.

Martin glanced toward his partner. "Eddie," was all he said.

The little man scurried away, sideways like a crab. He must have had a flashlight with him, because I could see beams of light stabbing up and down in the dark. I turned toward the ex-soldier.

"I hope it didn't sound like I was showing off. My favorite subject is poetry. I can recite all of "First Day Thoughts" by John Greenleaf Whittier. *The still small voice which reached the prophet's ear.* That's a famous line."

There came, from the direction in which Eddie had gone, a loud gurgling noise, a sucking sound. Then the pipes clanked and clanged.

"Does that mean," I asked, "there's no more water again?"

The giant nodded.

"Until when? When you stop tonight?"

"Not 'till we're done."

"Well, how long will that be?"

Martin didn't answer. He pulled a strange-looking saw from the bottom of a toolbox and, still lying on his back, began cutting through the water main above him. Eddie, angling back, had heard my question.

"You tell me," he said. "You know how many toilets you got in this house?"

"Three upstairs: for Lotte and Norman, for me and Bartie, for Arthur and Mary; and I guess there are two downstairs. So five.

Eddie: "No, sir. Six. You forgot the one in the room over there, by the garage."

"Yes, that's right."

"You sure going to remember it now. It's got a line of its own to the septic. What I'm doing, I'm running a hose so there's just enough pressure to make a flush."

"I don't understand. Is that the only toilet we'll be able to use?"

"That is right."

"But for how long?"

"Well, six bathrooms, and all the work in the kitchen: two, most likely three days."

"But that's the toilet for the gardener!"

"And that's three days depending—depending me and Martin work overtime every day morning to night."

"That isn't possible!"

Martin ceased the back and forth movement of his saw. "Ditch machine coming," he said.

"That's right," Eddie went on. "Gonna dig from here over to that Romany Drive. Big machine. Like a Ferris wheel, except instead of seats it's got buckets that cut like a knife."

"But that's where the flower beds are!"

"Be that," said Eddie, "as it may."

"Oh, no! Oh, no!"

"Why do you want to carry on? You just plant another garden."

"It's not the garden! It's Tuesday night! Lotte's party! We have a big party every time there's an election."

There was a pause. Martin placed his saw against the underside of the pipe and yanked it toward himself with a screeching sound.

"Ha! Ha! Ha!" I was the one who was laughing. "Where are they going to pee? All those big shots! The politicians! Ha! Ha! Ha! The movie stars! In the garage!"

There was a grunt, a bellow, a guffaw: Martin was laughing too.

Then Eddie joined in, yapping like a dog. The three of us howled together. Martin held out his hand; Eddie slapped it. Then Martin extended that vast pink palm toward me. I hesitated a second, a half of a second, then brought my own hand down.

The men set to work. It was a terrible job. Mostly they labored flat on their backs, groping up at the pipes. A constant mist of dust filtered down around them. At times they rolled over and, with a miniature pick, a half-sized shovel, dug at a line of trenches. Wordlessly I watched, holding my knees. Once Eddie, without looking, thrust his hand toward me; instinctively, I gave him his hammer. At another point I pulled the hooded light down the pipe, so that it shone unobstructed on the site. I was not wearing a watch. I guessed an hour had gone by, but it might have been two or, for all I knew, three. I think, with the sweet swamp smell of sweat, of sewage; the swaying dust and the darkness; the closeness of the half-seen men, I fell into a kind of reverie. We might, the three of us, be miners hacking away in the darkness at a vein of coal. Yes, we might be members of the United Mine Workers, whom John L. Lewis was leading in the fight for a decent wage and a decent life. He had even defied Harry Truman by taking his men out on strike. What we shared was the camaraderie of working men striving for a common goal.

"Wait! Wait, Eddie! Wait, Martin! Stop. Stop working. I thought of something."

"What's that?" said Eddie. He had paused in his labor and was pouring the contents of a metal thermos over his steaming head.

"You *can't* work every day, the way you said. Not morning to night."

"Why's that? Why you saying that?"

"You forgot about tomorrow."

Martin was on his back, heaving on the handle of a wrench. "What about tomorrow?" he asked.

Eddie tilted his head at me. "This a game to be cute?"

"No, no! It's Election Day. You'll get time off. There's a law, I think. Our school is closed the whole day. You've got to vote."

"Vote? For what? The president?"

"And for Congress. Don't you want the Democrats to come back in? Don't you want Harry Truman to be elected?"

"I don't practice all that, young man. Truman never did nothing for me."

"But look at the conditions you have to work in. This heat, this darkness. There are millions of others who have to work like this at the bottom of mines. For a pittance. Besides, President Truman believes in civil rights for your people. That's why Strom Thurmond is running. There's no such thing any more as the solid South. Do you know what I say? I say good riddance! They're not even Americans. They do the lynching. They make colored people drink from separate fountains. They're like the Nazis! I hate them! Hey, I know what! You guys are pulling my leg. Are you voting for Wallace? Is that it? I understand. My family was tempted, too. But my dad, he's Norman Jacobi, the writer and producer, he said the perfect is the enemy of the good. He meant that a vote for Wallace is a vote for Dewey. For big business. The status quo. Martin, you were in the army. Weren't you fighting to change things? To make a better world?"

The huge black man released his double-handed grip on his tool. He shifted about, turning his yellow eyes upon me. "I look at you," he said, "I see the apple rotten to the core."

I gasped. It was as if that same great palm had slapped me. What had I said? What had I done?

"Ain't voting Dixiecrat," Eddie said. "Ain't voting Democrat. Ain't voting Progressive. I read the newspaper and I know the names. You live in this estate. I seen through the window a piano, a piano that's bigger than the room I was born in. This is a plain fact. If I came at night and took a fork of your silver I'd eat like a king—except I'd soon be in the jail again and your Harry Truman, he'd be the jailer. That's politics, my young master. Your momma, cutting her pretty flowers. You, with your white-skinned girlfriend. The nigger who puts a cap on his big black head and drives you to town in that car. All that, you eating the cake, so to say, and you ain't going to share the crumbs with the like of me."

"She's not my girlfriend!"

"Furthermore, you ain't telling me or Martin a thing when you mention Mr. Norman Jacobi. I know all about the folk been moving to this neighborhood. I been under their houses, too. Last job was at the man who made that *King Kong*. We seen that, ain't we, Martin?"

The silent Negro lay on his back, eyes rolling, lips drawn back; he could have been the giant ape who fell from the Empire State Building. His chest, like an expiring animal's, rose and fell.

"When Martin was to war I went to the theater just about every day. Used my head so I didn't once have to pay. I'd say that it seems I saw just about every film that was made. Feels good in the dark when you're lonely. You hate the people in the South, you say. You say they are degenerating. You listen. I had friends there in my boyhood white and black. Drinking fountains? I put my mouth to the same bubbler as did they. They are friends for life even though we don't see each other and don't never speak. Of course they grew up to desire the white girls when they became ladies. But they are inside me nevertheless. In all the years I sat alone in the dark theaters I tell you I never saw on a picture screen a black man to be friends with. Only servants like your Arthur, your Mary, and dancing niggers now and then. Mr. Thurmond of South Carolina? He don't know *nothin'* about the discrimination compared to the people who make the moving pictures. Don't speak to me about voting. Ain't interested in politics."

The sudden thought I had was, *How does he know the names of our butler and maid?* And then, *How does he know about the Steinway?* But those concerns immediately sank in the wake of my alarm at what had gone wrong. Where was the camaraderie? The solidarity of the workers? What had happened, and so quickly, since I had helped with the lamp and the hammer? Since I had touched the black man's hand? Already they were literally turning their backs on me as they set to their tasks. Martin gave one last tug on the wrench handle, so that the embedded nut gave way. The pipe above him parted and a thin stream of liquid, red with rust, ran out. Eddie, meanwhile, had crawled off to deepen one of the trenches.

I crawled after. My mouth had gone dry again. I tried to speak, but the words were choked. I took another breath. Then in a rush I said, "We've got a pool in the back. Would you fellows like to go for a swim?"

Eddie didn't reply. He kept digging into the ground with the point of his pickax. But Martin dropped his tool and rolled onto his belly. Wordlessly he began to crawl over the ground toward the distant exit. Eddie in his crab walk came after. I was the last to come out into the light and air. I knew at once from the shape of the shadows that it was late in the afternoon. The heat beat more strongly out of the asphalt driveway, the bricks of the house, than from the colorless sky. The new Buick, too, was gone from the garage.

"It's this way," I said, pointing to the arcade. But the men were already under the arch. I followed them out to the yard. The sun hung low over the lemon grove. The green lawn was on the left, the blue pool to the right. I came up behind the Negroes. "You can change in the cabana," I told them, indicating the small, whitewashed cabin. "There are swimsuits and towels and caps if you want them."

But Martin pulled off his shoes on the spot where he stood, then dropped his pants to his ankles. With one hand he ripped away the wet rag of his shirt. Eddie removed his clothes as well. Then both men walked to the edge of the pool. Eddie's thin legs poked out of a pair of boxer shorts. Martin wore tight briefs that, next to his skin, were as dazzling as alabaster. Slowly, like a sawed redwood, or sequoia, he toppled sideways into the water. He dropped well below the surface, hanging there in a great black blur; it might have been the piano that had been lowered into the deep. Up he came, spouting, and with a kick of his legs descended again. Eddie leaped into the shallow end and began to jump up and down. He waved his arms, sending up a spray. Then he began to holler and whoop.

The screen door off the kitchen opened and closed with a bang. Mary in her white uniform stood on the step. The door half-opened again. Arthur leaned a shoulder out.

"What's this foolishness?" he asked.

"These are the workers," I answered. "From under the house. I invited them."

Mary said, "Your mother is not about to appreciate this trash."

But it wasn't my mother who drove round the house and came to a stop in the circle. I could tell by the slam of the door that the car in the drive was the Packard. A moment later Norman stepped through the arcade. He was dressed in a sports coat and slacks. As always, a white handkerchief spilled from his breast pocket. "Hi, Dad!" I called. "This is Martin. This is Eddie. I invited them to swim in the pool."

Norman was already tripping down the steps. He strode across the flagstone to the water's edge. He stretched out his hand, which Eddie, his moustache dripping, reached up to take.

"I am pleased to meet you," Norman said. "It must be hot as blazes under the house. I'm glad you've had the chance to cool off."

Eddie grinned and flopped backward. At the far side of the pool Martin, his arms stretched behind him, clung to the tile at the rim. He nodded toward my father.

Norman held up his briefcase. "I've got work, Richard. We're going to have to shoot overtime tomorrow. Nobody's happy about it. And over what? A picture about who's in love or not in love with whom. All those misunderstandings, they're actually based on two plays by Shakespeare. Keep it a secret. We'll be murdered if that comes out." He grinned and moved to the kitchen door, making a point of ushering the servants ahead of him.

The workmen resumed their play. Eddie, I realized, couldn't swim a stroke. He kicked and cavorted three or four feet deep. Martin now launched himself like an underwater missile, a blunt-headed torpedo, from one side of the pool to the other. A minute went by before he came up for air. I took off my shoes and rolled up my trousers. I meant to dangle my legs in the water. That was when Bartie came out of the house. He had his drawing pad and his easel.

"Get out of here, Bartie," I shouted.

"It's my time to paint."

"No it's not. Not here. I'm with my friends."

"They're my friends, too. I'm going to do them in watercolor." He set up the three-legged stand and smoothed down a fresh page of his pad.

I ran over and seized his tin box of paints. "Go away, Bartie. You don't belong here. You don't know them."

My brother lunged for the watercolors. "You're just jealous! Because you're not an artist!"

"You're not a painter. Everything comes out all crazy."

"I am too! I'm talented! Everybody says so. Give me my colors!" He jumped for the black box. I held it high out of reach. He jumped again. I laughed at his efforts, as if he'd been a dog leaping for a bone. Suddenly he turned and ran toward the archway. "Mommy! Mommy! Mommy!" he screamed. Lotte was standing there in a bright, summery dress.

"What is going on here?" she demanded.

Bartie threw his arms around her. "Richard is playing with those kikes!"

The shame of those words filled me as a liquid does a vessel. I couldn't, drowning in that chagrin, utter a sound. My mother turned toward me.

"What is the meaning of this?"

"It was hot. Under the house. It was burning. Norman knows. I gave them permission."

Lotte stood unmoving. She held a hand like a visor against the sinking sun. She saw Eddie stand upright and, as if he were chilled, clutch his cashew-colored shoulders. Further out Martin was doing the Australian crawl, rolling his back with every stroke, so that the water split to either side.

"Very well," Lotte said. "I see." She stepped from Barton's embrace and walked back through the arcade.

I was standing next to the easel. Before Bartie could react I seized the pad and turned to the colored-pencil sketch he had made that morning. I ripped it away. Then I ran to poolside.

"Hey! That's mine!" Bartie cried, dashing toward the water.

Before he could reach me I held up the drawing for the swimmers to see. "Look at this, guys! Did you ever see anything like it? It's insulting. An insult to your people. You'd have to be crazy to paint anything like that." Then, as Barton fell upon me, kicking and scratching, I tore the portrait of Mary in two.

3

Canyon Elementary was closed on Tuesday, but I did not stay long in bed. I wanted to spend the whole of the day under the house. *Mole-asses*: now I could laugh at Roger's joke. I'd be a mole, blind and burrowing, making my home in the ground. I lay a moment longer, listening to the banging of the pipes as a churchgoer might the call of his church bells. Then I dashed to the bathroom and spun the taps, delighted to find that not a drop came out. I bolted down my breakfast, not pausing to savor the two spoons of hot coffee that Mary had allowed me to pour into my glass of milk. Arthur came into the kitchen. The sight of him, in black pants and black coat, wearing his chauffeur's cap, did not alarm me; I thought he'd be taking Norman to work. Then I saw that he held my striped jacket in his hands.

"Can't procrastinate no more, Mister Richard. Put on this coat."

"Why? Why put it on?"

"We going out for the day."

I clenched both fists and brought them down on the table. "I'm not going with you! I'm not going anywhere. You can't make me."

"Now don't be that way. Mister Barton is waiting in the car."

I jumped up and slipped into the hall. I looked out the window. The Packard was in the circle. A wisp of exhaust came from the tailpipe. I could see Bartie, his head of blond curls, rocking against the plush of the rear cushions. Arthur drew up beside me. He held out the coat. "I believe you going to enjoy what we got in store."

"Fine! You go! You go with Bartie! There: that's a good idea."

The chauffeur was implacable. He seized me by the arm. "Please. I need you to help me. Please, now."

"No! Damn you! I'm not going!"

"You watch your language." That was Lotte. I was amazed to see her, at this hour, on the spiral staircase. Her hair was down. She wrapped the folds of a nightgown around her. "Put on your jacket, Richard. You are not spending this day at home."

"The hell I'm not! I know why you want me to go. You don't want me to be with my friends. You're ashamed of them. Don't deny it. Eddie was right. You're a prejudiced person."

Did she fly down those stairs? Float through the air? All I knew was the next instant she was magically before me, and the instant after that she slapped my face.

"That's all right, Miss Lotte. That's all right. The boy is coming along with Arthur. Ain't that right?"

"Yes," I said. "I'm coming. That's right."

What Arthur had planned was a day at the beach—not the beach exactly, he explained, once we had turned onto Sunset, but fishing at Santa Monica Pier. We rented our equipment from the shack across from the merry-go-round, where a line of preschoolers and their parents had already formed. A band was playing there, trumpets trumpeting, drumsticks drumming, violins sawing away—all without living musicians, as if we were watching an orchestra in a Disney cartoon.

Arthur led us out to where the men were fishing. Their rods were propped on the railing, the lines well out in the water; baskets and buckets stood at their feet. We were the only children, though I did see a few other Negroes among the fishermen. One of them was forcing a fish into a pail of water, holding it down as if he wished to drown it. Another, barechested save for a vest, took three steps and whipped his rod forward, making the line, with its sinkers and its row of baited hooks, whistle through the air. A third man sat on a stool, hands on knees, staring. I hung back, as if I had nothing to do with the spectacle of the blond, bucktoothed boy who toddled along holding his black servant's hand.

The mackerel, it seemed, were running. The men, and women too, were pulling in the squirming fish. I hated the experience at first—the dead minnows whose backbones we had to pierce with our hooks; the earthworms that wrapped around our fingers; the blood that ran in rivulets. All I could think of was our house; I was counting the moments until I could return to the shadows beneath it.

Arthur, seeing my distraction, my distaste, baited the line. But Barton had thrown himself into it, scooping up worm after worm and holding them up as though he were going to feed himself the way a mother bird feeds her nest. He dangled the tip of his rod over the edge of the pier and swooped his line upward, as basketball players in those days used to shoot free throws.

It did not take long, however, for our positions to be reversed. I caught the first fish. The pole dipped, the line grew taut, and I reeled in my catch and dropped it flopping at our feet. It flared its gills and stared with its open eye. Its back was green, shot through with black, like the most beautiful of my marbles. Arthur removed the hook from its rubbery lip and slipped it living into our pail of seawater. I caught the second fish, too. And I caught the third. Bartie's line lay limp on the heaving sea. There was a fourth strike. The next thing I knew I pulled up two desperate mackerel on the same cast.

Was it the smell of the black man's hands, his skin, that drove the fish into a frenzy? Or was there something about Bartie, his smell, the sight of his golden head leaning in perplexity over the rail, that kept them away? No matter: I was in a frenzy now myself. There were too many fish to keep in our pail. Gleefully I smashed their heads against the piling. I ripped the hooks from their gills. I was covered with slime. Scales stuck to my arms, my knees, my face, as if I were a species of reptile. It was blood lust. I wanted every fish there was in the ocean, wanted to stun them senseless and watch the slow, stiff, final turn of their tails.

Bartie was in tears. I saw that he'd wet himself. Arthur noticed the stain at the crotch of his pants and led him off to the washroom. I left my own line taut and humming in the ocean and reeled in my brother's instead. The bait hadn't been touched. I dug a live fish from the bucket and managed to stab Bartie's hook through the side of its snapping mouth. Then I threw the animal back to its element. Butler and boy returned. I let Arthur make the discovery. "Look, Mr. Barton. You got one, sure enough."

Bartie was ecstatic. He danced a jig. "Look, Richie! Look, Arthur! I got one! Bartie's got one!"

"That's great, Bartie. Reel him in. Look, like this." I wound my own line up on the reel. There was a mackerel, thrashing and writhing, attached. Barton only continued his dance. "Got one! Got one! Got one!"

Arthur drew in the fish, which was by now a little peaked. He swung it over the railing, so that it gave a few listless flops at my brother's feet.

"Pick him up, Bartie," I shouted. "Knock his damn head off."

Barton gasped. The little bump, the knot of emotion that throbbed between his eyebrows, was an ominous red. "Oh, no. He's mine. He's mine!" He dropped to his knees and plucked up the mackerel, hook and all. He cradled it against his chest.

"Kill it, Bartie! Kill the bastard!"

"No, no, no. My fish. Mine." He held the gasping fish against his cheek.

"But we're going to eat him. Right, Arthur? We're taking all of them home for dinner. That's the law, Bartie. You know, the law of the jungle. Big fish eat little ones too."

Arthur said, "Don't believe there's no way we going to have these fish to the house."

I stood stunned; it was as if my own head had been knocked against the pilings. "What do you mean? What are you saying? What's going to happen to them?"

"Don't know that I want to say, exactly."

"Don't *know*? Won't *say*? Can't we give them to poor people, so they will have something to eat?"

"Them fish, Mr. Richard, are going into the trash."

I was of a sudden swept by a wave of sorrow. I looked at the heap of mackerel, glistening and green. I saw myself, scale-covered, bloodied, as they must have seen me through the black pupils of their dying eyes. Now the tears spilled from my own. I wanted to tell them that I was innocent. What I actually said was, "You have to take us home now."

"Can't do that, Mr. Richard. Got to keep you boys out for the day."

"No, no, no. This is Election Day. Aren't you going to vote? What about that?"

"Truth is, I would like to vote for Mr. Truman."

"You can do it! There's still time. Just drop me off and take Bartie with you. No one will know. It's your duty. I promise not to tell."

The butler hesitated. He took off his cap and then put it on again. "I never did miss the chance to vote for Mr. Roosevelt before him."

Suddenly Bartie ran to the railing. "Run!" he cried. "Run, fishie!" Somehow he had disentangled his only prize. He held it skyward, then hurled it end over end tumbling into the foam-filled spray of the Pacific.

Barton and I washed up as best we could in the bathroom behind the carousel; then Arthur dropped me off at the corner of San Remo and Sunset. I crossed our front lawn and walked round the far wing of the house. I ducked under ground and squirmed to where I could hear, and then see, the two black men at work. I crawled forward until I was within the cone of light cast by the hooded lamp.

"Hi, Martin. Hi, Eddie. Would you like to take a swim?"

Without waiting for an answer, I turned and made my way to the exit. I knew they would be crawling behind me. We walked through the arcade and onto the grass, which the gardener had recently watered. Both men, as they had done before, dropped their clothes to the ground. Eddie was wearing what looked like the same baggy shorts he'd worn the day before. Martin wore the skin tight briefs that blazed in the sunlight. Like a shining scimitar they seemed to cut his dark body into two equal parts. Eddie gave a yell and jumped in. Martin climbed slowly down the ladder at the other end and then sank—like a continent I thought, like Atlantis—to the bottom. They swam for a time, perhaps half an hour. I took off my shoes. I took off my socks. I sat on the curved stones at the rim, dangling my feet and my pants legs into the water. Then the screen door slammed and my mother came out.

She was wearing, I saw, the little two-piece bathing suit, a bikini it was called, that she'd brought back from France. Her breasts were hardly covered by the purple cloth. Anyone could see the points of her hips, the private flesh of her thighs. She stood for a moment, pushing her curls under her white rubber cap. Then she stepped down to the grass, crossed over the flagstones—not hurrying over those hot, flat rocks—and lowered herself into the water.

Both men had seen her. Eddie stopped cavorting. He watched as Lotte did the breaststroke toward him, her head and bare shoulders flashing upward, her legs scissoring, her buttocks on the rise and fall. As she came nearer, the little Negro did a kind of crazed dog paddle; and, when she drew nearer still, he hopped from the water and stood trembling in his own puddle. Martin swam on undeflected, propelling himself from one side of the pool to the other.

Now my mother kicked off from the shallow end and did a backstroke in the other direction. Her face and chin, breasts and knees, made little islands in the water. Her feet kicked up foam like a propeller. Martin was waiting mid way. He treaded water until she reached him and then fell in beside her, matching her stroke for stroke. They were like the figures in an Esther Williams movie. But Lotte was not smiling for the camera. She swam on, never turning her head to look at the man swimming beside her. She reached the deep end and began her return in a crawl. Again, the black man joined her. They took their breaths facing each other, opening their mouths in unison. They traversed the length of the pool and kicked, simultaneously, off the rows of tile. Now Lotte was in a sidestroke. So was Martin. There were only inches between them. Their knees might have knocked. Her breasts, with their ribbon of cloth, might have brushed his barrel chest. They swam slowly, moving ahead in spasms, until they reached the far end. Then my mother dove down and came up in a shower of foam. The water flew from her gleaming cap the way light is shed from an incandescent bulb. Martin was waiting for her, his own head streaming.

"What are you doing in my pool?" Lotte asked him, as if she had seen him for the first time. Then she resumed her swim to the shallow end.

Martin did not follow. He lay floating, rolled onto his side. Eddie came running over. His partner bobbed and reeled, like a whale that has been struck by a ship. Eddie held out his hand. The swimmer lunged for it, but missed. He gasped, open-mouthed. Then, perhaps because he sensed Lotte once more swimming toward him, he lurched toward the hand and caught it. With a struggle Eddie managed to pull his friend from the water. Then they walked toward where I was waiting at the side of the pool. The Negro's underwear was no longer white, no longer shining. The cloth was damp and as dark as the flesh that was secreted inside.

The workers put on their clothes before they descended once more below the house. I pulled on my shoes and socks, and followed. The lamp was hung over a pipe by its cord. The Negroes crawled forward and squatted in its light. They didn't pick up their tools. They were both looking fixedly at the spot where, under their gaze, I'd come to a halt. No one said a word. For a reason I could not fathom, my heart began to pound in my chest. *I can go back,* I told myself. But I went forward.

When I reached the two men Eddie turned off the lamp. The three of us lay together in the utter dark. My heart now beat so loudly in my ears that I was certain both of my companions could hear it. From just behind me Martin said, "Go ahead."

In the space before me I could hear Eddie draw in a breath. Then he said, "You a Jew, ain't you?"

I was on my left side. I thought I could feel the ground rise beneath me, just as I had during earthquakes. "Yes," I replied. "I think I am."

"Martin, you know, he was in the war. He saw some bad things. Things he don't like to say. The worst of those things were about what happened to your people."

For a moment I felt relieved. "Oh, yes. I know what the Germans did to the Jews. I saw the pictures in *Life* magazine. It was terrible. They didn't spare even the children. They—"

"Shut up!" Eddie commanded. "You don't know nothing. I ain't talking about no pictures in no magazine."

At that moment I felt a hand, an enormous one, fall upon my hip. Of course it was Martin's; I thought I might choke from the heat, the darkness, the lack of air. When the black man at last spoke, he was so close behind me that his breath washed over my skin. "What I seen tore me up."

With a quick moment of finger and thumb he snapped my belt buckle apart. Eddie picked up his narrative:

"It was a camp, you know. What he saw was the walking skeletons. Bones that was moving. You could not tell the dead from the living."

As the little man spoke the huge hand hooked my waist band and pulled my pants down. Then the tips of the fingers touched the top of my underwear and slipped inside. I was struck by the contrast of the hand's size—it might have been that of a colossus, it might have been that of the mighty King Kong—and how lightly the thick pads of the fingers moved across my smooth, hairless belly.

"Here's the thing," Eddie went on. "Here's what's going to break your heart. Over at the corner of a field, inside the wire, there was what looked like a mountain. It was the human feces, you know. All the Jews' shit. Martin had to go there. Those were his orders. And what he saw. Oh, young man, what he saw!"

Martin's hand closed over my penis. He held it in his fingers. His hot breath stirred the hairs on the nape of my neck. The heat of his body went right through the back of my shirt. We were as close as the swimmers.

"The Jews there were the living Jews; living dead, I ought to call them. They were climbing on that mountain. They were digging through that shit. They were seeking out—I don't know what. Corn kernels, maybe, that had not been digested; or seeds; or a bread crust. Poor people! Starving people! They were that hungry for food."

I didn't know whether to believe Eddie's words. His story did not sound right to me. It sounded more like what would happen in a place like India, or China. But what if it were true? If the starving people had been reduced to searching through their own excrement? I felt a surge of pity—for them, I suppose, and their suffering; but even more for Martin, who had had to endure such a sight.

"That's right," sighed the black giant behind me. "That's the way." He meant, I understood, my penis, which had grown hot and as stiff as if there had been a bone inside. That was it. What my friends meant. *A boner.*

"Hey, big brother! Where are you? I can't see you! I want to play!"

Barton! And under the house! He could not have been more than twenty or twenty-five feet away. I jerked aside. I fumbled with the top of my pants.

"Where is everybody? Are you hiding from me? Please! I've got something to show you. You won't be able to guess. You won't ever! It's dark down here. Why are you hiding?"

Eddie snapped on the lamp. Martin had pulled away from me and lay on his stomach. I closed my buckle.

"Over here, Bartie. We're all over this way."

I could see his head, with the halo about it, crawling through the darkness. He came up to where the three of us lay. His face was flushed. The welt above his eyebrows bulged. The eyes themselves were glittering, as if they'd been splashed with liquid. He held up something that the lamplight covered with spangles.

"See? They're mine. Arthur bought them for me. With his own money. But you can play with them. You can hold them, if you want."

He stretched out his arm, so that we could all see the water-filled sack. Inside it three goldfish hung suspended, not swimming, not so much as flicking a fin, merely huddling together as humans might when something threatened their lives.

4

That night I lay in bed listening to the election returns from around the country. Truman, as predicted, was doomed. We were stepping backward, allowing the plutocrats to rule. The health of the poor would suffer. The working man would toil in vain. And Negroes would remain second-class citizens. I turned off the radio. I clicked off the bedside lamp. Blue fairy light from the pool slid over the walls. From below I heard the sound of Lotte's party. It was smaller than usual, surely because of the president's dim prospects. The fact that the guests had to line up at the gardener's bathroom became a great joke, or a lesson in democracy perhaps. In the darkened room, I touched myself experimentally.

Late in the night I heard my mother's step in the hallway. The door opened. I smelled her perfume and heard the rustle of her dress. She put her arms around me. Her cheek was against mine. "My darling boy," she whispered. "You know I love only you." She kissed me once, finding my mouth. Then she retreated. If I had dared to speak, this is what I would have said: *Don't forget Bartie. Go to his room too.*

I woke the next morning to the glorious news that Harry Truman had won. Even the L.A. *Times* had to admit it. Norman and Lotte were awake in the kitchen. They were hugging each other, hugging me and Bartie, and calling all their friends on the phone. Wednesday, of course, was a school day like any other. *A writing instrument; a bag; a bottle of Coke*: "PENSACOLA!" Even Mrs. Static, apparently a Democrat, smiled at Roger and me. During recess I played dodgeball with my friends. In Mr. Stegelmeyer's class I made a little speech about the pendulum of history and how true Americans did not judge Jackie Robinson by the color of his skin but by how he played the game.

On the school bus home, chugging up the steep hills of Amalfi, Madeline asked to see my hands.

"They're awfully dirty," I said, displaying the crescent of grime, a mixture of soil and fish flesh, that still resided beneath every nail.

"I don't care about that," Madeline said. "They're the hands of an artist. You could be a pianist. You could be a painter."

When I walked into the driveway on Sam Remo Drive I knew at once the workmen were gone; in their place the gigantic wheel of the ditch-digging machine was tearing through the pansy bed, the lilies, the rhododendrons. Each of its revolving buckets was like a mouth, the teeth chewing up petal and root, devouring every shrub. My mother stood stone-faced, clutching Mary's hand. Mary herself lifted her glasses to swipe aside her tears. The entire operation, from the curb at Romany to the edge of the house, took a little more than an hour. Well before that time was up the gang from the neighborhood—Tim, Warren, Sandy, the Coveneys, and the rest—had gathered at the gate. They watched as the wheel turned without stopping and the diesel engine whined and groaned, sending up billows of oily blue smoke.

That night, when Bartie was taking his bath, I snuck into his room and took his box of colored pencils. I tore a sheet from his drawing pad. Then I went to my room and began what was to be the first of a lifetime of sketches and paintings. The subject was the sad-faced pansies. I wanted to make a gift of the picture to my mother. It did not matter that I could not go to the ruined garden. I worked from memory. So it is, I discovered, that all art is created: not from the actual objects or the life we see around us, but from the images of our childhood, with its early sorrows and many joys, that we carry undamaged within.

PART TWO

SAN REMO DRIVE

(2000–2001)

I

There used to be lemon groves up and down our street and on many of the surrounding blocks of Riviera. When my brother, Bartie, and I were kids we'd play cowboys and Indians about the trunks of the trees. I'd shoot him and he'd shoot me, and each time we'd jump back up, resurrected like a dog or a cat or a flattened fox in one of our favorite cartoons. Finally we'd pluck the lemons from the lower boughs and bite a hole in the tops. The idea was to turn the fruit in your hand, squeezing the juice into your mouth like a Spaniard with his goatskin—which we did, sphere after sphere, until our teeth ached and we lay back drunk on the stuff. "Ha! Ha! Ha!" Bartie laughed. "Look! At your skin!" The sunlight, filtering through the grove, had been gilded by the ripened fruit. The flesh on my arms, and on my panting chest, was yellow. "You're a dirty Jap!"

Norman, our father, had tried to include the abutting grove when he bought our house, a pillared colonial like something from *Gone With the Wind*, in the Forties; but the owner wouldn't sell. It wasn't a matter of money, I've come to realize, but the age-old question of—well, they didn't call us Jews, not outright; in those days the term was *movie people*. For a year or so we stared at the lemons through a row of whitewashed slats. Then our mother, Lotte, with the help of her Japanese gardeners, turned the fence into a hedge, a tangle of rhododendrons, forsythia, and vines hung with improbable figs. The smell of citrus wafted over just the same, and up went, like a canary flock, their chromium sheen. I tried to acquire the same lot when Marcia and I—her cash, my inclination—bought the house back after a lapse of thirty years. This time the issue *was* money, a great deal of it, as if these last lemons were in fact as golden as their glow.

My wife made out her check to the same family to whom Lotte had sold the house three decades before. I saw at once that the hedge was still there, dotted, in its recesses, with the pouches of the purple figs. The gardeners now are Mexicans or, lately, from Guatemala. I like to set up my easel next to the wall of vegetation, with its smell, its stickiness, its bees. That's the shadow you see moving on the diagonal, upper left to lower right, on a hundred of my canvases. The blue above it: the sky? Sure. But also the levitated contents of what Marcia calls *la piscine*. Mikado yellow, in streaks and blobs, an echo of that old sourness, I squeeze directly from the tube. There is a line, a squiggle, that no one can interpret: it is the memory of where crazy Bartie would gambol down the awning and launch himself airborne over the unrippled surface of the pool.

In the Eighties, when I moved back to San Remo Drive, the lemon groves had almost disappeared. But the house was just as we had left it. Somehow the family that bought it from us had managed to raise five girls—and they'd climbed the cork trees and dug divots out of the lawn with a seven iron, just as Bartie and I had, and as my own boys do now—and not move a stick of the furniture.

On the evening of our return I moved by instinct through the living room—could those be the same filmy white curtains? Not possible! They'd *have* to be as tattered and yellowed as Miss Havisham's—and turned left, and left again, to the bar. I threw open the cabinet doors. The Capehart was just as we'd left it, its arthropod arms immobilized in midair. And not just the Capehart. Here were our old 78's, album after album, Schubert and Schumann and Brahms; Toscanini's version of the Beethoven symphonies; Furtwangler even; Robeson's *Ballad for Americans*; Rodgers and Hammerstein, Rodgers and Hart. I piled *Pal Joey* onto the spindle, and while the machine huffed and puffed its way through the discs I let the cheap music, like some dime novel villain, have its way with me.

"Richard! What are you doing here, sitting in the dark?"

I barely recognized my wife—and not just because she had a scarf like a peasant over the beehive of her hair. She switched on the overhead fixture.

"Marcia. Listen. These are our old 78's. *I could write a preface on how we met*— Do you remember that? Jesus! Nothing gets erased. *So the world will never forget.* That's not all. Here. Johnny Walker. Black Label. These people, they owned a milk company, right? Teetotalers! I'd bet anything on it: this was our bottle of Scotch."

"You should see what they've done to your pool," she answered. "It's lit up like a tourist attraction. Like the Blue Grotto of Capri."

"Do you know, when we bought the house from Mary Astor, there was no pool. Norman and Lotte put it in. They dug it out of the lawn. Norman would only sunbathe. He got a tan with a reflector. The pool was really for Lotte. For Lotte and the Sunday guests, I mean. I told you about them, didn't I? Elizabeth Taylor? Tony Curtis? The whole Fox and Lox Society, that's what they called it. Before we came there was nothing but lemon groves. Block after block of them. You could smell them, the budding lemons. You could—"

I stopped. Marcia was staring at me, as if I were a stranger. Truth to tell, I hardly knew her either. The natural order of things had been reversed: we living people were fading like ghosts; only the phenomena of the past—the lyrics, the drapery, the light bulbs hidden in the lozenges of the chandelier—were solid and real. *Bewitched,* you said it. *Bothered*! *Bewildered*!

Marcia said, "Are you drunk, or what? Come on. We've got junk to throw out. And we ought to drain that pool."

"Look at that," I said. She followed my gaze to the bottle.

"You've already brought that miracle to my attention."

"Can it be?"

"Can it be what?"

I thought it better not to explain that, like a clue in a very bad mystery, the level of the liquor was precisely where we'd left it when we abandoned the house. Instead I struggled out of my chair and seized the whiskey. With my shirttail I cleaned the rims of two grimy glasses. I poured each to the brim.

"To us," I said. "A new start. In a new house."

"But it's an old house, isn't it?" answered my wife.

The last song came to a halt. The Capehart raised its mechanical arms, as if praying for more. I didn't budge.

"What are you listening to now?" Marcia asked. "It's over."

It wasn't the music I was hoping to hear. It was the plash of limbs in the water—not myself or my cannonballing brother, but Lotte, undoubtedly in her Forties bikini, the sun gleaming on the helmet of her rubber cap; or else, on occasion, on Thursdays, maid's day off, butler's day off, wearing nothing at all. She'd turn like a seal in the water or pose naked on the tiles, the biblical Susanna at her bath; but it was not the elders who were peeping.

We did drain the pool, and kept it empty for seven years. Then, in the fall of 1992, we filled it again so that our boys, adopted Navahos, could learn how to swim.

"Big lake!" shouted Michael, the moment he caught sight of the blue water in the backyard. He ran pell-mell across the fresh-cut grass.

"Me too!" shouted Edward, and if I hadn't swooped him up he'd have jumped right in.

The boys were three years old. We'd brought them back from the reservation that same afternoon. With their black bangs and flat faces, the twins might have been Chinese. The tribal council had insisted that we take a weekend course of study, which was held in a classroom hung with strips of flypaper dotted with struggling flies. We took notes, Marcia and I, on the Long March and the meaning of sand paintings; on Kit Carson's cruelty and the birth of all mankind from Esdzanadkhi, the mother of the earth. But here at San Remo Drive were our new sons, in their brown jackets and brown knee pants, their ankles disappearing into pairs of brand new Nikes. All I knew for sure, lessons or no lessons, was that their ancestors had arrived on this continent well before another sort of long march had delivered mine.

"No, no, no!" squealed Edward, as I continued to spin him in the air.

"Me, me!" shouted Michael. "My turn!"

"Oh, for God's sake," said Marcia. She was coming down the back steps from the kitchen. She had changed from her business suit into a blouse, slacks, and a straw hat to keep off the sun. She had a tray with three glasses of lemonade and, for herself, a wine spritzer. "It's a hundred degrees. Why not let them into the water?"

"Yay-y-y-y!" cried the Navahos. They ran up for the lemonade, which they drank eyes closed, two hands on the glass. Then they began to tear off their clothes.

Marcia pulled a chair under the striped canvas awning that ran from the back of the house halfway to the edge of the pool. We'd met after she'd already spent a small fortune on six of my abstractions. "It'll be cheaper to collect you," is what she'd said when I proposed. It had taken a long time, the whole of a first marriage, to convince her that she couldn't have children; it took a good part of this one to get her to stop toying with the idea of a career in real estate and agree to adopt the twins instead.

"That's better," she said, tipping her head toward where the bare, brown bodies of her new sons were jumping up at the hedge. "That's how they like it."

It was a surprise to me to see that their penises were uncircumcised. They resembled the purple figs, which, in glee, each boy was hurling at the other.

I took off my shoes and socks and rolled up my pants. I stood on the semicircular steps that dipped into the shallow end of the pool. "Come on, guys!" I shouted. "You can wade here."

Michael—I think it was Michael, since they now looked as much alike as two brown eggs in a carton or the proverbial peas in a pod—took me up on it. He came bounding across the grass and leaped from the flag-stone. At once he ducked to the bottom, only to come shooting upward in a fountain of foam.

"Watch me!" cried Edward. To my dismay he made his leap where the water was six feet deep. Like his brother, however, he bobbed quickly up. The two of them, unsinkable apparently, began whooping and splashing. Their screams were so loud, there was such a hullabaloo, that I hardly heard the ringing of the telephone. A moment later Isolina, our pretty maid, brought out the receiver at the end of a long extension cord.

"Mr. Richard," she said. "A lady for you."

Marcia said, "Oh, that must be Lotte. I promised her I'd call as soon as we arrived with the boys."

I took the telephone and sat down at one of the iron deck tables. Marcia called over: "She's never been over once in all these years. Tell her to drive out and see Edward and Michael. Tell her we've filled the pool. It's not too late for *une nage*. How that woman likes to swim!"

But it wasn't my mother. It was my model. "Are you there, Richard? Can you talk? Or are you surrounded by your new family? Your papoosi? Your pepperoni? Your papyruses. Whatever."

Against the shouts, the cries from the children, I pressed a finger against my ear. "Yes," I said, as neutrally as I could. "I can hear you."

"I see. Oh, I see. Marcia's there too. Don't say anything. Just absorb what I'm telling you. You think you can dump me? Now? After all these years? You think you can buy yourself a whole new family? Husband and wife and the adorable paparazzi? What if I decide to make a fuss? A, a— rhubarb! I'm capable of it. Richard? Hello? Are you there, my love?"

"Yes, I hear you," I answered. "We arrived about an hour ago."

"You shit. I gave you my heart! Oh, I hear them laughing! Those war whoops! They sound delightful. Why did you have to show me their pictures? I can't get those little brown faces out of my head. I envy you. I'm burning with jealousy, you lucky son of a bitch. Wish your old friend some luck, okay? It's a little late, don't you think, for her to have a wonderful life?"

There was a click. The dial tone came on. I said, probably too loudly, "Yes, well it was kind of you to call. I will. I'll tell them. Goodbye!"

"Who was it?" asked Marcia, pulling one pale leg from a patch of the sun.

"It was Mrs. Williams. Wasn't that her name? From Black Mesa? Sheila Williams. She wanted to see if we had a safe trip. She said to give her best wishes to the boys."

Marcia raised her pointed chin, her pointed nose, as if she meant literally to sniff me out. But all she said was, "That's very thoughtful."

I didn't reply. The wind, the Santa Ana, whipped perspiration from my forehead and the back of my hand. I couldn't see either of the Navahos in the pool. Then I looked again. Had they learned already? Had they already been taught? Or, like animals thrown into water, did they instinctively know how to swim? I followed the brown blur of their bodies as they moved under the surface, second after long second, until at last in simultaneous gushers they came up for air.

When, some years later, the two of them decided they wanted to play tennis, they didn't take to it as they had to water. It turned out this was an activity that had to be learned. In the days when Norman was teaching me how to play the game, he'd always say, "It's a sport you can enjoy all your life. Look at the king of Sweden." A generation later I was not above holding that example up to the eleven-year-old Navahos, no matter how far they might be removed from the land of the Northern Lights.

"What Swedish king?" Michael demanded. "That country is a democracy."

I marched the two of them into the clubhouse, where a portrait of Gustavius V—it must have been from just after the war, when he'd arrived in Hollywood for some understandable fence-mending—hung on the wall. The twins stared upward a moment. Their white shorts and white shirts were as dazzling as teeth against the dark, sweat-streaked skin. Then Edward turned aside.

"Oh, he's dead," he said.

True, technically. Though the monarch has remained alive in my imagination—not as the father of his people, or the naval officer in his ribbons, or the secret hero of what were then clandestine gays; but as he is on the wall of the Beverly Hills Tennis Club: a bewhiskered old duffer in flannels, squinting through glasses at the approach of the white, not yellow, ball.

The king isn't the only one still alive and kicking. There's something about the sun in California, the way it bears down in winter at much the same angle as in July, that has preserved half the population. If you'd been at the club on the afternoon I spent hitting ball after ball, first to Edward and then to Michael, and had glanced over to court six, you couldn't have missed my childhood friend Mosk doing the same thing with his grandson. "Concentrate, damn it," shouted the Penguin. "Read the word *Wilson.* Attaboy!" The uproar on court one? That was the Pumpkin, who in the course of time had been a Davis Cup player and Wimbledon quarter-finalist, thrashing the latest phenom from UCLA. At a quarter of four my cousin Jimbo, the son of Norman's younger brother, arrived; from his slumped shoulders and the sweat that beaded his near-hairless pate, I could see that he'd already resigned himself to losing the three-set match we'd been playing for fifty years. Mummies, all of us! As perfectly petrified in our attitudes and gestures, not to mention the tendency to drop a forehand volley into the net, as the frozen Swede or dried-out old King Tut.

Jimbo and I changed sides on the odd game; over his panting I could hear the steady splash of someone traversing the pool. Impossible to see over the hedge, but I knew only Lotte would dare take laps in the middle of December. She lived practically around the corner, at Beverly and Oakhurst, but insisted on driving her '82 Honda into the alley behind the club, where she'd rattle the rear gate to catch somebody's attention.

"Thank you, Timo darling," she'd say to the ancient Filipino—he'd been a ball boy for Gustavius, for Christ's sake, and rumor had it he spent the next three nights in the Royal Suite at the Ambassador—and pinch his cheek; he never failed to blush, in spite of age and inclination.

I'd once offered her the master bedroom of our old place on San Remo, where she could swim as she always had, hours on end. "Oh, no, sweetie. I don't dare set eyes on it. I don't dare think of it. All my old things! Like a fleet in mothballs! My credenza! My Steinway! I don't want to look backward! I've got to look ahead. Next you'll want to put my old portrait back on the wall. Like Dorian Gray!"

"We *have* put it back, right over the fireplace. If you'll come with the Oscar I'll put it there too, right on the mantle beneath it."

At that she gave an exaggerated shudder. "See? The very idea makes me quake. It's like a shrine to the dead. Look, you've made me cry. Kiss them away, my prince! Ha! Ha! These tears! Oh, to be seventy again!"

Lotte had no idea that I paid her monthly fees. She thought that because Norman had been a founding member, she was entitled to the privileges of the club, including phone calls and the tab of her bridge group, for free. This was the third Sunday of the month, which meant she'd invited her children and grandchildren for the buffet of baby-back ribs. Bartie, of course, was not going to pass up a free dinner. The twins liked to gnaw on the sticky bones. I shooed them off their court, so that they could shower and change. Then I finished off Jimbo with a back-hand down the line. When I followed the boys around the row of bushes, I saw that Lotte was just getting out of the pool. Timo stood by, holding a terrycloth robe.

Lotte approached him, the flesh loose on the bones of her arms, the way the Greeks prefer it on a shank of lamb. The Filipino enveloped her. She gave a bird's peck of a kiss to his chin.

That's when Bartie arrived. His forehead, now, was all creases, and his smaller eye, perhaps against the wash of his cigarette, was drawn almost closed. It looked as if the nicotine from all his other cigarettes had left the yellow tinge in hair otherwise gray. "Hey, Bro," he said, and came out of his stoop to extend his hand. "I'm here to refuel."

Michael stepped forward. "Hello, Uncle Barton," he said.

"Hello, Edward," Bartie answered.

"I'm Michael."

"That's all right. What is in a name, eh, Bro? To quote the bard. Have you seen Spielberg? Is he around?"

"I haven't seen him, Bartie. Maybe he's playing cards upstairs."

"I hope so. He better be. Lotte said he was reading my novel. She loved it. It's called *A Girl of the Streets*. She gave it to that friend of hers, Pearl. She's married to Shire, you know, the big agent. Pearl said there was definitely a movie in it. First a book and then a movie. A tie-in deal. She's very excited by the prospect. She told Lotte this was a Spielberg vehicle. It's based on a real-life situation. I met this person. I got her life story here, in my head. Your heart could break from the pathos in it. But there's plenty of hot sex, believe me. That's what the masses want these days. I've got the chicks coupling like monkeys. Balls and cocks and tits and ass. You aren't listening, Edward. You boys are innocent. You don't know how to please the public the way I do. Anyway, Bro, Lotte called it a brilliant satire. Don't be jealous, those were her actual words. Pearl is definitely going to bring this to Spielberg's attention. Shire will be my agent. I've got an idea: you could be the art director. I'll make sure my big brother is written into the deal. This book is going to get the Jacobi family back in the movies. Wait! I forgot! I am always forgetting! You are going to France."

"I'm only going for a week, Bartie. I'd be honored to work on your picture."

"*La Belle France!* That's where I'll go if I hit it big. I've lived a Spartan life. According to the precepts of the Buddha. He knows I'm a person who will cross the street so I won't step on a beetle. Now it's the Riviera for Bartie! I see him in a villa overlooking the beach. Those *filles de la nuit*, eh Bro? Those *damoiselles!*"

The boys had already turned to go indoors. I watched through the glass door as they pulled down thick towels for the shower. When I turned back, Barton had his head in his hands.

"There's a problem," he said. "A problem. They don't let you smoke on those flights. Six hours! I can't go for six hours! Do you think it's the same on Air France? Reagan should have crushed those environmentalists. They want to make us prisoners! Before you know it we won't be able to smoke in our own homes. Six hours: three, four, five, six. Bartie will be unhappy. He'll start to cry. Are you laughing at me? It's not so unreasonable, you know. It could be the spirit of Pericles, reincarnated in the form of that beetle. Hee, hee hee! Or Otto von Bismarck."

A half hour later we were lined up at the buffet. I brought Lotte's plate to her, a tuna fish salad, since, for all her miles in the pool, she found it difficult to stand. As I leaned over her I saw the patches of scalp beneath her hair's damp strands. She put her lipstick on, smacking her lips in the mirror of her compact.

"I gather Marcia's not coming? Not coming again? I don't know what to do about that girl. I try and try but that's one heart I can't win over."

"Lotte, you know Sunday is her busiest time. She wants—"

"Oh, *look!* Look!" She leaned back, peering over to where the boys stood in white shirts and flannels, holding their empty plates. "I want to eat *them* for dinner. They are scrumptious. Just look at those black bodies. Black as Negroes'. Tell me, darling—" And here she said something that, though I'd shared the earth with her for more than six decades, made me gape. "Are the penises big and black too?"

"You know, Lotte. There are times when—"

"All right! I knew it was a mistake even before the words were out of my mouth. You have to forgive a person of my age. We become forgetful. Yes, I forgot you were such a prig."

Bartie came up with what seemed fifty ribs stacked on his plate. He'd gone to the bar, too, for a highball.

"Tonight Bartie's not eating his brussel sprouts," he said as he pulled up a chair.

"Goodness, Barton, you are making a spectacle. You can always go back for seconds."

"I intend to, ha-ha-ha! Do you see the humor in what I said?"

Lotte let out a peal of laughter. "Oh, Bartie, that's *funny!* It's *hilarious.* You are such a witty person when you're feeling happy. We're all feeling happy. We're having such a good time. Here come Michael and Edward. Come closer, boys!" She reached for Michael, who was clutching his own plate of ribs. She caught him by both ears and, as if they were the handles on a pitcher of milk, pulled him toward her. Then she dipped her napkin in her ice water to rub the smear of lipstick that was superimposed on his mouth. "But no one is happier than Lotte Jacobi. I am a grandmother. Of two wonderful boys. Now *that* is an accomplishment!"

Edward got a kiss too. He sat down next to his brother. Bartie rose from his seat, simultaneously feeling in his shirt pocket for his pack of Kools. "Well," he said, already moving toward the sliding glass doors. "Excuse me while I drive a nail in the coffin."

Lotte beamed. "Isn't he wonderful? And clever? When Barton is like this you can have an intellectual conversation."

Michael was kneeing me under the table. He leaned over and put his fingers, slick with grease from the beef, around my ear. "Grandma loves me too much," he whispered.

"Mel! Oh, Mel!" Lotte, half-rising, was calling out to the aged, blue-blazered man who had once been our family doctor. Then another gentleman caught her eye. "Yoo-hoo! Judge! You come over here, too!" This happened to be the Penguin's father, even at his age a member of the State Supreme Court. What stuck in my mind was the afternoon, poolside, when his task had been to join Lotte and the phony Frenchman in marriage, a command performance not repeated in the Mexican divorce. It always amazed me how happy men were to see her. Both came beaming at an octogenarian trot.

Women, too: Estelle, Marjorie, Genie—the whole of the bridge group, with alternates, was coming down the spiral stairs. Even the ones that descended a half-step at a time, clinging to the banister, stopped to wave. The last in line? Pearl Shire, with Bartie bending her ear. In a moment or two they had all gathered around. Various husbands hobbled up at the outskirts. I couldn't help but think how, after Norman's death, no one came to Lotte's election-night parties; it turned out that all the politicians and movie stars had been his friends. But these—why, Jed Masmanian, the famous psychoanalyst, was actually on his knees before her, as if he were about to be knighted by her blown kiss: these were hers.

"Estelle, Genie, you know my grandsons. Aren't they *handsome?* That is Michael. That's Edward. Bartie plays the cutest game of mixing them up. And of course everyone knows Richard. Sweetie, you tell them the exciting news. You haven't heard? In just one week my oldest son is going to have an exhibition at the *Louvre!*"

I cut as quickly as I could into the chorus of exclamations. "Not the Louvre, Lotte; you know that."

"Well, of course I know that. It's the Jeu de Paume. What's the difference? It's the modern wing of the Louvre, that's all. You didn't expect they'd hang your paintings in the same dirty old building with the Venus de Milo."

Marjorie said, "I love the Jeu de Paume. That's where I saw the water lilies."

Genie said, "It means they rank you alongside Monet."

Lotte: "That's exactly what Betty always said. She said that Richard worked and reworked our pool on San Remo the way Monet did the light on his haystacks or the facade on the Cathedral of Rouen. She was the first to appreciate him. Dear Betty! Of course the element is the same, the pond with its beautiful, beautiful lilies, and the blue pool and the blue sky. You know, in that series, the funny little zigzag in white? Like a kind of question mark? It's Bartie! Bartie jumping off the awning! Scaring me out of my wits!"

There was a burst of laughter, and even applause, as if one of the paintings had just been unfurled. Then Barton, with a fresh drink in his hand, pushed his way through and sat down. This time the Scotch was in a wineglass, without rocks.

"He's not there," he said to his mother.

Lotte, instead of answering, turned to her circle of friends. "Here's my good-looking little boy. I always said, watch out for him—he's the one with the talent. Did I tell all of you that Bartie's finished a wonderful new novel? *The Streetwalker*, it's called. It's just a gem. And so beautifully written."

"Where the hell is Spielberg? You said he was upstairs. He's not upstairs. I looked myself. I looked and I looked. There were just a lot of old people playing gin rummy. Ha! Ha! Ha! When the Big One comes, they'll still be playing. They'll never die. You people just go on forever. Under the burning buildings, out of the cracks in the ground, we'll still hear the cry of the Angelenos: '*Gin!*'"

"All right, Bartie. You're just a little excited."

"I'm not excited. Pearl said she was going to show my book to Steven Spielberg. Didn't you, Pearl? Didn't you say it was a work of genius? A Spielberg vehicle? It's got everything, right? It's got verisimilitude. That's because truth is stranger than fiction. I saw the veins in her arms. The way she has suffered. So you have to show it to him. You made a promise."

The agent's wife pushed her sunglasses atop her head. "I hope there hasn't been a misunderstanding, Bartie, dear. Your mother showed me the manuscript. I told her it had promise. It does! But that's not the same thing as *making* a promise. I couldn't show Steven the manuscript in the shape it's in—"

"What do you mean? Isn't it brilliant? 'Brilliant.' Isn't that a direct quotation?"

"I mean, Bartie, things like the presentation. Those crumpled pages. And the mistakes in punctuation. You can't just run the words together without commas and periods or capital letters and expect the reader to understand the story."

The red welt, a bulge between Bartie's eyebrows, began to darken. "This is very disappointing to me. You shouldn't tell a writer that. It takes away his enthusiasm. Bartie doesn't use fancy computers. He doesn't have a secretary to do his typing. You have confused me. I thought it was a work of genius. So why are we talking about commas?"

The crowd had begun to draw back. Most of the men, some pulling at the sleeves of their wives' dresses, had drifted away.

Lotte said, "Where are you going? Don't go! I didn't tell you why my boys, both my darling boys, invited me here today. We were just talking about it when you girls came down the stairs. They said, 'We know it's six months away but we wanted to start the plans early.' The plans for my big birthday! They have had the most wonderful idea. You tell them, Richard. You, Bartie."

I stared at her dumbfounded. Barton, in his bafflement, cocked his head like a dog.

"That's right. They want to fly me around the world! To far off places like Shanghai! To Bangkok and Bombay!"

The faces of the women lit up.

"How exciting!"

"That's splendid!"

"Richard! And Bartie! That's so generous!"

"Of course just as you ladies arrived I was telling them that alas I'm too frail and old. Oh, to be eighty again! But they said, 'We thought of that. You should take a companion. We are going to buy you a ticket for two.' Isn't that *wonderful*? Well, girls, who would like to go? Oh, look: a forest of hands! It is going to be like the old days. I'd go everywhere with Betty. To Cairo! To Moscow! To Zanzibar! Poor Betty is gone. I think we'll just have to have a raffle!"

There was a whoop. All the women pressed forward. Laughing, each cried, "Take me! Take me!"

Lotte sat like a queen. "You see, children. My friends understand. Living to ninety is an accomplishment."

This time the crowd broke into applause. It was as if the cake were before her and she'd blown out all the candles.

In the midst of the celebration one voice piped high. Edward's. "But Grandma," he said. "We weren't talking about that. Uncle Barton wasn't even here."

"Goodness," said Lotte. "*Look* at the time." She began to fumble before her, wrapping uneaten rolls, even a rack of the ribs, in napkins and sweeping the food into her bag. Then she stood and began to move from the table. "I've got a meeting of the Plato Society tomorrow. Bright and early! That's practically our motto. And I haven't finished my research. Do you know what they assigned me? The Ottoman Empire! And I'm just a girl from New Jersey! But it turned out to be fascinating. I had no idea how ignorant I was. I only said 'Turkey,' you know, and 'Turks,' but the truth was that empire stretched over half of Europe and half of Asia. I think my personal hero is Suleiman the First. The more you learn about his words and his deeds the more you understand why they called him The Magnificent."

And she was gone. I heard, or imagined I heard, the clang of the back gate and the cough of the Honda's untuned engine.

The club members went back to their tables or out to their dinner engagements. I sent the boys off to get their racquets and bags from the lockers. For a moment Barton and I sat without speaking. Finally my brother said, "I do this once a month. It's more than I can stand. She wants to turn me into an infant. I can see that. But I grin and bear it. I know I've done my duty. That is the way I gain good karma. What about you, my Bro? What will happen to you after you die?"

2

Marcia was halfway through her Waldorf salad when we got back to San Remo Drive. She ate in the dining room at the end of the vast cherry table, under the glow of the crystal chandelier. She looked to me like a cross between the proverbial jungle Englishman who has dressed for dinner and, with the napkin tucked under her chin, the black bangs flat on her forehead, and the spectacles slipping down the slope of her nose, a precocious schoolgirl.

"Well, look who's back. And so early."

The boys dashed forward. "I won!" cried Michael. "I beat him six-three, six-four."

Edward: "Liar! He cheated. All his serves were foot faults."

"You never know the rules. You're just making excuses."

Marcia put her fingers to her temples. "Can we keep it to a roar, please? I have been showing houses all day long to very unpleasant people and their very unpleasant children. I was hoping for a half hour of peace. One. Half. Hour."

"I'm sorry we're early," I told her. "I couldn't wait to get out of the club. Lotte was in fine form. The plan was to stop for ice cream. I drove by Toscanini's, but for some reason it was closed."

"Get yourself a glass. Very well, get three glasses. We shall drown our disappointments in wine."

"That's not a serious idea. The boys—"

"Oh, the *boys*! You are going to France, aren't you? They pour Beaujolais down the throats of their babies and they all grow up to be frog writers and frog philosophers and frog painters, *n'est-ce-pas,* with their frog pictures in the Louvre. Edward, why haven't you gotten the glasses, as I asked?"

"The Jeu de Paume," I corrected, "in case you are referring to anyone present."

Marcia leaned forward, so that her pretty pointed chin rested on her balled-up hand. She spoke in a stage whisper, "Unless you are afraid that because they are not actual Frenchmen, only poor Indians, they won't be able to hold their liquor. Their *firewater,* I mean."

"Oh, don't be silly. They've got homework to do, that's all. They farted around all weekend."

She pushed up her spectacles. "Well, that's a relief. For a moment I thought that you, of all people, were doing some racial profiling."

Edward came back with three tumblers.

His mother said, "These are not wine glasses. You see? This is a wine glass. That is a drinking glass. Never mix milk and wine; don't you learn such things when your father takes you to that temple?"

Marcia saw, as did I, how the boy's face fell. "*Except* in working-class

France." She reached for her bottle of burgundy and filled half a tumbler before the wine ran out. "Oh, dear. Well, this one belongs to me." She transferred the liquor to her own curved glass and tossed it off, perhaps in an imitation of a laborer in Pigalle. "*Salud*," she said, as an afterthought.

Michael said, "I know where you keep the bottles. I'll get one." Before I could say a word he was off. Marcia said, "Now don't look at me so disapprovingly, you two. A number of things have occurred this day. My head happens to be splitting. I'll tell you what happened at the Montana house. You know, Edward, the one that your father always calls the Cotton place. Oh—here we are. What a smart boy! You have chosen an excellent year." To me she said, "Open it, will you?"

Against my better instincts I set about loosening the cork.

"What was I saying? The Cotton Club. Ha! Ha! Ha! You boys are going to enjoy this story. *Attendez!* I was showing this family around. In just one moment you will all be asked to guess what sort of family it was. So there they were: a mommy bear, ha-ha-ha, a poppa bear, and a little boy cub and a little girl cub. So the poor broker—we call them that because while once they were rich they no longer have any money; the poor broker, already with a headache, takes them upstairs and takes them downstairs and takes them all around."

"This is a long story," said Edward.

"Don't be impertinent. Just for that I am going to make it longer. It's quite a lovely house that old Joseph Cotton built. I rather like how the sun comes through the ivy that has been allowed to grow over the windows. To continue: we went next to the kitchen, *la cuisine*."

Michael and Edward, who had just started French, dutifully repeated, "*La cuisine*."

"Then the dining room, *la salle à manger*."

"*La salle à manger*."

"Then the den. *Le, le*—what-the-fuck is the word for it?"

The gagsters in unison piped, "*What-the-fuck*."

I laughed.

Marcia said, "Very funny. Extremely funny. So at last we come to the living room, never mind the translation; it is an exceptionally beautiful living room, with hardwood floors and a magnificent Persian rug. What are you waiting for? Richard, pour."

I gave her another half glass and a thimbleful for each boy.

"Now at last I shall tell you the great event. I happened to glance down while in this living room and there was the little girl, almost as old as you, Michael, and you, Edward. At *least* eight years of age. Let us agree upon nine. There she was with her pants pulled down peeing on the 19th-century kilim."

The boys, at this, hopped up and down, screeching with delight.

"Ha! Ha! Ha! She was taking a piss!"

"On the carpet! The kill-him carpet!"

"Quiet! Quiet, please. Oh, my poor head. A needle is going through it from ear to ear. You have missed the point. The point is the parents—"

"The momma bear! The poppa bear!"

"Were they peeing too?"

"No, no, no. Worse! When I expressed to them my shock and my dismay they only, well, they only chuckled; and when I bent down to yank the little bitch off the floor, he, no, it was she, actually said, 'Allegra isn't done.'"

Now I thought the boys would pee in their own pants. They were doubled over, holding their bellies.

"Allegra wasn't done!"

"She hadn't finished her pee pee!"

"Her sissy!"

"Her number one!"

"Yes, I thought you would enjoy that story," said Marcia, who was frowning down into the dregs that sloshed in her glass. "But you still haven't got the point. The point is—well, I told you that you would have to guess. What kind of family were they? I don't mean were they Jewish or Catholic or black or white, but were they poppa bear and momma bear lawyers? No-o-o-o."

"No-o-o-o," echoed the twins together.

"Were they doctors? Certainly not."

"Not. Certainly not, not, not."

"Were they business bears? I don't think—"

I cut her off. "All right, Marcia. I get it even if the boys do not. They were psychoanalysts."

"Yes! Gold star for Richard! Psychoanalysts! Oh, good lord in heaven: the stain was a big as Russia on the map, right through the priceless kilim, and they didn't even go *tut! tut! tut!*"

Michael and Edward staggered around the room, half in hysterics, as if the mere fumes from their tumblers had made them drunk.

"Okay. Okay, guys. Go on upstairs. You've got to finish your assignments."

They stopped their gyrations. "No, Father," said Michael. "I don't want to."

Edward said, "We want to stay here."

I could have finished their sentences for them. *We want to stay with Mom. We never have such a good time.*

But Marcia was staring into her salad bowl, at the lettuce, the walnuts, the yellow yolks of the eggs. "It has been a difficult day," she said, without looking up. "Go upstairs. You are getting on my nerves."

"Come on. Get going. Let's hit the books."

Michael: "That's mean. It's not fair. We already did our homework."

"I know everything I'm supposed to," Edward chimed in. "Ask me. Ask me about Dr. Maulana Kerenga."

"Oh, Lord," moaned Marcia. "Do I have to listen to this?"

"Yes, you do, Mom! We all have to appreciate the culture of Afro-Americans."

"And of all peoples," his brother added.

Marcia let her fork drop to the table. "Listen, Richard. Are you listening? We are raising human parrots."

Michael drew himself up, chest out. "Maulana Karenga was a brilliant professor; he was upset by the riots in Watts—"

"That's here," said Edward. "It's why the festival has special meaning for all of us who live in Los Angeles."

"—He decided that Afro-Americans needed a festival to honor their culture and their traditions."

"This is Kwanza, which means first fruits of the harvest: a spiritual celebration of the oneness and togetherness of the people."

Michael's turn: "We begin the seven days of Kwanza on December 26th. The first day is Umoja, or unity, as reflected in the African saying, *I am because we are.* The second day—"

"Me," said Edward. "The second day is Kujichagulia, or self-determination—"

"*Kujichagulia!* Marcia brought the base of her glass down hard against the table. It did not shatter, but wine spilled in a wave over the polished surface.

"I'll get a towel," I said, turning to go. Behind my back I heard Michael intoning, in the singsong way with which children perform, "*Ujima:* that means collective work and responsibility."

In the kitchen I grabbed the dishtowel from its hook. Then I paused. I think I was hoping for the sound of laughter, Marcia's whoop, the snort of her merriment, like a drug taken through the nose; and the yip-yap from the Indian boys. Nothing. I leaned against the Arrowhead cooler, which dislodged a hidden capsule of air from its depths. I wondered, at the first pinprick against my temple, whether by some form of airborne contagion Marcia had transferred a migraine from her skull to mine. Outside, the pool light was on and the pool itself, from the vantage of the kitchen window, looked like a turquoise stone in a piece of jewelry. Yes, the kind the Navahos had sold, along with blankets and punchcards, at the side of the road that Marcia and I had driven along to pick up the boys. With the towel over my shoulder I pushed like a waiter through the swinging door.

Marcia had lowered her head to her hands, so that the discs in her neck stood out like those of a Käthe Kollwitz sculpture. *Starving Woman.* The boys were still chanting, but the smug smiles were gone. They looked as if they were trapped on a carousel that had gone amok. There was a frantic note in Michael's voice:

"The colors of Kwanza. The colors are Black, Red, and Green. Black for the face of our people—"

"Red for the people's spilled blood—"

"Green for the hope in our motherland."

"*Our people. Our motherland.*" Marcia was mouthing the last words of each line. She raised her head when I came in. "This is how our children have prepared for Christmas in the public schools of California. *Umoja! Kujicha-watzis!* Why don't they just dance around like Druids?"

I dropped the towel over the spill of wine and began to mop up. "Why the histrionics? It's only a Christmas pageant. They're making a gesture to diversity."

"*Diversity?* That's what they call it. But it's the return of paganism."

"What's that," asked Michael. "That paganism?"

Marcia: "It's the absence of belief in God. Or the belief in many gods—gods in the stones, in the trees, the leaves of trees; oh, for all I know in the hum of the refrigerator—"

"Like Uncle Bartie believes," said Edward. Both boys began to giggle.

Marcia turned on them. "Are you mocking me? How dare you? Where you come from they believe in witch doctors. Witch doctors with rattles. That's what we have tried to save you from."

"Don't, Marcia," I said. "It's not necessary."

"Listen to me, boys." Marcia pushed her chair away from the table. "I am not from Los Angeles. Watts, those riots and all that bad feeling, have nothing to do with me. When I was your age, do you know where I was?"

"In St. Louis, Missouri," said Michael.

"That is correct. In the best part of St. Louis. And in those days, at Christmas time, we put on a play. One year I was a wise man, one year I was a shepherd, and one year I was the Virgin Mary. Do you understand this? *Where is he that is born King of the Jews? For we have seen his star in the east and are come to worship him.* And the wise men followed the star, and the shepherds followed the star, and they came to Bethlehem; and there in a manger—do you know what this is, my boys?"

"The man who runs the team?" ventured Edward, in a tone too low for his mother to hear.

"It is *not* the barn," she went on, "which is what everyone thinks, but the trough from which the animals eat in the barn; and the baby Jesus was laid there in his swaddling clothes because there was no room for this poor family at the inn. Think, darling boys, of how our audience in St. Louis was transformed. A twinkling star, the wise men with their beards and their gifts, and the animals—one year we had real sheep, but mostly we had schoolboys on their hands and knees, and cardboard pigs and cardboard cows. Oh, those sweet cows! Their noble faces! Yes, Bartie may know the truth: the dumb beasts have in them a spark of divinity. That is why they bent on their knobby knees, and so did the wise men and so did the shepherds at the sight of my baby and the sight of me." She looked up, her glasses flashing. "I was eleven. Eleven."

There was a pause. I thought of how Christianity, with the power of its symbols, trumped all other religions, from the bloody Aztecs to Zoroaster, where light fights it out with the dark.

"Don't cry." That was Michael. His own face was twisted in sympathy with that of his weeping mother.

"Please, don't. Please," begged Edward.

"We have to be happy," Michael cried. "I'm happy. Remember: I beat him in straight sets."

"Didn't!" said Edward in a shout. "You cheated! Look, Mom! I'll show you!"

In an instant he had retrieved his racquet from his sports bag and leaped with it onto one of the dining room chairs. "You can't step over the line with your foot. Not before you hit the ball. That is what the geek does. Now you are watching the geek." So saying, Edward threw up his left hand, as if tossing a serve, and swung his racquet—down, then up, and then overhead into the center of the crystal chandelier.

Marcia let out a high, piercing scream.

"No! Oh, no!" cried Michael. In a flash he ran from the room and up the curving stairs.

Edward stood for a moment, gazing down at the shining fragments. Then he jumped from the antique chair's rosy cushion and fled in the wake of his brother.

Marcia was screaming still, and still on the same note, like a soprano who never seems to take a breath.

"Stop it!" I commanded. "You'll frighten them. It's only a chandelier."

She did stop. The lozenges, the shards of crystal, were spread about her. Pieces of glass glistened in her lap. "That foolish child! That ignorant boy! There are so few beautiful things in the world."

"You aren't hurt, are you? Don't move. I don't want you to cut yourself."

"Don't you understand? This belonged to Lotte."

"All right. We won't tell her. She never sets foot in the house. She'll never know."

"But I know."

"Just sit still. I am going for the broom."

In an abrupt movement she stood at her chair. The prisms and octagons fell from her. Diamond dust winked in her hair. Out of nowhere she announced, "You didn't open yesterday's mail."

I halted. "I guess I forgot. Was there anything in it?"

"Yes. A letter from Air France."

"Good. My ticket."

"I opened the envelope."

"So?"

"Two tickets. Not one. Two."

"How stupid. I told Ernie you weren't coming. He knows perfectly well you don't fly." Again I turned toward the swinging door.

"Wait. Never mind the glass. Isolina will get it in the morning. The ticket wasn't made out to me. It was made out to Madeline."

"Oh. I see. Then there was no mistake."

"Are you standing there and telling me you are going to your opening at the Jeu de Paume and the reception at the embassy and the state dinner with Chirac and all the rest of the froggies with their rosettes or whatever they call them in their lapels—that you are going to these things with your mistress instead of your wife. *No mistake!* Is that what that means?"

"Just calm down, okay? In the first place Madeline is not my mistress—"

"She used to be! For years! For most of your life! No wonder you never married. You didn't have to. You *had* your wife."

"Don't be ridiculous. Haven't you ever heard of childhood sweethearts? That's how we began. And we've ended as—I guess you could say as collaborators. What I do is paint her. Period."

"Don't lie! Lying disgusts me. You swore when we adopted the boys—"

"And I kept my word. Religiously. Let me finish. For eight years Madeline has been my model and only my model. The people in Paris wanted a roomful of my figurative work and in their opinion, hell, in everyone's opinion, these last portraits of her are the best. If you'd take the time to look at them you might even agree. And if I don't finish them in the next week I'm going to have to crate them and carry them on the airplane myself."

"I've taken the time. I've seen them. French postcards! With her legs spread wide open and her boobs hanging down and her fat ass shoved in our faces."

"Look, I asked you to come. Repeatedly. So did the president of the Republic, for Christ's sake."

"Yes, you asked me, because you knew for a fact that I'll never get on a plane again and there's no way to get there except on a tramp steamer. Ha, ha! Appropriate for *her*!"

"I swear to you I hoped you'd make an exception. If *you* were the one with the exhibition and *I* were the one with the phobias, believe me I'd—"

Marcia lifted the back of her chair and slammed it down. "You didn't lose your best friend in an airplane crash! Oh, now I've got such a headache! You've no idea! I've told you, Richard. Robbie had a nature like no one I've ever met. He was just a boy but he was *wise*. Childhood sweethearts! I had one too! What was that decent man thinking as he fell through the air? *For over a minute*! How *dare* you talk to me about phobias?"

"I'm sorry. I apologize. But it seemed perfectly natural for me to bring Madeline. It wasn't my idea. They asked for her. They're paying for her. I couldn't—"

"Where is she staying? At the Crillon?"

"Yes at the Crillon. In quite different rooms. If that's a problem—"

"Oh, no. Why should that be a problem? They ought to give you the bridal suite."

"I told you, I kept my word. I haven't touched her. Not since we brought home the boys—*the papooses*, as she calls them."

"I can't believe you don't understand. Are you that big a moron? It's *not* the sex that I mind. You two can fuck your fucking brains out for all I care. I wish you would! Maybe you can fuck yourself out of your addiction. This lifelong dependency. God! The whole world is going to look at this scatalogical shit, *Tart on Toilet Seat*, and see that you are besotted with the woman. You'll be a laughingstock."

"Now you really do sound like someone who has lost her mind. How can you be jealous of Madeline? For Christ's sake, she's almost sixty."

"Yes, and you depict it. Every ounce of flab. Oh, Richard, to an outsider like me even the wrinkles look so much like love."

"Do you know what I feel for her? It's gratitude. She was the first one to inspire me. And the last one too."

"I can't in the middle of a migraine attack bear this high-mindedness. The artist and his muse! As if you haven't lusted after her all your life."

"I haven't. I don't. You can't see what's in front of your face. Okay, I'll make it simple. I'll spell it out for you. The woman I love, Marcia, is you."

She stood clinging to the chair back. The look of pain on her face was so great I thought that I could see the zigs and zags, like an art deco motif, of her headache's aura. She said, "You are not taking her to Paris."

"Marcia, let's think this through. Let's try to find a solution. Can't you—forgive me for saying it: can't you find a way, a hypnotist maybe, like that Russian on Melrose who just snaps his fingers; or else a half bottle of Valium and your whiskey sours? What I'm saying, Jesus I feel like I'm making a wedding proposal—what I really want is for you to join me in the green dress I bought you and for me to introduce Monsieur Chirac to the wife I adore."

Marcia gave a little wave of her hand. "Even if I believed you—no, let me amend: I do believe you mean what you are saying; you have a gift for being momentarily sincere. But I am not going and neither is Madeline."

"My God, I can't believe how much you hate her."

She turned and opened her eyes, which had been half shut against the thrust of the light. The dust in her hair glittered, as it might have had she been at the American Embassy and wearing a tiara. "I have tried to explain this to you. I have tried for years. You willfully misunderstand me. It is not Madeline I hate; it is the paintings you do of her."

She sank back onto the cushion of her chair. "Now, my thickheaded husband, do you get it? She won't be going to Paris."

I started. "The paintings—?"

She nodded.

I ran from the room and took the stairs by twos. The overhead lights shone through the studio's open door. Breathless, I walked inside. I felt, upon seeing the carnage before me, the way a man must when discovering the whole of his family slain. Every painting was slashed through left and right, as if by a machete. It was as though a village of Tutsis had been surprised by Hutus. I went from canvas to canvas. I couldn't find one that could be resewn or restored. This had been two years' work: Madeline naked on her sofa, on her balcony, frowning as she wiped herself on the toilet, smiling as her breasts floated on the water of her tub. That last, the bathroom grouping, had particularly appealed to the custodians in Paris, who wanted to make a connection to Bonnard. I felt, at the sight of these dismembered limbs, the ripped breasts, the torn threads of the genitals, a sexual pang that I had not experienced while gazing at the sheath of skin wrapped round the living subject. The French ought to put up a placard: *Une oeuvre de Monsieur Manson.*

"All right." It was Marcia, standing in the doorway. "I'm here for my punishment."

I whirled. "You crazy bitch. You ought to be in an asylum. Did you think this was some kind of voodoo? That you could wound Madeline by stabbing her image?"

She stepped forward, into the wreckage. "I wasn't after Madeline. I was after your love for her. And that's where it was: in the paintings."

"You don't know me, Marcia. And you don't know art. There is no more love in these paintings for Madeline than there was between Cezanne and a bowl of fruit."

"That may be. Perhaps I am in error. But at least that fat-assed whore won't be going to Paris."

"What are you talking about? What *can* you mean?"

"There's the tickets." She pointed to a small shredded pile at the side of a toppled easel.

"You make me want to laugh in your face. We're going into the twenty-first century. I can get another ticket by pushing a button."

She flew at me, fists raised. "You thought you'd get away with it. Like with Lotte's chandelier. Just don't say a word! A love tryst! You bastard! At the Crillon! That crappy Crillon!" She was pounding on my chest. I did want to laugh—not at her reasoning or her anger but at the square white patch of napkin that still dangled beneath her chin. "What's the matter with you?" she cried. "What kind of man are you? What I did was unforgivable. Why don't you punish me?"

What might have been a film of blood dropped over my eyes. A roar, an animal's roar, came from my mouth. With all my strength I threw her backward. This room had been Norman's library. The exterior walls, overlooking the cork tree to the south and east to the front lawn and curve of San Remo Drive, were now little more than frames for the outsized windows that we'd punched through them. But the two interior walls had not been touched; they still held Norman's books, shelf upon shelf, volume after volume, rising from floor to ceiling. Marcia cowered in the corner where I'd thrust her, at the right angle of those stacks. I leapt forward, onto an oak cabinet. Then I reached up and began to pull the books down on my wife.

She screamed, she bent over; but she did not attempt to escape the cascade that fell on her. I swept off an entire shelf. Chest heaving, with a hoarse rattling in my throat, I hurled down another. The large tomes broke over her. I watched in delight as the pointed corners dug into her flanks and struck the center of her spine. She did not say a word, though I thought I heard her groan. Stretching higher, I hurled down a row of dictionaries and an old Rand McNally. They fell with a rumble and thud. She dropped under the force of the avalanche.

Then a shot, or what sounded like one, rang out.

I ceased. I stood panting. She rolled sideways; she pulled herself from the clutch of the pile. "The children," she said.

I knew she was right. It wasn't a gunshot. It was the slam of a bedroom door.

"You go to them." Marcia forced herself upward. Where she'd been pummeled her face had already started to swell. I started to speak, but she cut me off. "No, no. I'm fine. Go to them. Hurry."

I dropped to the floor. I strode into the hall and made my way down it. For some years now each of the boys had had his own bedroom; but when I opened Edward's door, he wasn't there. I crossed the bathroom that had connected Bartie's old room and mine: and there, where I used to sleep, huddled together in a single bed, the covers drawn over them, were the petrified shapes of my sons.

From under the blanket there came a cry: "I didn't mean to do it! It was an accident!"

A second cry: "Leave him alone! Don't hit him!"

I came up to the bed and squatted beside it. "No one is going to hit you, I promise."

"Get back! Get away! We hate it here! We want to go home!"

The words chilled me. "But, Michael, you know this is your home."

"No it's not! Not really. Our home is where they have witch doctors. She said so."

"She's upset. She's not feeling well. You know what she's like when she gets her headaches."

Edward, still invisible, said, "Then why did you hit her?"

Before I could answer, Michael said, "Don't lie. We heard you."

"I won't mislead you. I didn't hit her. What I did was just as bad. Because I wanted to hurt her. I feel awful. The worst part is, I am setting a terrible example for you. Don't ever do what I did. No matter how angry you get—and I was very, very angry: never hit anyone smaller or weaker than you. Never hit a a woman, okay? I'm not sure there's anything more important I can teach you."

There was a pause. The light from the pool swayed like a beaded curtain on the walls. The shapes on the bed had been like two stones, without even a sign of breathing. Now they began to move. The blanket grew slack. A brown foot, a brown ankle, protruded from the lower edge.

Edward: "Are you going to marry Madeline? Are you going to live in the bridal suite?"

I couldn't help but laugh. *"What big ears you have,* said Red Riding Hood to the wolf. You heard the whole thing, eh? No, I'm not going to marry Madeline. I don't love her. It's your mother I love."

"But you are taking her to the exhibition. To live in the crayon."

"The Crillon. It's a hotel."

Michael said, "But what will happen to us?"

"We'll be here alone."

"You won't be alone. You'll be with your mother."

"No! She screamed and screamed, even though it was a accident. She hates us."

"That is complete nonsense."

"No it's not. We're Navahos. We don't believe in the baby Jesus. You heard what she said."

"Now look: let me tell you what I heard. I was crazed in there. I pulled down a whole shelf of books on your mother. More than a shelf. She really took a beating. Her pretty face, it was already starting to swell. But when I stopped, do you know what she said? The very first thing she said? *Go to the children.* She was thinking more of you than of herself."

A head came out of the woolen blanket. That was Michael, with his chopped head of hair, the two black paisleys of his eyes. "Then you shouldn't be here. You should be with her."

I had to look aside, because my own eyes were filling. I saw their clothes, their flannel pants, their shirts, even the white rags of their shorts, heaped in a corner. I rose from my haunches. "You're right. I've got to go to her. You guys all right? No one's angry. It's just a lot of glass, that chandelier."

Edward, the culprit, pulled down his side of the blanket. "I'm really, really sorry about that."

"Your apology is accepted. I'll see you both tomorrow when you get home from school. Good luck with that report."

Michael sat up, his ribs showing through his tautly stretched skin. "Wait, wait a minute. You didn't tell us about the Jewish Giant."

"Murphy to Mulrooney," said Edward. "Murphy to Mulrooney!"

What they wanted, what they needed, was to resume our post-buffet routine. I suppose I needed it too. "Okay. But I'm going to have to make it short. You know I've got to get back to Mom."

"Because she's got a black eye!"

"A puffed up face!"

"This is very nice. This is swell. Your humanity lasted for two minutes."

"Tell," said Michael. "The 1934 season. The pennant race."

I sat on the edge of the bed. "It was the end of the 1934 season. The Tigers were locked in a pennant race with—who do we love to hate?"

"The Yankees!"

"And rooting for the Yankees is like—?"

"Rooting for U.S. Steel!"

"Except maybe it's time we changed that to—okay, Microsoft. So then, just when every game counted, here come the Yanks to Detroit."

Was it even true? I no longer knew if what I saw in my mind's eye was actual history or the glittering patina of my own embellishments. The Yankees? I think it was the Red Sox. And the Tigers, that September, were four games up. Poetic license, then.

"Obviously, boys, the Jewish Giant had a dilemma. The High Holy Days were coming at the same time as the hated foe. What was he to do?"

"What? What?" said the twins, as if they had never heard the story before. Thus we sit in anguish as Hamlet duels with the poisoned sword, while another part of our brain, held in abeyance, knows that his body will soon be piled atop the other corpses.

"You know the answer. On September 20th—"

"Yom— Yom—"

"Kippur, when all of the city of Detroit was calling on him to play, where was the Jewish Giant?"

"In the sin-a-gog."

"Can you beat that? The pennant is on the line, and instead of showing up at Tiger Stadium, the Jewish Giant, once a member of our Beverly Hills Tennis Club, has a shawl wrapped around his shoulders and is praying in shul. It's a disgrace! It's a betrayal! It's a plot by international Jewry to destroy the national pastime. But what were the American people saying—in their homes, in their workplaces, and in the barrooms of Detroit?"

"We have to ask Mulrooney!"

"We have to ask Murphy too!"

Then the three of us began to recite the Edgar Guest poem:

Come Yom Kippur, holy fast day wide-world over to the Jew
And Hank Greenberg to his teaching and the old tradition true
Spent the day among his people and he didn't come to play
Said Murphy to Mulrooney, "We shall lose the game today!—"

Edward broke off, itself a kind of sacrilege. "Father, you are a Jew, aren't you?"

"We're not done here."

"No, really; aren't you?"

"I guess I am. No, I am."

"Then why don't you go to the sin-a-gog?"

The question brought me up short. What I said was, "Well, I wasn't raised that way."

"How come not?"

"I think Grandpa Norman and Grandma Lotte, when they were children—they had to go through a lot of that rigamarole, and they wanted to spare me and Uncle Barton from having to do the same."

"Are we Jews, too?" asked Michael. "At school they say so."

"I think that's your choice, whenever you want to make it."

"Did you choose?"

"Look, what about Mulrooney? And Murphy?"

"*Did* you?"

"Yes."

"Why?"

"Because I found out when I got older that some very bad people wanted to kill all the Jews—"

"Hitler, you mean—"

"Yes, a long line of people from Haman to Hitler, and I guess without really thinking about it I made up my mind that I wasn't going to be another victim. Oh, too fancy! I just wanted to keep this tribe, which had been around for a hell of a long time—well, I wanted to help keep them around a little longer."

"Bad people wanted to kill all the Indians, too."

"That's right."

A small silence fell. I watched the water from the pool, the reflection of the water, dart like herring across the walls and ceiling.

Michael said, "Let's finish."

The three of us chanted in unison:

We shall miss him in the infield and shall miss him at the bat,
But he's true to his religion, and we honor him for that!

There were no lights in the master bedroom when I went in a few minutes later. I flicked on the sconces. "No!" came Marcia's voice. I flicked them off. But in that instant I had seen that she was not in her bed; she was in mine.

"Your headache?" I asked.

"No. I don't want you to see me."

Extraneous light beams came from the streetlamp on the drive. By that illumination I walked to the bed. I reached for Marcia. I ran the palm of my hand over her face. "Poor darling," I said. "Does it hurt?"

I felt her hand touch my belt, the buckle of my belt, and pull loose the clasp. "Not too much," she answered. "It would have hurt more if you had done nothing."

My loosened trousers fell to my ankles. I stepped out of them. She fumbled for the waistband of my shorts. She said, "I was so afraid you wouldn't do anything. That you'd just stare at me with contempt. That would have stopped my heart." She stretched the fabric away from my erect penis and drew it down. I put one knee next to her on the mattress. I moved my hand from her face to her breast, holding it beneath the slippery silk of her nightgown. She lifted herself. She put her arms around me. She kissed my face—my forehead and quickly my cheeks, my throat, my mouth, my chin. I collapsed on her. Her legs were open. Her gown was hiked. Her hips were already in movement. My penis rode through the wet hair and in to her.

"Oh, Richard! My Richard!" she called. "Where have we been?"

We made love minute after minute. My pupils grew wide. I could make out, in the half-candlepower, her face: her open mouth and puffed lips, her eyeballs moving in a swoon beneath their swollen lids. A smell rose from her, deep, dark, and distinct, like the tar in a roofer's vat; I sensed my penis extend itself, until it bumped against some inelastic barrier. Then the strings and bands and threads that held my body together, like the ones the people of Lilliput had wrapped around Gulliver—all these restrictions gave way and I poured myself out.

3

We all become our parents, through the action of genes of course, but no less through the accumulation of habit and example. Thus I did not rise the next day until noon. When Lotte said she had a meeting of the Plato Society "bright and early" the following morning, what she actually meant was two o'clock in the afternoon. Norman was much the same. Often enough he read the sports pages and sipped his coffee in bed; then he'd trundle down the hallway to the couch in the library and—"I think best in the prone position," he'd say—lie down on that too. But not when they were shooting on the lot; on those days, if he went to sleep at all, he rose before the first light of dawn. Now and then he'd take me, and later on Barton, with him. I know that my brother likes to say I became an artist by ripping up his drawings and appropriating his box of pastels—and it's true I drew my first little still life with his materials. Long before that, however, I had taken the tortuous journey on upper Sepulveda, through the black tunnel and down into the valley to Burbank. From the high hills I could make out the large red crosses that Jack Warner had painted on the roofs of the soundstages, to mislead the Japanese zeros into thinking his studio was a hospital. That was the first of the illusions I encountered there, a collection of trompe l'oeil that prepared me to be a painter.

For example: I remember looking up from my pint-sized vantage and seeing the white handkerchief that always flowed from Norman's breast pocket; I noted how it mirrored the painted clouds on the cyclorama that loomed above him, which in turn replicated the cumuli that moved slowly across the authentic sky. That dizzied me, much like barbershop mirrors, or as the paintings of Magritte—a landscape before which stands an easel that may or may not contain a canvas—still do.

Another example, from one of my very first visits: Norman and I entered a soundstage hand in hand. The building was as large as a hangar, so perhaps I was not surprised to see an aircraft, or at any rate a cross section of an aircraft, inside. To my practiced eye it looked like the cockpit of a Grumman Hellcat or a P38. It sat on a pair of sawhorses, and there was a man inside. He wore a leather helmet, goggles, and a flying scarf. The makeup people were crowded around him, applying last-minute touches of paint; the lighting people took readings; and the camera people stretched a tape to his nose. Then the crowd stepped away, and the pilot reached upward to slam the canopy shut. I squeezed Norman's hand. From somewhere a voice said, "Okay, everybody, we're ready to go. And *action!*"

Flames shot up around us. Thick smoked filled the air. The poor airman, at this catastrophe, was banging on the inside of the Plexiglas.

His mouth opened and shut. That meant he was screaming. Again he pounded, his fists turning raw and red. He was trapped! The flames leaped higher, seeming to engulf him. The black smoke curled over the truncated wings. I stood trembling. Norman's hand gripped my shoulder. If he had not restrained me I might have flung myself forward, lunging at the cockpit in order to pry the pilot free. At the same time I was fully aware that three stagehands lay on their backs beneath the dive bomber, making the smoke and flames. Nor had I failed to notice that the actor's legs dropped out of the center of the rocking fuselage and rested comfortably on the ground. I was, without knowing it, split in two—part of me wanting to break out in laughter at the comedy of the scene, even as my heart pounded in anguish for the doomed man. I didn't know then what I know now: that every artist must seek to draw these separate halves of himself, and of those who view his work, together.

I have taken this long digression—Matisse! Jack Warner!—to put off the memory of how, when I woke the next day and strolled downstairs at a quarter past twelve, the children were gone. Not that there was anything unusual about that; they never returned from school until midafternoon. "Marcia!" I called. But she did not answer. I glanced toward the garage. Only my little Boxster was there. Shopping, I supposed. Gallery hopping. Lunch with Vanessa or some other friend. Yet for some reason my skin was covered with a film of sweat. Then I heard, from afar, the sound of sobbing. Isolina, the maid. Even that was familiar, since she gave way to tears whenever she thought of her father and her little boy in Guatemala. I tracked her to the window by the bar, dust cloth in hand.

"Isolina," I began, but she ran by me and out of the room.

I ran myself, back upstairs to the bedroom. The clothes in the closet were strewn helter-skelter, and half the lingerie had been scooped from the chest of drawers. Marcia's makeup, her toiletries, even her high-tech toothbrush had disappeared. I checked the hall closet, fully aware that her large Samsonite suitcase would be gone. I raced back to the boys' rooms. The same shambles. The same chaos. Was there a struggle? A fight? Why hadn't I heard it? That bottle of wine: had she slipped me a drug? What frightened me most was that the baseball I'd gotten Koufax to sign was missing from Edward's room: that meant the boys knew they were in for the long haul.

"Isolina!" I roared. "Isolina! Come here!"

No response. Still calling, I went through the whole of the house, even down to the basement that had by then been entirely filled with stacks of Bartie's manuscripts. No Isolina. Then I simply held still. The sound of her weeping came from outdoors. I found her crouched in the cabana by the side of the pool. I asked her when Marcia had left. I didn't have to ask her anything else:

"This morning. She drive away in the morning. She take the *niños*. All with suitcases. I help to carry them. She didn't say where she going. She didn't say when in this day she going to come back. She didn't say nothing, only gave me a hundred dollars and tell me to say nothing too. Here, I don't want it. The *niños*, they crying. They say they want to go to the school. She was like to me crazy because she was laughing. I don't know what Isolina to do. No wake you, not even if the house is on fire. That is what I remember. *No wake Mr. Richard.* So I dust and I dust always the same top of the table. She going to hurt Mr. Michael? Mr. Edward? I don't want no hundred dollars. I don't want no million dollars. You tell me what Isolina to do."

What I did was send her home in her rusted out Olds. Then I returned to the bedroom, to the studio, to the mantel over the fireplace— wherever I thought she might have left a note. There was none. I sat down in the kitchen, where we kept the address book, and started a series of calls. To Vanessa, who didn't answer; and to a lot of her friends and my friends, who sometimes did. Everywhere I left the same message: call me if you hear from Marcia. I told the same thing to her hairdresser and her colleagues at the realtor's office and the desk of the club. Then I called her doctor. Then I called her shrink. It was her yoga instructor who blurted out, "You mean, she's kidnapped the boys?"

The thought, the word, had not occurred to me. But now that it had, I dialed the number of my business manager and soon enough said, "Listen, Ernie, don't you think we should call the police?"

He said, "Don't be silly. You can't kidnap your own children."

"Of *course* you can. I read about these cases all the time. It starts as a family dispute and the next thing you know the father or the mother has taken the kids to Florida or some place like that and changed all their names, and then they marry a rich widow or a rich widower and that's the last I'll see of my kids."

"You're letting your imagination run away with you. You're not getting a divorce. This isn't a custody battle. She's angry over a specific thing—"

"That's right, Glickman: why the *fuck* didn't you make sure they mailed Madeline's ticket directly to her—?"

"Because you never asked me to."

"I pay you to anticipate problems, not make them."

I heard plainly enough the fat manager sigh. "Let me finish my thought. She has a specific grievance and I am predicting that in a day or two you'll get a phone call demanding a specific remedy."

"All the more reason to call the police. They can tap the phone or trace the phone, you know what I mean, and that way they can find her. Oh, Jesus! And if she doesn't call? Or call for weeks? They have to be in school. We're going to France—"

As soon as I said the words I realized what Marcia wanted by way of a specific remedy. But Ernie was already replying: "It won't take weeks. If you'll forgive me saying so, Marcia's not what I would call a doting mother. I don't mean she's not fit. I just mean from what I've seen Michael and Edward will be a handful for her; I don't see her stretching this out very long."

"What if she has help? She's got family in St. Louis. She's got her ex-husband in San Francisco. Her bitch of a sister—where is she? I think she lives in Encinada. God, *Mexico!* What if she's taken them over the border?"

"That's your imagination again. Be a mensch, which is what your boys are going to need you to be. I'll track down the family in St. Louis, okay? Just to put your mind at ease. What's the sister's name? Diane, pronounced Dee-Ann? I'll try to track her down too. Just stay calm and by the telephone. And watch the mailbox. One more day, two more days—she'll be in touch."

I hung up. Instantly the telephone rang. It wasn't Marcia. It was the guidance counselor from Canyon Elementary asking why the boys hadn't shown up at school. Out of masochism, I suppose, I told her the story. Again, the moment I hung up, the telephone sounded. It was the first of the Schadenfreude Brigade, those I hadn't yet called, and some that I had, eager to hear the latest turn. After an hour of that I got into my sports car. I drove aimlessly around Riviera, peering left and right, as if my wife and my children might be hiding behind the neighborhood hedges or the one or two remaining lemon groves. Then I swung across the old polo fields and headed out to Toscanini's, thinking what Marcia might think: buy them off with the ice cream they'd missed the previous night. It was such a dumb notion I didn't bother to stop.

Instead, I swung back to Sunset and pulled in first at the Bel Air and then the Beverly Hills Hotel. I asked if anyone like Marcia and the boys had checked in. I did the same at the Beverly Wilshire. Next, in the failing light of the December afternoon, I drove to Vanessa's. I realized she wouldn't tell me if my family was there, but the parked car on Bedford would. That curb was empty. For a mad moment I contemplated driving all over town, from house front to house front, in search of the silver Lexus. Then, in the stream of six o'clock traffic, I headed home.

As I drove past the front pillars I was suddenly certain that Marcia would be parked at the back circle, just as I always expected that our old pecan tree, long since chopped down, would still be rattling the castanets of its pecans. But when I took the second corner I saw that neither the tree nor the car was there. Inside, I sat with my head in my hands to listen to the messages on the phone. None was from Marcia. One was from the French consul, asking me to drop in. Two were from Lotte:

"Richard? Oh, hello, sweetie. It's your mother. I just came back from Plato. I had to give a paper on the Turks. Anyway, darling, I'm so sorry to hear the news. Charlotte called me. You must be *frantic!* I can just imagine what you are feeling. Those poor darling boys! It's a damned shame she has to act out this way. Of course I know everything will work out just fine. I don't believe she'll go back to her husband, do you? I can't say I am surprised. People will do desperate things when they are depressed. Didn't you tell me she sits in front of the television until all hours? Watching *The Tonight Show?* But I never dreamed her psychosis would involve the boys. Do you remember how she'd clutch her head and say, *Stop that screaming!?* Well, I raised two boys, all on my own after Norman's death, and I got my degree and rolled up my sleeves, and helped other families with their children. It's no bowl of cherries for anyone. Where are you, for heaven's sake? Are you just sitting there listening to your mother in the *amused* way you have? That is rude, Richard. It's like eavesdropping. Or are you out? I wish I could help you. The timing is really rotten. There's your exhibition and my birthday. That's what she wants: to throw a monkey wrench into our happiness. Oh, I can't help thinking about what those handsome boys are feeling. They love—"

The machinery cut her off. She'd placed her second call only a few minutes before I'd walked in the door:

"Richard? Are you there? It's your mother. I don't know why you haven't called me. And now I'm about to run out. I'm having a bite with the girls before the Philharmonic. Oh! That's the doorbell! Marjorie is picking me up. Shall I tell her to go? I could send her away. An evening with Mahler! I could do without that! If you want I could come over in the Honda, though you know I don't like to drive at night. Not since I went up the wrong ramp of the freeway. Lotte, my girl, as far as driving is concerned the handwriting is on the wall. But I would if you want the company. Who is going to cook your dinner? I know intuitively you haven't eaten all day. Oh that bell! Coming! Yes, we could sit in the dark together and wait for that girl to come to her senses. Wouldn't that be nice? To sit side by side the way we used to. Darling Richard, I would hold your hand."

Click. Off to *Das Lied von der Erde.*

But she had reminded me I hadn't eaten all day. I walked to the kitchen. Without thinking I took out a package of cereal and a carton of milk and sliced a banana. I sat down to the breakfast my boys had not. What next? I took two aspirin. I drank some coffee. Then I went upstairs and into the studio. Like my mother I rolled up my sleeves; I did what I could to set things right. I returned the books to their shelves. I restored the toppled easels and gathered the scattered brushes and pencils and tubes. As I had feared, there was little I could do with the paintings. I tried to tape their torn backs, but the sides of the canvas kept drawing apart. I prepared a needle and thread—despite Lotte's fantasies, Bartie and I had long ago learned to darn our own socks—and like a plastic surgeon set to work on Madeline's face. Alas, the rows of stitches made her look like Frankenstein's monster. At two in the morning I threw in the towel.

I staggered down the hall to our bedroom. Impossible to sleep. I thought of Marcia, tugging at my belt, her hips moving before I lowered myself between her legs. A poor way to count sheep. So was climbing into her bed in an attempt to inhale a few molecules of her *eau de toilette.*

After an hour of this I rose, pulled on a pair of jeans, and returned to the studio. I took a smallish canvas, an easel, and a fistful of brushes and paints. I set up shop in Michael's bedroom, overlooking the pool that, all ashimmer, spread out below me like a cocktail dress. I painted it—for what? the five hundredth time?—from one edge of the canvas to the other, like a seascape. Then I turned the easel around. I took pains to capture the whitecaps that pulsed over the wall like rays inside an oscilloscope. No one would ever know that these spikes of decomposing light, just flickers, just wisps, were the dragonfly wings and the bumblebee wings, once sodden, but now thanks to my brother taking flight.

I got into bed at five in the morning and might have slept through the whole of the day had not the telephone, shrilly ringing, awakened me at noon. Rain, I noted, was pelting down. I reached for the receiver, but when I picked up no one was there.

"Hello? Hello?" I shouted. "Who is this?" No voice. No dial tone. Then I said, "Hi, Edward, my special friend. Take care of the Koufax, okay?" More silence. Not even the sound of breathing. The receiver almost slipped from my sweaty grasp. Finally a voice, not Edward's but Michael's, and not at the mouthpiece but, or so it sounded, a half room away, said, "Let me. Father? I want—" The line went dead. I yelled into the receiver, but it was as if I were shouting at the spot in the ocean where a man had gone under. I hit *69, but of course there was no trace of the number. I sat for an hour, staring at the phone. When it did ring again, I jumped. But it was only Jimbo, trying to be helpful, asking me out to his place for poker. I told him no. This time I left the receiver off the hook.

I wandered a bit, from room to room. I built a fire in the fireplace and poured myself a Scotch. The rain fell even harder. There was a rumble of thunder. The sky grew as dark as the shadow of a solar eclipse. Fooled, the acorn bulbs of the streetlamps came on.

I went down to the cellar, as I used to do whenever I heard thunder as a boy. I looked at the columns of Bartie's prose, a lifetime's work, that stretched from floor almost to ceiling. The iron furnace came on with a roar. I went to what looked like an old stack of boxes. The cardboard was rotted by mildew. I pulled at the stained seams. The sheets inside were an odd size, like foolscap, and covered with the loony loops of Bartie's hand. I managed to yank out a story so ancient the paper clip that held it together had rusted. The paper itself looked as if it had been eaten by worms. "Trouble in the Suburbs," that was the title, printed out in capital letters, across the top. There was a thud of thunder and the sixty-watt bulb dimmed on its cord. "Depth charges!" Bartie and I had called to each other, pretending that a destroyer on the surface was attacking our submarine.

"A school bus stopped at the corner," was how the story began. "When the driver opened the door a procession of semi-happy faces crossed the crowed street." That's right: *crowed*. And, not such a bad touch, *semi-happy*. I squatted on my haunches to read the piece through.

The hero, Dave Conway, gets off the bus with the others. He is looking forward to his date that night with his girlfriend. The trouble is, he's got a straight F report card in his pocket and knows his parents will ground him ("Go to your room, young man," he anticipates his father saying). He takes out his frustration by throwing rocks onto the cars that pass on the freeway below. Then he goes home to have a beer. He is interrupted by his mother, "a lean dry woman with cold piercing eyes like a cobra." Sure enough, Dave and his mother have a terrible fight, in the course of which she slaps him in the face and digs her nails into the flesh of his arm. Dave retreats to his room, from where he hears his mother pick up the phone and "tell his chick that he couldn't make it tonight for reasons of behavior." After brooding for a time, he goes downstairs, plucks up an axe, and tiptoes up behind his mother, who is—"chump, chump went her jaws"—eating an apple. He hacks her head off with a single swipe. Another nice touch: "The head rolled beside the apple core, the eyes shutting immediately." Then, in what may or may not have been a deliberate nod to Oedipus, Dave sits in his father's leather chair and calls his girl back to tell her he will pick her up later that night. When she asks him if this is all right with his mother, he replies, "Oh, yes, we've buried the hatchet." *Finis.*

The thunder had finished its drumrolls. I looked round at the pillars of paper that rose on every side. Was the Buddha smiling at this? And at the way Dave, after hurling rocks onto the freeway, kicks the hindquarters of the neighbor's dog? I thought of how Bartie would spend hours in the pool, splashing the waterlogged insects onto the flagstones, so that they might dry their wings in the sun. Did St. Francis of Assisi also want to set fire to the family cat? What about Prabhavananda, Bartie's guru? And those Jains who are loath to take a step, or a breath, lest they destroy an unseen caterpillar or microbes by the million? Did they, too, wish to chop off their mothers' heads while they, like Eve, chump-chump-chumped on an apple? With a pang I suddenly remembered how Lotte—yes, a cobra on occasion, a serpent, a seductress: how she used to read all of Bartie's stories. Had she read this one? And mussed his hair, saying, *It's so beautifully written! It's just a gem!*

When I came upstairs, it was no longer raining. I started for the kitchen but stopped at the sound of the front-door chimes. *They're back!* I thought, running through the foyer. The chimes sounded again. "Marcia!" I shouted, even as I fumbled with the doorknob, the lock. "I'm coming! I'm here!"

But it wasn't Marcia, and it wasn't the boys. Ernie, rumpled as ever, stood in the doorway. He was wringing his hands. "I'm sorry to disturb you. I didn't know you'd be working. But something has come up."

I saw that he was glancing at the speckled jeans I'd climbed into bed with, and at the tank top, also bedabbed. "No, no. I tried to start a canvas last night. Come in, you're getting wet."

But in truth the late afternoon sun was shining, though raindrops still fell from the tree limbs and off the portico's edge. Ernie, however, was soaked by his own sweat.

"I won't come in. It's just that I thought I'd better tell you the news in person."

"What news? Has something happened? Is it the boys?"

"First of all, I want to apologize. I made light of the situation. I said it would all blow over. And that's what I thought. I didn't think she had the heart for it."

"Okay, Ernie. I never doubted you are a well-meaning man. What happened?"

"I got a call from a friend. Well, there's a chain of acquaintance here, which ended up in Judge Mosk's office. He feels for you. He's an old friend of the family."

"Will you get on with it? I want to know if the boys are all right."

"Yes, yes, as far as I know. The thing is, she's brought charges. Wait, I'm not sure she has. I think it was Vanessa who called the district attorney. She's the one who brought Marcia in. Both her eyes were shut, Richard. Her throat was purple. The problem is, this is going to come before Judge Schoenberg's court."

"Ronny? I used to play tennis with him, for Christ's sake."

"I wouldn't count on past relationships. We're in a post-O.J. world here. The whole city is spooked."

"But if Marcia didn't bring charges—"

"I don't think that matters. Right now the issue is, will you be charged with a felony or not."

"A felony!"

"I think that's what Judge Mosk is doing. He's trying to have it reduced to a misdemeanor. The world is upside down, you know. It doesn't help that you are a famous artist. The press will howl about favoritism. In this case your talent actually hurts."

"What *is* the case? What is it I'm supposed to have done?"

"The charge is assault with a deadly weapon."

"Are you crazy, Glickman? We're talking about books! The weapon was a book!"

"An atlas, I heard. A heavy one. Look, a shoe can be a deadly weapon. A toaster, I think. People get smothered with pillows."

I stepped out onto the brickwork of the portico. The great white pillars loomed above, like the phony Greek columns on a courthouse. A bird, I saw, was hopping over the lawn, looking for unlucky worms.

"All right. I get the picture. What is it you want me to do?"

"I think you ought to go in and shave and get into a suit and come downtown with me."

"What the hell for, Ernie? I'm not going anywhere."

"The thing is, even if the charge is misdemeanor assault you're going to have to come to court to be arraigned. If it's a felony, there's going to be a bench warrant for your arrest. I made all the calls. I've arranged for your surrender."

"I love that, *surrender*. What if I don't? What then?"

"The police will come here and make the arrest."

The two of us were pacing—too fast for Ernie, who was already wheezing—the length of the covered porch. I stopped, directly beneath the spot where the glass-enclosed lantern hung suspended on its chain. "Ernie, I can't go. I've got to wait this out. The boys are going to need me. Michael tried to call last night. I've got to be here for them. Call Jimbo, will you? I'll call Ronny. We've got to get this quashed."

"Well, I've got more news. Not good news. About the boys."

I whirled on him. "You said they were fine. I asked you and you said they were fine."

The fat man held up his hands, as if he thought I would hit him. Rivulets of sweat—and this was a cool day in December—ran down his cheeks. "They *are* fine. Just listen: I got a call. From a Ms. Williams. She was in Arizona—"

"Wait a minute. *Sheila* Williams? Was that her name? Was the call from Black Mesa?"

"Yes. From Black Mesa."

"I remember her. She made us jump through hoops when we adopted the boys. She and a Mister Toombs."

"He got on the phone, too. The two of them. I don't know how, but they knew all about the assault. They knew Marcia had taken the boys."

My knees weakened. I caught hold of one of the green shutters to stay upright. It had suddenly dawned on me that Marcia had flown the boys to Flagstaff, or had driven all night to the reservation, and had dumped them there, the way a shopper trades in defective goods. "Ernie, you can tell me. Is that where they are?"

"No. I don't think so. But it's clear they are interested in getting them out of your custody."

"What do you mean, *custody*? They're not in my custody. These are my sons. Jesus! Toombs, he and Williams came out here a year after the adoption. We all had a good cry. Do they really want the boys back with their mother? Can she still be alive? She had cirrhosis even then. She was as yellow as a Chinaman. No one knew who the father was. She gave us nine names. Is that what's going on? Has the father shown up? Someone claiming to be the father? Are we going to have to pay him off the way we did the mother? And we furnished the goddamned dormitory. Twenty-five thousand dollars. What now? What now, Glickman? Do they want us to computerize the whole reservation? This is bullshit! We did everything by the book. The mother had six weeks to change her mind. She didn't. She gave up her rights. The tribe gave up its rights. There is no further review. Michael and Edward belong to Marcia and me."

Ernie struggled out of his jacket. His breasts showed through the damp front of his shirt. He crooked an elbow in one hand as he stood there; he used his other hand to prop up his heavy head. "Shoot the messenger if you want to. Nail me to the cross. They read me the documents. The boys are minors. As long as they are, the council has the right to petition any local authority to determine if they are being abused."

"Better and better! Abuse, now! I'm a pervert! I beat my children with a belt!"

"They don't claim that. Not physical abuse. They raise the question of whether you are a fit father. Listen, Richard: a lot of it was nonsense—that you are denying Michael and Edward their heritage and telling them stories about witch doctors and, well, leading what they call a bohemian life."

"What's *that* about? Because I'm a painter? The most respectable people I know, the most straight-laced and utterly bourgeois, are painters. Including, alas, myself. My god! They claim, these Indians, that we stereotype *them!*"

"Look, it's all a lot of crap. You don't have to convince me. But a felony charge, battering, an attack—that is a problem for us. Even a misdemeanor won't help. And—I hesitate to mention this. You are so straight-laced! Well, I shouldn't joke. They also heard about Madeline."

"Heard *what* about Madeline? Heard what?"

"They talk about an adulterous affair. A habitual pattern, over many years. They also mentioned some new pornographic paintings."

"These are outright lies. They were beautiful paintings. And I haven't been with Madeline since the day we brought the boys home. I want to scream. I want to tear my hair out. Nothing is true here. Everything is distorted. No. Not what happened with Marcia. I don't deny that. I feel disgraced by it. Of course it's a terrible example to the boys. But it never happened before. It will never happen again. Ernie, I'm not going to lose them, am I? Is this really happening? What am I going to do?"

"You're not coming with me?"

"No, no, I can't. What if they call again? What if I'm not here? They might lock me up for the night."

The big man sighed. "Okay. I gave you my best advice. I feel responsible. I mean, about not acting sooner. I'll do what I can. I still think I can track the boys down."

"I'm a faithful husband. I love my wife. I'm a good father, Ernie."

"I know that. You hang on. Stay here. I'm going to try to head off the police. It's contrary to type, my saying this, cynic that I am, but things have a way of working out."

He gave a little wave, a flap of an arm, and stepped off the bricks, onto the asphalt of the driveway. I watched him duck, gasping, into the blue sedan he'd left at the curb.

What now? What next? I knew I ought to eat, but the first bite of the sandwich I put together filled me with nausea. I fixed another Scotch and held it in one hand while I put the telephone back in its cradle and lifted it again to check for messages with the other. Nothing. The goddamned French Consul. Lotte, too eager. A handful of friends. I took Ernie's advice and shaved, missing more spots than I hit. I felt hotter than the water that poured from the tap. The sweat poured from me as it had from the body of my manager. I tried lying down on Norman's old couch. I must have slept for a time, because when I opened my eyes it was pitch-dark. My skin, my body, were burning. Was I coming down with a fever?

I peeled myself off the leather and changed into a pair of trunks. I thought I would try to cool myself off with a swim. When I got to the back yard a mist was rising into the chill air from the surface of the heated pool. I got in. I did the dead man's float. William Holden on his back instead of his belly. I stared up: there were the moon and the stars, smeared together like an erased equation on a blackboard. A bird, which should have been sleeping, trilled from the branches of the eucalyptus. Not a bird. The phone.

Edward! Michael!

I splashed to the edge of the pool and hauled myself onto the flagstone. No Isolina. No receiver at the end of a cord. Impossible to run in a pair of rubber thongs; I was trotting headlong, you could say, when on the sixth or seventh ring a deck chair materialized against my shin. I understood then, slapping about wetly like a duck, that the rest of this night was likely to be a comedy.

And why a comedy? Because I knew who was on the line even before I picked up the phone. "Hello, Madeline," I said.

"How did you know it was me?"

"I've heard from everyone else. I figured it was time I heard from you."

"I'm sorry. Sorry I didn't call, Richard-boy. I didn't know what to say. Everything I thought of sounded self-serving. I knew you'd think I was an opportunist. Not that I don't want you back. There's no point pretending I don't. But I know all too well you won't come."

"You're right about that."

"More's the pity. I'll settle for hearing that you're all right. I'd bet a new car you haven't eaten a real meal in days. Is it true? Is she gone? Don't answer! Aren't we old friends? Why don't we just have a nice chat, like friends are supposed to. Did you hear I've got a new part? A real part? Not television. Not the voice overs. Not that damned UPN. It's Madame

Ranevsky. You know, in Chekhov? *The Cherry Orchard*? I am amazed at how much this has meant to me. Franklin is mounting it at the Playhouse. We're going to start rehearsals—oh, listen to me! I haven't gotten anything. *If* I get the part, and it's a big if, *then* we start rehearsals right after we get back from Paris."

"Madeline, about Paris. There's something I have to tell you."

"Uh-oh. The voice of doom. I've been expecting it. Go ahead, tell me. I've got a cyanide capsule in my cheek, like Eva Braun."

"Which makes me Hitler, huh? I wish you'd—"

"Oh, for heaven's sake! I'm a big girl. I'm sitting quite firmly down. Why don't you just tell me what happened? Starting at the beginning."

"What happend was the fools at the airline sent your ticket to the house. Marcia opened the envelope."

"Oh, boy. Oh, boy. Poor Richard."

"She thinks it's a love tryst. That's her language. She was wild. She was crazy. So was I. I pulled a bookcase down on her. The next morning she was gone."

"Gone, eh? Really gone? Once upon a time that would have constituted a happy ending."

"There's no happy ending. She took the boys with her."

There was a pause. Then Madeline said, "And she'll bring back the porpoises if I don't go to France?"

"Ernie thinks so."

"And what do you think?"

"I don't know. Marcia tore up the tickets. Now the tribe is making trouble. About the paintings. About you and me."

"*My nursery, dear delightful room! I used to sleep here when I was little.* Those are my lines. Madame Ranevsky's. *And here I am, like a little child.* Do you know why I called? The audition is tomorrow morning. Early. Eight. I thought maybe you'd give me a ride."

"Madeline, you have to admit this isn't the greatest time."

"No. Wait. It wasn't really for the ride. Richard, Richard-boy, I have a problem. All of a sudden I can't remember my lines. They are in my head and they just fly out. I pick up the text and for a moment I can't remember which role is mine. Varya, the young one. Ranevskaya, the hag. A half hour ago I had the paperback of the play in my hand and I didn't know what it was doing in my house. Richard, am I going mad? Is it a breakdown? Did I imagine you said I am not going to Paris? *Is* that what you said?"

"Okay, listen. I better come over. Jesus, I'm dripping wet from the pool."

"No, no. Don't come over. I'm fine. Don't think I had a stroke. I think it was petit mal, or whatever they call it. A transient episode. Let's say good night. Let's be civilized people. You should sit there and sit there and sit there and wait for your wayward wife."

"Ten minutes, okay? Hold on, sweet. Ten minutes, I'm there."

I was pulling on my pants before I hung up the phone. I threw on a shirt and stuck my feet, sockless, into a pair of loafers. I ran down to the garage and pulled out the Boxster, the *voiture de sport à l'Allemand,* as Marcia, always Frenchifying, called it.

I gunned the car onto San Remo and didn't slow up at the stop sign for Sunset. On the straightaway, with the Riviera Club on the left, I hit eighty-five, then, after the turn onto Amalfi, eighty-five again. I skidded around the downhill turns, tighter than San Francisco's, that dropped toward the shore. Madeline owned a tiny top-floor flat on Sumac, at the ridge of the canyon. From the windows you could see a chunk of the ocean. I pulled up behind her beat-up Volvo and took all four flights of the outdoor staircase by twos.

Madeline was waiting on her balcony, among the potted trees. "Goodness, what a racket," she declared.

"You're the one disturbing the peace," I answered, between gasps, "dressed like that."

For all of her age, Madeline had only a few silvery strands in her otherwise jet-black hair. It was loose at the moment, as if for bed, and fell over a salmon-colored sweater. What had startled me was the flimsy piece of purplish lingerie that barely covered the fold at the base of her buttocks. *Was* she, in fact, about to go to bed? Didn't think, for all my protestations, that I was coming? Or had she thrown it on for my benefit? The thing was no longer than the skirt on a bathing suit, or the fairy-fluff on a tutu. *Brazen* was the old-fashioned word that came to mind.

She ignored my remark, pushing her sweater to the elbow and pointing over the ocean to the soft soapstone of the moon. "Look. Aren't we lucky. It's full. With a reflection, like in Munch."

"It's been hung very nicely. Is that what you asked me here for? Stargazing?"

"I'm surprised you came at all, considering you've lost your parabolas. Your parachutists. I know where I stand in that line."

I seized her wrist, above the silver bracelet I'd bought her two decades before. "I wish you'd drop that gag. After eight years it's getting stale."

"Ouch! Let me the hell go!"

"All right. Don't shout. They can hear you all the way to the Jonathan Club."

"Do you know what I think, darling? I think we should start over. Hello, Richard. You look thin. You look famished. I've opened a bottle of wine. I was right: you haven't eaten in ages. I'll make you some chicken. I'll make you a salad."

She'd taken up the untucked hem of my shirt. She fumbled with it, tugging a little. Behind her, the door to the flat was open. Now I heard the music, Vivaldi's oboes, on the loop of her carousel. I smelled the perfume evaporating from the hollow of her clavicle and from behind her elfin ears. She gathered her hair in her free hand and swept it from the curve of her throat. "You set a record," she said. "You and your Boxster."

I followed her inside the one large room that made up her flat. The windows on the far side were open over the crest of the ridge; floodlit moths were hurling themselves against the twanging screens or hanging motionless, green wings extended, on the glass. I came to a dead stop in front of her sofa bed. Next to it, two candles burned on the coffee table, flanking two bottles of wine, one not opened, one half empty. The chicken she mentioned, her crummy chicken Marsala, and the salad on salad plates, had been laid out already. What else? In the fireplace, a fire. Of course the music. Of course the Chanel. I had to smother a laugh. It was like amateur theater. The set for a seduction.

"What the hell is this?" I demanded. "Soft lights and music. Perfume and wine. Don't tell me you threw all this together in ten minutes."

She sank onto the sofa, feet doubled beneath her, like the old-fashioned White Rock girl. "Well, I was hoping you'd come. Based on my knowledge, I thought you would."

"There isn't any audition, is there? You didn't have a panic attack over your lines. You heard about Marcia. You probably heard about the boys. *Start boiling the rice.* Jesus Christ, Madeline! Didn't you think this would be—well, a little transparent?"

"Richard. Darling. Give a girl a break. It's been eight years."

"And you trick yourself out like a whore!"

"Who are you to give lectures? *Ten minutes?* That's how long it took you to drive here from Riviera. We both know what you came for. You came for a lay. No one drives eighty miles an hour for anything else."

I considered this. "Maybe I did—"

"*Maybe!* I heard your tires squealing on Amalfi!"

"Because you scared me. With false pretenses."

"Are you just going to stand there like a wooden Indian? Come on," she said, patting the cushion beside her. "Come get a feel of my papillons, my papillas."

Here Madeline stretched backward so that I could see she wasn't wearing a bra. The tightened sweater might have been the cape before the bull.

"Can't you turn off that music?" I strode to the stereo and punched futilely at the buttons. The volume only got louder. I pulled a plug from its socket. The lamp went out. From behind my back I heard her laughter. More comedy. I yanked a wire from the back of the machine. The oboes stopped.

"Next we put out that phony fire." But when I turned I came face to face with the only painting she kept on her walls, an early study, mostly of her back, in charcoal. Her face was half turned so that you could see the blur of a nose, of an eyebrow, of a myopic eye. Her sharp, jutting pelvis was lost in the drapery of the bedclothes, which rose in a series of little wavelets, like the points of a stiff meringue.

All she said was, "A masterpiece. By a thirteen-year-old child."

"I think," I said, "I can remember the day I painted it."

Sheepishly, then, I went to the sofa and sat beside her. She continued, "I live with it and if I don't want to break into tears every five minutes I have to avert my eyes." She picked up my hand. She started to kiss the web of skin between my fingers. She licked at my wrist. She took the whole of my middle finger into her mouth. It gave not pleasure but a pang, the way the lines at her puckered lips revealed her age. She pulled back, wiping a stand of spittle.

"Do you like that?" she asked.

"By analogy, I guess."

"I adore it. I adore the hand that held the chalk, the pencil, the stick of charcoal; the hand with the brush."

Here Madeline flung her head over the back of the sofa, so that her hair fell almost to the floor and that same throat, plump, white, and bulging, lay exposed. It was like the gesture, I thought, of one wolf in submission to another. I stared down at her bare foot and ankle, then seized it, where it disappeared under her buttock.

"What are you doing?" But she raised herself, so that her leg came free.

"Not a charcoal," I answered. I slid my hand to the meat of her calf, then under the bend of her knee. The sole of her foot was against me. I worked my fingers along her inner thigh, up to the hollow at the top. I could see the darkness at her groin. She continued to stare at the ceiling, but took a deep breath and held it. I felt, against my knuckles, the heat that came from her.

"Madeline, sweet. Do you really want this? Shall I go ahead?"

Her other leg spread outward, which made the pale folds of her lingerie fall open. I glimpsed the beginning of the rise of her mound.

Without lowering her head she said, "I have wanted this every day for the last eight years. And more! Since Marcia bought you and you bought your paprikas. Sorry! Sorry, sorry, sorry! Edward. Michael. What happened to *Dog-with-Tongue-Out?* To *Cloud-in-Sky?* Oh, God in Heaven! Those round heads! Those black eyes. I am going to hell because of the sin of envy. Oh, and covetousness. And hatred. How I wished they would die!"

"You don't mean that. You're more exhausted than I am. Maybe I should put you to bed. You've got an audition tomorrow morning. At eight, isn't that right? You're going to need your sleep."

She reached for my trousers; she fumbled at my zippered fly. "*Oh, my sins! I've always thrown my money away like a lunatic. I married a man who—who—*Do you see? I can't remember! *Who made nothing but debts. My husband died of champagne.*"

Madeline had worked my pants down. Her hand rested on my crotch. I pushed my own hand through her stubble and cupped it over her. She went on, as if we were discussing the theater in a taxi.

"How can I read those lines? I once saw a woman from the Moscow Arts Theater. A woman directed by Stanislavsky."

"You'll perform them as well as she did. Everyone sounds great in Russian."

"No, no. I know who I am. The range of my talents. Oh, that painting! If I weren't enjoying sitting here with you, and your hand on me, I'd get up and turn it to the wall. Richard-boy, can't you see I am in despair? Didn't I have really beautiful breasts? Can't we agree on that proposition? Look at this! Oh, dear God, hairs are growing out of them! Like out of an old man's ear. Fool! I'm a fool! Why did I fall in love with you? Why did you make me? Can't you just love me back?"

"You know I love you. Even the fucking French can see that. Madeline, you can't believe our whole lives have been some kind of fling."

"Do you remember, Richard-boy, the first time I kissed you?"

"Yes. At Halloween. After Bartie attacked the little jockey."

"And those boys, the Coveneys, all those boys were in the lemon grove. Spying. I felt you. You were hard against me. Just the way you are now."

Her words, or the memory they evoked, stiffened me. I leaned forward, wanting to kiss the spot on her throat where a vein was throbbing. She started to laugh.

"What's so funny?"

"You!"

She was gazing down at my loins—rather, at the red and white stripes stretched tightly over them.

"I was in the pool. I forgot. I pulled my pants on over my trunks."

"Ha! Ha! Ha!" She couldn't take her eyes off the bulge of a half-hearted erection. "It's like a candy cane! Ha! Ha! A barbershop pole!"

"All right, Madeline."

"A peppermint stick!"

I crammed my shirt into my waistband and zipped myself up. "I had a feeling this night was going to be a lot of laughs."

"Oh, forgive me," she said, with her legs now primly shut. "Don't be angry, darling."

"Don't be angry? You know what this reminds me of? When I came back from Yale delirious with desire and you led me on and said only five more days, four more days, three more days, and then, what the hell happened? You locked yourself in the bathroom."

"I've reproached myself. I've cursed myself for that night."

"Yeah, well now I know what I hated about what you're wearing. They're the same damned panties. Lavender!"

"But wasn't it for the best? What if we'd gone to your bed that night?

Everything might have ended."

"Listen. I've got some news for you. It's what I came to tell you. Marcia didn't just tear up the tickets. She tore up the paintings. Ripped them through. The whole series. Everything we've done over these last few years."

Madeline's face went completely white. As though I'd done her portrait in barium sulphate. She rose from the cushion and took one step backward. Leaning sideways, she took another. I didn't move. A primitive part of my brain had connected the way she looked now—bloodless, lifeless, listing—with what Marcia had done to her image. The voodoo had worked after all.

"Madeline—"

"Don't talk. All right? Just don't talk. I feel disconnected. As if you'd pulled the wires out of my life, the way you did to the music. My life! You never understood what a conventional view I had of myself: three papooses, six papooses, a picket fence, apple-fucking-pie. And I tried. Two marriages! Poor Franklin! And dear old Ned. Do you remember him that night? Hiding in the lemons? And believe me there were plenty of your fly-by-night flings. And do you know what I thought? As my consolation? I thought, well, Richard gets everything: a wife that—don't kid me—you adore. In middle age the miracle of children."

As she spoke she continued backward, a deliberate step at a time. "But I had something. I was not—not bereft. Oh, Madeline is not going to pass on anything to posterity. No platitudes. No pontoons. And it's not as if I'm going to be remembered for the soap operas and tearjerkers I've been doing for the last forty years. Very well. So be it. This was my solace: I have known a great man. I have been his—Dora? Wait a minute: is that Freud or Picasso? Olga! Jacqueline! Saskia! That was Rembrandt's wife. Naked in a pool of water. Older, even, fatter even, than me. You never in your whole life painted yourself, darling. *I* would be your self portrait. My God! What an honor! I felt honored to be in your work. Even if Picasso was a shit, rather like you."

She took a last step back. She was at the doorway. Her eyes were now nothing but pupil, as if all brain function had stopped. Then she turned, walked onto the balcony, and leaned over the rail. "My life!" she cried.

Was it a cry of longing? Or a line from her play? For a terrible moment I thought she might hurl herself onto the stones of the patio below. I moved onto the balcony. There was, through the windows, more than enough light to see the line of her crack and the maidenhair curling from her linen. I kicked off my shoes. I dropped my pants. I stepped directly behind her and tore off my trunks.

"Oh," she murmured, as though surprised. "Is it you?"

I bent at the waist, thrusting both hands under her sweater and up the length of her backbone. Then I reached around her ribcage, searching for her swaying breasts. I gathered them. I felt the nipples spring taut, like, in miniature, the tophats of a magician.

"We'll do them again," she said. "Every one of them. I'll lie in the bath for you. I'll piss in the toilet for you. I'll hold my legs in the air. Will you make my breasts beautiful? As beautiful as a Russian actress's?"

I stepped back, hooked a finger into the lavender drawers and drew them down. Her buttocks floated before me. There was the periwinkle of her anus. The rim of it opened and closed, like the folds of cloth that surrounded the shutter of a camera. I thumbed either side and moved the under part of my penis against it.

"No, not there," she said, hoisting herself, so that the pod of her sex organs, slick already, was exposed. I placed myself inside her.

She said, "At last."

I moved inches into the canal. With a groan, she thrust back at me. Then we began to slap loudly, repeatedly, against each other. I was leaning forward, braced on her back. Her hair fell down like black laundry. I raised my gaze to the ocean and kept it there. All this while the earth must have been turning. Because the moon, with its silver reflection, had long since gone down.

"Ah, Richard-boy! My only love!"

Which was when I spent myself fruitlessly inside her.

She stood upright. She stepped from the blue blot of her underwear. Then she turned, putting her hands in front of her body, like the knock-kneed *September Morn:* no, like a Renaissance painting, Masaccio maybe, of Eve after she has discovered evil and good.

I pulled on my pants. I stepped into my shoes. Then I went inside and set to work. I cleared the table. I scraped the uneaten food into the disposal and rinsed the silver. I corked the opened bottle of wine. I turned off the overhead lights.

"Such a busy hausfrau."

Madeline had lain down on the sofa. She had covered herself with the lime-green coverlet she kept at one end. It was up to her chin.

I moved toward her and squatted next to where, in the light of the candles, she squinted up at me.

"Going home now?" she inquired.

I nodded.

"You aren't coming back, are you? In the morning?"

"No, dear. I'm not."

"And France——?"

I didn't answer.

"I understand. The disgrace of this night is all mine."

"There's enough of that," I answered, "to go around."

"Do me a favor?"

"If I can."

"Under the couch. The book. My lines."

I saw the paperback. I fished it out and let the pages fall open to near the end.

"*Oh, my orchard!*" I prompted.

She didn't look at the text when she said, "*My sweet, beautiful orchard! My life, my-my*— Wait. Don't tell me. I am going to remember. Yes, I *do* remember. No wonder I repressed it. How pat. Ha! Ha! Ha!

How apropos. *My life, my youth, my happiness, goodbye! Goodbye!*"

She closed the book.

"Shall I put out the candles?" I asked her.

"Put them out," she said.

I did.

4

I wasn't going back to the Palisades, in spite of what I'd told Madeline. How much time was there to kill? Of course I'd run off without my watch. The clock in the Boxster, which I hadn't switched from daylight savings, read 6:02. A little past five, then, in the morning. I eased down Channel Road and turned left on the Pacific Coast Highway. I drove south, past the Beach Club and the Jonathan Club, *movie people* grudgingly allowed. In the dark, amidst the lit-up dials, I remembered a letter Norman had written to the *Times*. "It is unfair to accuse our fine country clubs of anti-Semitism," he began. "Why, recently both the Jonathan Club and the California Club have asked me to become a member. The Jonathan Club invited me to join the California Club, and the California Club invited me to join the Jonathan Club." They didn't print it.

I drove back and forth along the coast until it was light, and then I drove some more. At midmorning I headed north to Santa Monica Boulevard and took it all the way into Westwood. I parked behind the offices of the French Consulate. The consul, a tall, bald man named Trouvé-Roveto, greeted me at the door and led me down a corridor to a large, oval-shaped room. Curtains covered the windows. A number of screens—computer screens? video?—were built into the wall, which created the impression of a visit to the aquarium. At one spot a number of photographs were hung in a cluster. I recognized one of them.

"That's Romain Gary, the writer, isn't it?"

Trouvé-Roveto looked up from where he'd settled himself, one leg over the corner of his desk. "Yes, he was the consul here in the past. You know his work?"

"A friend of my father's," I answered. "He used to come to the house for dinner. I do remember him, though I was only a child."

He looked, in my memory, much as he did in the photo. He would pull letters from his pockets and read them to us, first in French, then English. Norman explained they were from his mother, a Jew trapped in North Africa. Even I could see how he seemed to live for these messages, which came week after week, all through the war. "I've never forgotten how he used to read aloud to us from his mother's letters."

"Ah, yes," said the diplomat, across whose hairless head the reflection of the overhead lights glided like streetlamps over the hood of a car. "It is a fantastic story. All the time she was dead, you know. She wrote them before the occupation. A friend mailed them with faithfulness to her son."

"No. I didn't know."

"But it is a fact. He wrote a book about it." So saying, the consul touched a switch on his desk and the room grew dim. He touched another switch and all six of the screens came on. "Now you will see, my dear Mr. Jacobi, why I have asked you to this room. I do not think I will leave you with disappointment." He fiddled some more at his desk top; suddenly each of the screens turned blue. I saw that they were filled with my paintings: the water of the pool; the cloudless sky; a dark shadow that was an abstraction of the fig-heavy hedge; the white scribble, like a toothpaste squirt, midway between the trampoline of our awning and the unrippled depths.

"Voila!" said M. Trouvé-Roveto. "This is the installation, just as you will see it in five days. Is it to your liking? One turns, and then turns again, and everywhere the manifestation, *en blue,* of your talent. Do you not feel at this moment transported to L'Orangerie? Yes! Definitely! One sees the well-known affinity with Monet."

The man stopped speaking. His jaw, a rare thing in a diplomat, gaped. He could not disguise that he saw that his guest was weeping. I did not try to disguise it myself. My shoulders shook. The tears came out in a flood. I moaned.

Trouvé-Roveto recovered and came to where, in sheer helplessness, I'd dropped to my knees. He bent over me, flourishing a handkerchief. "It is because of the beauty? Tell me: is not that the reason you have been moved?"

The reason? I didn't know the reason. Was it a deferred reaction to everything that had come before? The suggestion, by unknown lawyers, that I had intended to murder my wife? That other lawyers were busily at work to rob me of my sons? Or was it Madeline, those three gray hairs, the imperfect breasts, the flesh accumulating at her throat? Or maybe it was the paintings, *these* paintings, their cleanliness and their calm. Or was I weeping for poor Gary, when he found out about his mother? Or because of the foresightedness of the woman herself? It might have been all of these reasons, which, like Atlas, I bore simultaneously on my shoulders. No. To my own amazement, I heard myself tell the Frenchman the actual cause:

"I wish it were that, Monsieur. But it isn't the beauty of the paintings; it's that I shall not be able to see them—not in your exhibition. I shall always be grateful to you. And to the government of France. To President Chirac. Forgive me: I cannot attend the premiere."

The consul drew back. "What? This is impossible. It is too late. Everything has been prepared."

"I wish I could change things. I can't."

"But this is to us an insult. Really, a scandal. Are you ill? Is it grave?"

I handed him back his handkerchief which, as in a folk dance, had dropped to the floor between us. Then I rose and walked through the roomful of paintings. "Yes, that's right," I told him. "My illness is grave."

Nine hours later I was reunited with my sons. What happened was that, after returning from the consulate and sleeping through much of the afternoon, I was awakened by the ringing of the phone. It was Barton.

He didn't give me a chance to say hello.

"Richard. It's me. You've got to come down here now. The situation is serious. It's giving me a nervous breakdown. You know I have a virus in my stomach. I need peace and quiet. That's why I have a garden. I like to live with plants. So get out here pronto. They are screaming like banshees! Banshees, brother. They don't understand I am set in my ways. You know how I am if you use one of my towels. Now the sun is going down! It's going down! That's when I start to write. How can I? You tell me that. I'm not like you. You can paint in any circumstances. You don't have to think. I use words. Words are a superior medium. I'm not like those Frenchmen who write inside cafés. That's all a big act. You can't compare their work to mine. Oh! Did you hear that? They're running up the stairs. My fingers are trembling too much to light a cigarette."

"Bartie, calm down. Take a breath. Tell me what happened."

"It's Marcia. That woman you married. She shouted my name at three in the afternoon. That is like three in the morning for you. She pounded on the door. It woke me up. She pounded and pounded. I thought it was an emergency. I thought it was an earthquake. When I came downstairs she was there with the wild Indians. That's who they are, brother. You'll never get that out of them. It's in the blood."

"Bartie, wait. Do you mean Marcia was there with the boys?"

"Yes! She couldn't handle them. She said she was tearing her hair out. I knew she was petit bourgeois. A real Angeleno. That's why she left them with me. I think she wants to go shopping. To her yoga class. To have somebody do her nails. She doesn't understand I have an artistic temperament. What about the paper lanterns in my garden? What about the goldfish in my pool? My little plants! It's an oasis of tranquility."

"All right. You hold on, okay? They're not hurt or anything, are they?"

"Who? The boys? They're fine. But I can see the pink clouds! Pink clouds! I should be starting my next chapter. I can't—"

I hung up on him. I hadn't had time to remove my hand from the receiver before it rang again."

"Bartie, I told you I'm on my way."

"It isn't Barton. It is your mother. Isn't it *fantastic!* Isn't it *exciting*! I have been saying prayers every night. I got onto my knees, darling, like a *nun*! Now my prayers have been answered. Those dear boys are back. You ought to go right away. What if she changes her mind?"

"Mom, I was out the door when you called."

"Well, don't let *me* hold you up. I just wanted to tell you to be nice to your brother. He's having a little difficulty with the situation. He is such a confirmed bachelor. Do be kind. He's had a big disappointment with his book. Steven is being such a shit. A simple thing like reading a manuscript and he can't be bothered."

"All right! Christ, I'll be nice."

"Why are you shouting? I'm not accusing you of anything. A little thoughtfulness never hurt anyone."

"I didn't say it did."

"Good. Now when can I expect you? I'm running out for bagels and cream cheese. I called Timo to bring over some nice rare roast beef from the club. He'll do it as a special favor. What else do the boys like? Oh, my *flan!* I'd better get going. Goodness, I don't know if she left them with so much as a *toothbrush.*"

"Lotte, what are you thinking? I'm not bringing the twins over there."

"Of *course* you are! Where else could you take them?"

"Home. To their rooms. To their friends. To their school."

"Sometimes, Richard, I think you are *stupid.* School is over. The Christmas holiday has started. That's how much you know about raising children. It makes me laugh to think you could take care of them yourself. Do you think Isolina is going to do it? That silly little Mexican—"

"Guatemalan. She loves the boys, it so happens. And she has a child of her own."

"In a mud shack some place! Do you think I am going to allow my grandchildren to be brought up by a servant?"

"Why not? You let us be. Right? Before Norman died."

"I never heard of such an accusation."

"Knock it off. You're not in your dotage. Who took us to the Carlsbad Caverns? Arthur! Arthur and Mary. And in the Fifties. They were the only black people in the state of New Mexico. And who took us that time to the dude ranch? Arthur! While you were off with Betty in Timbuktu. I shudder now at the humiliation. *His* humiliation. And who cooked for us and fed us and put us to bed? Mary!"

"Oh, well, nineteen-fifty. That is ancient history. Everybody did things differently then."

"Oh, my god. You even let that poor man take us to Jack's-at-the-Beach. And in his uniform!"

"Ingrate! Your father treated you to the Hotel del Coronado. Have you forgotten that? The finest hotel in Southern California. And the Fairmont Hotel in San Francisco. You were so demanding! You made us stop at that awful Anderson's soup place. Every Thursday we took you and Barton to the Swiss Chalet. We were a loving family. People smiled in appreciation. You are like a Communist! Rewriting history this way."

"Let's not argue, Lotte. I've got to go."

"Listen to me, sweetie. I am sure you and Isolina will do the best you can. But who is going to watch them when you are in Paris? Give me the pleasure. It's a grandmother's prerogative."

"No, no. They're wild Indians. Real little savages. You've got all those figurines from Germany and Czechoslovakia. All the little cups from China. Don't worry, Marcia will be coming back in a day or two."

"Never! You can trust my intuition. She ought to be arrested for what she's done. And if I'm not concerned about my apartment you don't have to be either. Besides, we'll be out all day at the club. Be reasonable, Richard. Who else is going to do it? Your poker friends? Your tennis friends? And Madeline will be with you in Paris—"

"Madeline's not going to Paris."

"No? Not Madeline? Then who's going with you? You can't be thinking of me? Is that it? Have you been planning a surprise? Oh, and

I thought I was joking about a trip round the world. Paris would be *wonderful!* I haven't been there forever! There is nothing on earth like those flowers in the flower boxes. This makes it almost worth turning ninety. Oh, Richard, I just adore you!"

"Mom, maybe you *are* in your dotage. Don't you understand? No one is going to Paris. Not Madeline. Not you. And not me."

There was a brief pause on the line. I heard her swallow and gulp. "What did you say? It is a terrible connection. It sounded as if you said you weren't going to your premiere."

"I'm not. I've already told the French Consul. I can't leave Michael and Edward. They are going to need me. And so does Marcia now. I've got to be there for all of them."

"Richard, don't do this to me. You might as well stab me with a knife. *They* need you? *She* needs you? What about me? At the end of my life? This exhibition is the greatest thing that has ever happened to me. It is more important than Norman's Oscar! I didn't even care that Adlai Stevenson was going to invite me to the White House. Ha! Ha! Ha! I was a fool! I had fantasies of being a First Lady. Dolly Madison Jacobi! No, Richard. You are my heart. You are my brain. You are my soul. Go alone if you have to! I'll still be with you. Don't rob me of this. I've told all my friends!"

"You sound like that Frenchman. Don't make a scandal. I don't give a shit. I'm going to pick up my sons."

"A knife! You are twisting my entrails on a knife! This will kill me."

"I don't have time for histrionics, Lotte. Can't you see it's the right thing to do?"

"No! It's self-indulgence! It's sentimentality! I hate those things. You listen to me. I am going to Bartie's. I am getting into the car. I'll take the boys. I'll show you I can do it. We'll have a lark together! My house will ring with laughter! Then you will feel free to go."

"Don't be ridiculous. You can't drive at night. That Honda is older than you are."

"Ha! Ha! That's true, if there were dog years for a car! Oh! I've just gotten the perfect idea! You go, sweetheart. You pick up the children. I'll meet you at San Remo Drive. Isn't it *absurd* that I haven't been back in all these years? You told me you put up that oil portrait over the fireplace. I was so touched to hear that. Yes, it's just silly not wanting to see all my old things again. If I leave right away maybe I can get there before it gets really dark. I can pack a suitcase. That's my idea! I will watch them there! So they can be with their friends and climb on the cork tree just like you and Bartie. Two brothers having fun again! Do you know what? I'll bring my suit! It will be just like the old days, performing my laps up and down my very own pool."

"You can't come!" I shouted. I almost added, *They smashed your chandelier.* "It's dangerous. It's already dark. You stay home, all right? We'll talk it over tomorrow, okay? Bartie's going crazy right now."

"No, not if you don't promise. Promise me! I'll never ask for anything else. You'll be in every magazine. You'll be dining at the Palais Royal. I knew one day you would hang with Leonardo! I've known it for years. With Leonardo at the Louvre."

"Not the Louvre."

"Be quiet! It's the same thing!"

"We'll talk later. I'll call you when I get home. Okay, Lotte? Let me go."

To that there was no answer. She had hung up the phone.

Back to the Pacific Coast Highway. Through Santa Monica and Ocean Park. Before Venice Pier I cut over to Speedway and right on 29th Avenue, where I parked the car. Bartie lived in one of the old houses whose windows had untended geraniums drooping from the ledges and shutters either unslatted or askew. The doorbell, I knew, was broken. I edged down the alley to the rear. Ordinarily, he'd be sitting there, puffing his Kools and piling up the pages of his manuscript. This was, as he often explained, the Age of Shudra. All the men and women of our time were living under the veil of Maya. He wasn't falling for that. In other words, his working day was only beginning, just as all the Angelenos were settling in for an evening of opium in front of their glowing screens.

"Hey, Bartie," I called, over the pointed staves of the backyard fence. "You there?"

No answer. I moved to the wooden gate, which was askew. I stepped through it into what might have been a botanical garden. The walls were covered with mosses, with grape fern and lady fern, like some vision of the Old South. There was a pepper tree in the center, just like the one we'd had on San Remo, bursting with hard red berries. Bartie had set up three pools, with little bridges and little boats. I glanced down at the gulping carp. Gladiolus, iris, larkspur—I couldn't remember the names of all the flowers. Snapdragon, I thought. Jack-in-the-pulpit or jack-in-the-box. Naturally, there was an iron Buddha, smiling and serene, his upturned hands on his knees. What the hell? I touched his nose for luck.

My brother was sitting at his round metal table, with a lamp shining over his shoulder. The smoke from his cigarette hung over him like a species of moss.

"There you are! What's the matter with you? Didn't you hear me call you?"

He didn't look up from the pages of his manuscript. His lips moved as he sounded out his words.

"Barton!"

He raised his head at last. "Hey, Bro. I can't talk to you now. It's my time to work. I'm like a slave in a galley ship. A prisoner on bread and water. It's what you have to do for art."

"I won't interrupt your writing. I'm just going to collect the boys and we'll be off."

"It isn't writing. It's rewriting. I have to fix my punctuation. The masses demand that you cross your t's and dot your i's. That's why Spielberg won't read it. Because of semicolons, Bro! Because of commas! He's just like all the others. He gives them what they want. Car chases and shoot-'em-ups and hot babes. What else can you expect from a capitalist culture? Jonathan Swift called these people Yahoos. They don't know anything about refinement. All they do is watch television. They whistle Bing Crosby. It's the Shudra Age. No one's going to look at your paintings either. Norman was the artist. He was a sophisticated man. The Lubitsch touch. He must be spinning in his grave."

"Bartie, I don't have time for this. Just tell me where the boys are. Are they sleeping upstairs? I don't hear them."

"The boys? You mean Michael and Edward? How do I know where they are? They were a distraction. I told them I always begin work at sundown."

"What do you mean, you don't know where they are? They were here, weren't they? You called to say Marcia had left them. Where are they now?"

"I am not a babysitter, my brother. That's not my style. I don't have to put up with those irritations. They got in my hair. Up the steps! Down the steps! I told them I must have tranquility. But they threw stones at my Chinese carp."

I didn't wait to hear more. I pushed through the back door. "Edward!" I called. "Michael! It's me! It's Dad!" There was no one downstairs. I raced up the staircase. Could they be so sound asleep? I burst into Barton's bedroom. A candle was burning, filling the room with incense. There was no one on the bed. I checked the other rooms, calling as I went. The house was empty. I went back outside.

"Bartie, will you stop writing a minute, please, and pay attention?"

"Don't tell me to stop writing! Why don't you give me five hundred dollars? It's a pittance to you. Then I could hire a student from UCLA. From Pepperdine. They could do this shitwork for me."

"God damn it, Bartie!" I leaned over the table and swept his stack of manuscript pages off the metal surface, into the air. "Aren't you ever going to be normal?"

"Why did you do that?" he cried. "You know I have a stomach virus. That's why I'm not like you."

"My children are missing! Can't you grasp that?"

"The children?" Suddenly the red welt on his forehead, the seat of his emotion, ceased throbbing. It went as white as a blister. "I don't know, Bro. Uh-oh. Uh-oh. Bartie doesn't know. They were here. A little while ago they were here."

Then I remembered the garden gate. It had always been latched. This time it was open. "Bartie, stay calm. Try to think. Did they go out of the garden? By the garden gate? Did they? Did you see them? Which way did they go?"

He sat in his chair, rocking back and forth. "It's Bartie's fault. Crazy Bartie. He lost them. He made them drown-ded. In the ocean. They're drown-ded, drown-ded." He rocked to the sound of that word, which he pronounced as he had when a little boy.

"You stay here. Okay? I'm going to look for them. Don't you move."

"Bartie's afraid. He's afraid of Lotte. What will she say to him? What will she do? Bartie's bad. He can't do his commas. Why was this Bartie ever born?"

I started off toward the beach at a trot. By the time I crossed Speedway I was running. A rusted ramp led to the sand; I clanged down it. The beach was deserted. The sun, like a blacksmith's ingot, was plunging into the bucket of the Pacific. A gull flew seaward, seeming to pull behind it the black curtain of night. *Ow-ow-ow*, it called. I could see, far out, like a line of chalk, the row of breaking waves. Kelp lay in piles about me, as did heaps of broken shells. There wasn't, in the damp sand, a single foot-step, aside from my own. I ran northward, a hundred yards, a hundred yards more. Impossible, in the sudden gloom, to peer more than a few feet in any direction. And what was I expecting to see? The two of them playing catch? Playing tag? Or wrestling, as they had always wrestled, on the sand instead of the carpets at home?

"Michael!" I called. "Edward!"

My heart was pounding. My skin was covered with sweat, either from my own exertions or the windblown spume of the sea. Was it possible? Could they have wandered into the ocean? There were riptides. There was the chilling cold. What was Bartie's word? *Drown-ded?* The pun in it struck me with sudden horror. Was I going to find them lying cold in each other's arms?

"Michael! Edward! Answer me!"

I turned, heading back the way I had come. I stumbled. I staggered. I fell and got up again. *Please, God. Please, God,* I kept saying. Suddenly, off to the south, a thousand lights went on: Venice Pier, lit up for Christmas. Is that where they'd gone? Out to the pilings? But these days there was nothing to attract them. They'd long since torn down all the amusements, the Giant Dipper, the Some Kick Coaster, and the Noah's Ark Funhouse, which had giraffes in the windows and rocked like a boat. There were only fishermen now.

Then, in silhouette, against the twinkling backdrop of light, I saw a dark shape. It was as tall as one of the ark's giraffes, and just as spindly. I could see the pier, with its illumination, through what might have been the latticework of its bones. But this giraffe was alive; it was moving. Rather, something was moving on it. I heard a smothered cry, a laugh, a shout. I staggered forward. I blinked my eyes clear. What I had seen was a lifeguard stand, abandoned for the winter months. Someone had climbed up its crisscrossed boards and stood teetering at the top.

"Chicken! Chicken!" It was Michael's voice. "Jump! You've got to jump!"

I stood, too choked with tears to form words of my own. I watched as the dark figure, it might have been one of Noah's little monkeys, launched itself into the air and tumbled to the ground.

A second monkey scampered up the scaffold and took its place on the precipice.

There was a triumphant laugh. Edward cried, "Ha! Ha! Who's a chicken now?"

"Geronimo!" Michael leaped into the black of the night, landing on all fours.

I watched, as if bound by a spell, as another shape, gorilla-sized, rose up against the lights. The little chimps danced around it. "Your turn! Your turn! You said! You promised!"

"Oh, I'm scared. I'm old. I'll break my bones." Thus protesting, the big black figure hauled himself hand over hand to the tower's top. You could hear his cigarette-wheeze as he stood there panting.

The others taunted him. "Now! Do it! Now! Jump! Jump! Jump!"

Windmilling his arms, legs thrashing, my brother Bartie flung himself outward and, instead of landing safely in water, came crashing onto the ground.

I felt the concussion through the soles of my shoes. "Bartie!" I cried, running forward. "Are you all right?"

"Fa-ther!" cried Edward.

"Fa-ther! Fa-ther!" cried Michael.

The two of them came racing forward. They threw themselves on me.

Barton slowly rose. "Hi, Bro! You see? Bartie lost them. Then Bartie found them. I did it all by myself."

I dropped to my knees, embracing my children. I could feel them in the dark; they were kissing my hands and kissing them again, as if I were a potentate.

5

The three of us barely fit into the little Boxster. The boys, instantly asleep, lay tangled in the second seat. I drove slowly along the ocean, past the fat cannon and the cannonballs, under the transplanted palms. I took the twists and turns of Amalfi at a crawl. The arms of the boys were linked, their legs entwined, as they might have been in their poor mother's womb. After what may have taken half an hour, I turned off Sunset and made my way up the curve of San Remo Drive. As I approached the house I saw, reflected on the opposite stand of cypress, a blinking band of light. I took my foot off the accelerator; we coasted until the police car came into view. It was parked directly in front of 1341. An officer, cap off, was in the passenger seat; another, cap on, stood between the columns of the portico. I downshifted, roaring by the patrol car and fishtailing up the slope of the street. The boys awoke.

"What is it?" asked Michael.

His brother said, "Aren't we going home?"

I was too busy to answer. I took the corner of Lucca on two wheels and then turned again on Monaco. I didn't obey the stop signs. Back at Sunset I ignored the prohibition on a left turn and swung back onto the boulevard, heading east.

Edward's voice was breaking: "Father! You're scaring me. What's wrong?"

"Nothing is wrong," I told him, and braked for the Allenford light. But of course something was. The police could only be there to arrest me on a felony, or, worse, to seize the twins. Was everything upside down? Marcia kidnapped the boys and I was the one fleeing into the night. The light turned green. I started up again, this time at a steady forty. The last thing I wanted was to be stopped for speeding, or failing to signal, or changing lanes.

"I wasn't sleeping," Michael said. "You went right by the house."

"Where are you taking us? To Grandma's?"

Where else could you take them? Those were Lotte's words. But that was the last place I could go now. If the police weren't already waiting at the corner of Oakhurst, my mother would soon let them know of her proud possessions. Ernie's place was only a few blocks away, in Brentwood. Should I drive over there? Or check into a hotel? I could just keep on in a straight line, over the mountains, through the Mohave, and into the reservation lands of Arizona, which is precisely what I had feared Marcia had done. High up on the left, like a sailing ship stranded on a reef, or the earlier Noah's ark on Ararat, loomed the floodlit walls of the Getty Museum. I cut into the right-hand lane and looped around to the northbound conduit of 405.

"No," I said, by way of a belated response to my son's question. "We're going to Jimbo's. I left some papers there. Maybe we'll spend the night. You can play with Hannibal and Caesar. Okay? Do you remember how they used to pull you over the leaves?"

"I remember," Edward said.

Michael added, "We used to hold on to their tails."

I stayed on the freeway until Mulholland, then skirted the ridge of the hills until Calneva, where we went into something like free fall until ending up in front of the expanded ranch house on Garvin Drive. The Great Danes started barking before we got out of the car. Jimbo came out in that day's whiskers and a bathrobe. He plucked up a boy under each arm and ferried them through the gate.

"This is what the animals need for their late night snack."

The boys let out a squeal as the two dogs reared up, big as horses. They pawed the air like horses too. Then the four of them started a romp in the yard. I went indoors to the den. The walls were covered with my own paintings, and an occasional photograph of James's parents, my uncle Julie and Frances, the Irish actress he'd married back in the Thirties. The poker table was still set up from the night before, along with the remains of the beer and pretzels and vegetable dip that my cousin had put out for a spread.

"Ingracia's away?"

"For the week," Jimbo answered. "She's with her family in San Salvador."

"It's just as well. I'd like to stay a few days, if it's all right with you."

He scratched the few tufts of hair left on his head. "Sure. Love to have you. But what's going on? Isn't Marcia back? Didn't she bring the boys? And aren't you about to leave for Paris? I'm coming myself at the end of January."

Suddenly the dogs set up a howl. The doorbell rang. Jimbo glanced through the slats on the window. "It's the police," he said. "They're after you, right? You and the boys?"

I nodded.

"Don't move. They can't come in. I'll tell them I haven't seen you for days."

"No, no. It won't work. My car's out in front. How stupid! And look: the boy's are peeping over the gate. I'm sorry, Jimbo. I shouldn't have gotten you involved."

He strode toward the foyer. "Just stay quiet. Don't say anything. I doubt they've got a warrant."

The twins came in through the side entrance and tumbled into the room with the Danes. I put my finger to my lips. The boys fell silent. The drooling dogs stood panting. I could hear voices coming from the front of the house: Jimbo, a patrolman, Jimbo again. Then my cousin walked to the door of the den. His face was white.

"It's Lotte," he said. "There's been an accident. They had to cut her out of her car."

The boys rode with the police. What a thrill for them, I thought, following in the Boxster: the siren, the speed, the whirling lights. We got off the freeway at Wilshire and raced through Westwood. We went even faster through the stretch between the golf course fairways, and only slowed when we approached the intersection of Santa Monica. The sky there was lit, not only by the usual mauves and greens and yellows of the gushing fountain, but by the blinking blues of police cars and the steady beam of a searchlight that a fire truck was directing over the scene. Traffic backed up on both boulevards. A crowd stood on the grass and the cement. A car lay upside down in the basin. The water from the fountain splashed down on its undercarriage. I leaned from my window: the car was a hatchback, the color of the meat of a plum. Lotte's Honda! She'd lost control heading west on Santa Monica. She'd become airborne after striking the curb. Foolish woman! Silly old chatterer! What if she'd been heading east? What if, according to plan, she'd already picked up the boys? I struck my fist against the seat beside me. I got a last glimpse of the Indian brave, kneeling on his pedestal and still calling upon the Great Father, just as he had done since before Barton and I had been born.

Born, as it happens, at St. Vincent's. But it was Cedars-Sinai I drove up to now. I collected the boys and took the elevator to intensive care. Marcia was sitting in a chair outside my mother's door. She rose. We embraced. The twins held back, wide-eyed in the hall.

"How is she?" I asked my wife.

"Go in. You'll see."

"Where's Bartie?"

"He's here. He was the first to arrive. Try the visitors' lounge."

I moved to Lotte's door and went in. She was asleep, propped up on the bed. The usual tubes and wires ran in and out of her. She wore a clear oxygen mask, beneath which her makeup was smeared. There were no cuts. There were no abrasions. None of her limbs was in a cast. Even her reading glasses sat unbroken on the bedside table. I leaned over her and touched the brittle curls of her hair. Then I walked out and went in search of my brother. He wasn't in the lounge. He wasn't in the corridors. But I sniffed him out, standing in a corner of the bathroom, puffing on one of his Kools. He whirled around when I entered.

"They won't let me smoke!" he exclaimed.

"It's all right, Bartie. I won't stop you."

"This is a terrible situation, Bro. Just terrible. I begged the nurses. I told them about the shock to my nerves. But they are like the Gestapo. It's cruel and unusual punishment."

"You go ahead. Smoke all you want to. I'll stand guard by the door."

He took a final inhalation and ground the stub out on the side of the sink. "Never mind. I was upset. They exaggerated so much on the phone. I thought it might be fatal. What would Bartie do then? But you saw her, didn't you, Richard? There's not a scratch on her. Did you talk to her?"

"No. She was sleeping when I went in."

"Well, I did. She said she was feeling fine. She asked me to buy her a *New Yorker* so she'd have something to read. She's a tough bird. It's all that swimming. She's in tip-top condition. Absolutely tip-top."

"Jesus, she's lucky. There are no airbags in that car. I'm not even sure the seat belt worked."

"Don't blame the Honda. The Honda is a reliable machine. It wasn't her fault either. She hit a wet spot. We have to get a lawyer. It was the spray from the fountain. I've skidded through that lane myself. You'll sue them, Bro. An accident waiting to happen happened. That's what I told her. She thought it was witty. But she could have been killed. Thank God she's going to walk out tomorrow. They're only keeping her overnight for observation."

A man, strawhatted, as if for summer, came into the men's room. We went out and returned to the ward. Lotte was awake. The children were there, one on each side of the bed, holding her hands. "Oh, *here* you are," said Lotte. "I've had a little detour."

"Lean back, Miss Lotte," said the orderly, a plump young man in a green gown. "I got to put in your drops."

"This is Enrique," said Lotte, thrusting her head back, so that the drops would fall into her eyes. "He takes good care of me. Isn't that right, Ricky darling?" She blinked her wet lashes at him, dropping Edward's hand in order to grip the bare brown skin of the orderly's arm.

"That's right, Miss Lotte. Enrique going to treat you good. You already my favorite pinup girl."

"*There!*" said my mother. "It is amazing how everybody loves me."

"We love you too," said Michael.

"Oh, I know you do. We're going to have such a good time together. Richard will tell you. I was on my way to take care of you. Isn't it silly what Grandma did? I was driving along thinking of how I was going to sleep in my old bedroom and how I was going to play the Schubert sonata on my old piano, I could practically hear the chords, and the next thing I knew I woke up with these tubes in my arm."

"You hit a wet spot," said Barton. "We're going to sue the city of Beverly Hills through the nose."

"Is that what happened?" she said, a little dreamily. "Aren't you smart for figuring that out."

"It's an opportunity for us. We'll live in the lap of luxury."

"Yes, just like the old days, with our lovely servants and the Japanese gardeners and the pansy beds. Tomorrow you and Richard can drive me over to San Remo. Did they bring my suitcase? My suit's in there somewhere. So I can do laps. Guess what, boys? Do you know what I'm going to make you for dessert? That's right! Flan!"

She broke into a brilliant smile, which gave me a start. What I had taken to be a smudge of lipstick looked more like a smear of blood. "What's that?" I asked her. "On your teeth?"

"Oh, it's such a bother. Look, I have a tissue to blot it." She raised a reddened kleenex and dabbed at her mouth. *Internal injuries,* I thought with alarm. She must have read my expression, because she gave a little laugh. "Oh, Richard, you are *such* a worrywart. I had a tube down my throat. You know, a ventilator. It scratched me, that's all. Did you really think I was going to provide you with another excuse not to go to France?"

The door behind me opened. A nurse asked, "Which one is Mr. Jacobi? The son?"

"I am," I said, then caught myself. I motioned toward my brother. "We both are."

"The doctor would like to see you a moment."

Bartie said, "I know what this is. They want to get paid. That's the capitalist system. If you can't pay then you're refuse. They throw you on the garbage heap. You go, Richard. You're the one with the credit cards."

The nurse held the door. "I think Doctor Weiner would like to see you both."

Barton and I followed her out into the crowded reception area. A middle-aged man, younger than either of us, was waiting with an elbow on the counter. He had thick spectacles and damp, close-cut hair that looked as if it had just come out of the shower. He introduced himself: Doctor Weiner, indeed. Then he said, "We've just gotten your mother's echocardiogram."

I glanced quickly around the bustling room. The large sign of the coronary unit had been staring me in the face all along. "Echocardiogram? Was that necessary? Why is she in the coronary unit? She's been in an automobile accident."

The doctor looked from me to Barton, one of whose eyes was growing wide with surprise, while the other was drawing shut. "Gentlemen, has no one explained this to you? Your mother has had a heart attack. Whether it occurred before the crash or after it I can't say."

Just like Norman, I thought. The same accident. The same uncertainty.

Bartie was stammering. "No, no, no. That's wrong. She hit a wet spot."

I said, "I don't understand this either. She's never had the slightest problem with her heart. She stopped smoking thirty years ago. She swims a mile three times a week. She's done that for as long as I can remember. She eats a can of tuna fish for lunch every damn day."

Bartie: "Oh, well, lots of people have heart attacks. She's fine now, isn't she? What I call her is a tough old bird. She rolled over completely and you can see she didn't get a scratch."

"The fact is, it was a massive attack."

"You don't know her the way I do. She's an Angeleno. A sun worshiper. These people, they go on forever. A hundred is nothing to them. They're the status quo."

"Bartie, be quiet. Let the doctor finish."

"If you like, I'll call up the pictures. But look, I can show you on a piece of paper."

Weiner pulled out a ballpoint pen and clicked it. He leaned over the counter and in one quick motion I couldn't help but admire drew with an unbroken line the four chambers of the heart. "The difficulty," he said, "is here." He made a crosshatching motion over the line that separated the left and right ventricles. "I'm afraid she's torn a hole in the wall here. The blood ought to be received here and sent out here, through the aorta, and some of it is. But too much of it is just sloshing back and forth through the whole in the septum. Unhappily, it's pooling."

"Can you repair the hole?" I asked. "Can she go into surgery?"

"Certainly we can try heroic measures. But it would create a good deal of pain and distress and give her only another day or two of life."

At those words I felt my own blood drain, as if through an excavation, from my heart. I could feel it throbbing in my legs and my feet. I managed to say, "You are telling us she is dying."

"I am very sorry," he answered.

"How long has she?"

"She'll go before morning. A few more hours at best."

I thought I heard the doctor's voice catch in his throat. *Good for him,* was my crazy thought. He reached out and squeezed my arm. When he reached for my brother, Bartie jumped back and uttered a loud, echoing laugh.

"Ha! Ha! Ha!"

Then he said, so that everyone in the room could hear, "Well, if there's no life there's no death!"

I was able to catch a brief glimpse of the tears spurting from his one open eye before he whirled about and dashed into the corridor.

I returned to the room where Lotte was once again sleeping. The boys and Marcia looked up. I shook my head. Michael, at that, began to whimper. The door opened; Jimbo, in slacks and a shirt now, walked in. He was followed, strangely enough, by Gloria, my mother's hairdresser. She dropped to her knees by the bed. "Oh, the nice funny woman make me laugh!"

It may have been these words that awakened Lotte. She turned her eyes on my cousin. "Oh, Jimbo. Poor Jimbo. Can't you ever win a match from Richard? Richard, there you are. Can't you be a gentleman and let Jimbo win?"

"I try, Mom. It isn't so easy."

"Try harder."

"Okay, I'll play left-handed."

But she had lost interest in the topic. "Is it Tuesday already? I didn't know that. Gloria, are you here to do my hair? It's your last chance, you know."

"I know, Miss Lotte."

"That's right. I'm moving back to San Remo Drive. It's much too long a trip for you."

There was a brief pause. The machines beeped and gurgled. On the screens little balls, like tennis balls, leaped the series of nets in their path.

"Goodness! Why are you all standing around with such faces? I'm not going to die or anything!"

Marcia said, "Of course you're not. You just need some sleep. We'll go out. Is there anything you need? What can I get you?"

"I asked Barton ages ago to buy me a *New Yorker*. I was just starting the 'Talk of the Town.' You know my mistake? I didn't give him any money. He is a sweet child, my Bartie, but he certainly knows how to squeeze a penny!"

"I'll bring back the latest issue." Marcia herded the boys to the door. Jimbo held it for her and went out after the others.

Lotte didn't seem to realize they had gone. "On second thought, never mind. I have so much work to do. That Plato Society! They're like slave drivers! I worked so hard on Suleiman the First. I think I fell in love in a manner of speaking with that man. All his good works. Now what do you think they've assigned me? At my age? The Great Wall of China!"

"Are you tired, Mom? Would you like to sleep for a bit?"

"Of *course* I'm tired. That doesn't mean anything. It's the middle of the night."

Gloria reached upward to rearrange the dyed strands of my mother's hair. "You going to see. I take the bus if I have to. Going to see you every Tuesday."

"Thank you, Gloria. You are a good friend. That will do for now."

The hairdresser rose from her knees and left me alone in the room. Lotte's eyes had closed. There were spaces between every breath. Suddenly she looked directly at me.

"Oh, Richard! What a thing this is!"

"It's all right, Mom. It's just a bump in the road."

"Nothing is in order. Ernie will have a fit. You never stopped telling me to lock up Norman's Oscar. Or bring it to your house. Someone was always going to steal it. The caterers. *Gloria!* All those girls who cleaned my flat. Why didn't you want to give me that pleasure? I'd have had no pleasure if I locked it up in a vault. You think you're so smart. But you're not so smart. No one would touch it. It's only worth four-hundred and sixty dollars. It's just a lump of metal. But I got to enjoy the sight of it every day."

"I'm glad, Mom. I was wrong. I'm glad you had the pleasure." I went to the side of the bed and dropped down where Gloria had been kneeling. I took a hand, and almost gasped at how cold it had become. She put another icy hand on top of mine.

"You have to take care of Bartie, you know."

"I know."

"I just *hate* that Steven Spielberg! Couldn't he have looked at a page or two? You'd think he'd do it for Norman's memory. And then just send an encouraging note."

"Don't worry. Don't worry. I'm going to be a better brother. I'm going to be a better person too."

"As if that were possible! Don't you understand anything? I love the person you are."

"Well, I let you down about France."

"Don't be silly! We have an arrangement. I'm going to watch the boys. You know I must be losing my mind. I could swear I saw Marcia here. She's the one who's not such a good person, darling. I'll tell you a secret."

But she didn't tell it. Her voice trailed away. I looked at the green screens, like grass courts, where the game was still going on. I tried to make sense of the numbers that measured the oxygen in her blood. *Pooling,* that was the doctor's word.

Lotte spoke again: "My shameful secret is that I wish she would go back to that awful man in San Francisco. Oh, darling, then I'd have you all to myself."

She gave a small cough. With her right hand she pulled at the edge of her hospital gown, so that the white flesh of a breast was exposed. I turned my head away. I heard her say, "There's no one else."

I turned back and leaned over her. I saw that her face, in relaxing, was transformed. It was growing younger before my eyes, as in a film that was running backwards. *Oh, to be eighty again!* But she was sixty; she was forty; she was the girl who had stepped off the Super Chief at Union Station. I said, "What, Mom? No one else for what?"

A pause. "No one else to watch them. Those dear boys. While you are having your triumph in France."

"That's right, Mom. You'll have to watch them."

A longer pause. A gasp. Then she said, "What fun."

I put my ear to her lips. She did not say anything more. The door opened. My family came in. Gloria followed. Then Doctor Weiner. We stood on the three sides of the bed, while she snatched at the air a moment longer, and then to her own surprise I think was gone. The doctor confirmed this. And when he had done so I kissed my mother on the mouth.

6

Lotte was right: nothing was in order and Ernie did have a fit. "Jesus Christ, she always said she had a plot at Hillside, a plot next to Norman's. But there's nothing. I checked and double-checked. You can buy a plot now out in Siberia or have her cremated and put in with her husband. His grave is much too old to bury her whole. They're afraid it will collapse on the diggers."

That is why, at the ceremony, she ended up in a little bronze box that could not have held her shoes. The elderly ladies and gentlemen from the Plato Society were there, and her men-friends from the club—Judge Mosk; Mel, the doctor; Masmanian, the psychoanalyst—and all the girls from bridge. Her sister's daughter had flown in with her husband, and there were a few cousins I'd not met before. My own friends—the Pumpkin, the Penguin, the Cow, and the rest—sat in chairs before the pile of fresh dark earth that had been turned out of Norman's grave. My family was in the front row—the boys in matching blue suits, Marcia in a veil, and her sister in a little jacket and skirt like a stewardess. Ah, there was M. Trouvé-Roveto, dressed entirely in black. There was Madeline. And Ernie Glickman, trying to button the jacket of his suit. Barton stood, putting an unlit cigarette in his mouth, throwing it down, and then replacing it with another. When he finally had to bend down to start again on the discards, I was startled to see that his hair was combed all around a bald spot, like the tonsure of a monk.

When the rabbi cut our black ribbons I asked if I might speak and got up to face the crowd. At the fringes, sitting on a little fold-up chair, was an elderly black gentleman. The cap on his knees gave him away: Arthur! Our butler, our chauffeur, our fisherman friend. I saw Gloria. I saw the woman who did her nails. Timo, the little Filipino, stood at the back, his hands behind him, repeatedly rising on his toes. I hadn't the least idea of what I wanted to say. The day was a warm one for the weary end of the year. But the clouds overhead were tumbling and fresh, like clothes in a washer.

"I am trying to think of my first memory. Please give me a minute." My mind went back to the day that René had taken me out in a rowboat. How sure I had been that he wanted to kill me! For an instant I had believed in telepathy. But over time I came to realize that I had projected my own murderous impulses onto the so-called Frenchman. *You think you're so smart.*

"My first memory is of a rowboat," I told the mourners. And so it was. I was, I think, little more than one year old. My mother and I were in a lake. I think it was at MacArthur Park. I think it was a Sunday. My evidence for that was the colored funny papers that the man in the boat held before his lips, like a guide using a megaphone. Was that Norman? Fooling around to divert us? Or was it some stranger? Were there even multicolored comics in 1939? In all likelihood Lotte was pregnant; thus it is not beyond all possibility that I could feel my brother moving as she pressed me against her. Nothing was certain, save for the green grass, the blue sky, the white clouds, and the undeniable fact that my mother was holding me in her arms; and what I told her friends was that for the whole course of my life she had held me, and was doing so still.

I finished. We lined up to throw dirt into the grave. Marcia, I saw, had smuggled in a lozenge from the chandelier and used it instead of a stone. My boys came next, Edward and Michael, and then Jimbo and his sister, Liz, who was followed by the relatives on Lotte's side of the family. I looked for Bartie, but he was leaning against a tree, this time with a lit cigarette. Then I noticed a small group standing off to one side. At first I did not recognize them. I looked again. These were Norman's friends from the old days, the actors and actresses, the writers and directors, who had so dazzled me with their wit and beauty and bright spirits when I had been a boy in knee pants. Elizabeth Taylor, Tony Curtis, Lauren Bacall. And there our neighbor, Gregory Peck. They trembled now, they swayed, and clutched each other, as if to hold themselves up. They seemed to know they were standing on the edge of a cliff, at the palisade that marked the continent's end, and that the wind that was blowing about them would seize each and all and like pumice-stone dolls hurl them down. It was only then that with a shock I understood I too had grown old.

We took up our lives on San Remo Drive, Marcia and I and the boys. The school year resumed. I try, at night, in the stray beams of the street-lamp, to rediscover the pleasures of married life. I went to France not at the start but at the end of the exhibition. I did not see the ambassador. I did not see M. Chirac, though I received a note of condolence upon the death of my esteemed mother. The room that had been meant for Made-line's portraits was left empty. I saw the crowds hurry through. But I was pleased to see how they lingered in the room that had been covered with my paintings in blue. Yes, they were like the waterlilies at L'Orangerie. I watched as the visitors stood before the zigzag puzzle in each of those works, a worm in white that meant something to me but was as myste-rious to them as an ideograph in Japanese.

In the spring Barton got his letter from Spielberg—or at any rate a letter on genuine DreamWorks stationery. The check for the option on *A Girl of the Streets* was genuine too. Bartie worried that they were going to sign Julia Roberts or Gwyneth Paltrow for the lead part. "That's the star system, Bro. This company thinks they're artistic, but they're no dif-ferent than the others. All they want to do is rake in the bucks. These actresses are superannuated. They need a fresh face. A young girl. Some-one with charm."

He said this in high summer, while sunning himself on our deck furniture. The sweat poured off the flesh of his belly, his breasts. He was grinning over the top of his gin and tonic. "You've always lived off the fat of the land, Bro. Now it's time for me to start living the life of Riley too." I'd never seen him so happy, at least not since I'd tied the green-backed mackerel to the end of his line. I hope that, in this second act of subterfuge, I have kept my promise to be a better brother.

"It won't be long now, Bro, before I leave for the real Riviera. Not that I have to. Hell, those starlets are going to be lining up to get into bed with Bartie. Bartie, the artistic consultant. You read Spielberg's letter. It said I was a brilliant writer. That's what impresses these blondes, like Arthur Miller with Marilyn Monroe. But I can't stand this city! These Angelenos! I can't sleep—not in the day, not in the night. I wake up and I know she's in the room. I swear I'm going to have a heart attack myself. It's her restless spirit. She's not at peace. She's jealous, that's the reason; she knows that my ship has come in. She always wanted to take care of me. She doesn't want to share me. Watch out, Bro. You have to settle your accounts. If you don't have good karma you are going to wander like a ghost too. Poor Lotte. It must be hard for her. Those chicks will be all over me now."

There was a shout. Then a scream. The canvas awning, with its red and green stripes, writhed like a thing alive. But it was only Michael, only Edward. I could see the canvas bulge downward with each of their steps and then spring back into shape, launching them first into the air like playful sparrows and then into the waiting water of the pool.

ABOUT THE AUTHOR

Leslie Epstein was born in Los Angeles. His father and uncle were, respectively, Philip G. and Julius J. Epstein, legendary wits and the writers of dozens of films, including *Casablanca*, for which they received an Academy Award. Leslie studied at Yale and then Oxford on a Rhodes Scholarship. He has published eight previous books of fiction, most notably *King of the Jews*, which has become a classic of Holocaust literature, *Pinto and Sons*, *Pandaemonium*, and two volumes on the adventures of Leib Goldkorn. For many years he has been the director of the Creative Writing Program at Boston University. He lives with his wife, Ilene, in Brookline, Massachusetts. They are the parents of three children—Anya, Paul, and Theo.